The Rapunzel Murders

Julia Vaughan

Cahill Davis Publishing

First published in Great Britain in 2024 by Cahill Davis Publishing Limited.

First published in paperback in Great Britain in 2024 by Cahill Davis Publishing Limited.

Printed and bound by CPI Group (UK) Ltd, Croydon, CR0 4YY

ISBN 978-1-915307-14-9 (eBook)

ISBN 978-1-915307-13-2 (Paperback)

Cahill Davis Publishing Limited

www.cahilldavispublishing.co.uk

Prologue

The girl trembled as the hairbrush dug deep into her scalp, pulling back her hair. She tried to speak, but the tape across her mouth prevented words from forming, and only moans escaped.

'Hush now, just a few more minutes.'

Hands grasped her hair and a rubber band was snapped in place, the long hair now secured in a ponytail.

'How could you think you were the one?'

The girl tried again to speak but stopped when she felt her hair being sectioned and plaited.

'Rapunzel, Rapunzel, let down your hair.'

Harsh laughter filled the girl with a new terror as she realised what was about to happen. She tried to struggle, knowing her limbs were useless. She felt the scissors slice through her hair, the blades scraping the nape of her neck, and the plait fell away into her gaoler's hands.

'No rescue for you, dear princess.'

The hair snaked around the girl's neck and then the braid tightened. Her eyes searched out the two skeletons in front of her, a braid of hair wound around each neck. Hope left her body at the same time as her last breath.

|1|

7th October 2019

'I didn't wake you, did I?'

Kath swapped her phone to her other ear and poured water onto her instant coffee. 'Hi, Lane. No, I was up. How are you doing?' She smiled as she stirred the brown liquid. The combination of strong coffee and the Northern Irish voice of Lane Petreus was a good start to the day.

'I'm good, honey. Up before God, as usual. I'm just calling to say I'll be with you in a couple of days.'

Kath sipped her coffee and offered up a silent prayer. The next investigation for her cold case team was going to be challenging and she had been hopeful that she could get Lane on board.

'That's great to hear. Do you want to stay with me again?'

Lane had been her house guest during the first case barely three months ago.

'No, I'll book into one of the hotels nearby.'

Kath laughed. 'Was I that bad a hostess?'

'Not at all, sweetie. I just feel you need your own space at the moment.'

Kath was not going to question the psychic. 'Okay, if you're sure. We'll all be glad to see you.'

Kath had phoned her a few days ago when she realised which case they'd be taking on next. Lane had been excited and intrigued.

'Can't wait to see everyone, especially wee Marvin and Byron.'

'Well, although wee Marvin has a wee crush on you, he does actually have a girlfriend now.'

'Good for him. She's a lucky lass.'

'I still think you'll always be his fantasy lady,' Kath said, smiling.

Marvin had been seeing Kerry, a DC that they had worked with when Kath headed up the active case team. He had sensibly decided to wait until there was some space between them work wise before asking her out. The relationship was only a couple of months old but seemed to be going well. His divorce was almost finalised, his ex-wife quickly moving on to a new potential baby daddy with a fat bank account. Ruth had once said that Marvin was like a stick of rock—the word sensible ran all the way through him. Being a dad was a consideration much further along his career ladder, and he wasn't about to get himself into that kind of situation before he was ready.

Lane chuckled. 'I need to go, but I'll see you real soon.'

Kath ended the call and downed the rest of her coffee, a wave of relief enveloping her. Shirl had picked a real challenge for their next case. Three murders, a country estate, a family tied up with myth and folklore and stories of curses and witchcraft.

Kath flicked on the kettle again. 'Not enough caffeine in the world,' she muttered, reaching for the coffee jar.

***

Kath heard laughter as she climbed the stairs to the office. It was a warm, welcoming sound. It signified that the conclusion to their last case just a few days ago had been processed, the horrors now pushed a little further into the past.

'Morning, people.' Kath entered the room and looked at the smiling faces.

A chorus of greetings followed, and Kath could feel the positive energy.

Byron stood up and walked to the centre of the room, his right hand curled into a fist. 'I have something for everyone, from my mum.'

Byron Lord, the tech wizard who could tease any information from the depths of the internet, cleared his throat and went to each member of the team in turn, placing a crystal in each person's palm.

'Oh, a pretty rock.' Ruth raised her eyebrows and stared at the piece of rose quartz in her hand.

'You don't have to believe in this stuff, but just put your crystal on your desk or in your bag or pocket.'

'Thanks, mate,' said Marvin, turning over the piece of red jasper.

'What with Ruth doing her feng shui mad clutter clearing and this crystal energy, or whatever it is, we shouldn't run into any problems,' said Shirl, smiling.

Kath dug her cigarettes and lighter from her bag, with a look on her face that was half smile, half grimace. 'You've picked a case where we'll need all the help we can get, wherever it comes from.'

'I've done some prep work,' Byron said, sitting down.

Kath had left the file on his desk before she'd left last week for their well-deserved break. He was usually the first one in the office, and Kath was grateful every day for his addition to the team.

'Thanks, Byron. Okay, Marvin, have a look what's in the files, get up to speed. I'm going for a smoke and a think.'

Shirl had reached for her own cigarettes to join her but got the message. Thinking time equalled alone time. She pulled a KitKat from her bag and set about devouring it.

Ruth shook her head. 'Waistline, Piglet.'

'Shut your mouth, Eeyore,' Shirl replied through a mouthful of chocolate and wafer. 'Never too early for chocolate.'

'Never too early for Weight Watchers.'

| 2 |

Kath pushed open the door of the small police substation. She walked a little way down the bare-earth pathway that skirted the large grassy area in front of the woodland and stood underneath a tree. As she lit her cigarette, a golden retriever came bouncing towards her. Holding her cigarette high in the air, she patted the head of the excited dog. as it nuzzled her knees.

'*Timmy, come here.* Sorry.' A flustered woman in a bright yellow anorak came jogging towards her, the dog lead bouncing around her neck. 'Sorry, sorry. *Timmy*, come here, you mad dog.'

'It's okay.' Kath let the dog lick her hand. She had thought many times that a dog would be a nice addition to her life, someone to come home to who was always pleased to see you and was never in the mood for an argument. But it wasn't fair, as she was out all day and sometimes at night. No life for a dog.

'He's still young and excited about everything,' the woman continued as she clipped the lead to his harness.

'I was like that once,' Kath said before she could stop herself.

The woman laughed and ran a hand through her hair, which was a similar colour to Timmy's coat. 'Weren't we all?'

She sidestepped Kath, and Timmy gave Kath a lingering look as they walked away.

'Maybe that's what I need,' Kath said out loud, 'a bit more excitement.' She chuckled as she remembered the chaotic events of the previous few weeks. Enough excitement to last a lifetime.

Being a DCI on active cases for many years had given her a degree of excitement along with danger and frustration, but she had craved a quieter existence. When the chance to head up a new cold case team had been offered, she had thought that it would be the answer to some of her prayers. More regular hours, less pressure. But her last two cases had provided her with hostage situations, violence and a revival of a personal issue that she'd thought was dead and buried. Amongst the chaos had been the reignition of a love affair forty years in the making with her childhood sweetheart and current chief superintendent. Unable to keep her past from leeching into her present, it had left her relationship at stalemate and she'd had no contact from Lenny in ten days.

She crushed her cigarette end underfoot and went back into the station.

The PCSO behind the desk grimaced as he put the phone down.

'That's not a happy face, John.'

'Mmm. Bloody poachers seem to be active again in Restonfield Woods.'

'Oh? Tell me more.'

John looked down at his scribbled note. 'Chap by the name of Richard Bastion, at Lavender Cottage. Said he's heard voices in the woods for the past three nights.' He paused and gave her an enquiring look. 'You live that way, don't you?'

'Sneaky. You know I do.' Kath's village, her cottage down the lane from the main street, butted up to the woods. She held out her hand. 'Give me his details. I'll call in on my way home.'

He handed her the piece of paper, grinning. 'Only if you're sure...'

'Like I said, sneaky.'

'Right place, right time. Cheers.'

She went upstairs, smiling and picturing Mr Bastion as a tall elderly man who was bound to bend her ear. Never volunteer for anything, a friend had once said.

Ruth was at the whiteboard as Kath entered the office. 'I've booked a room for us to talk to the parents, this afternoon at the Mallard's Rest.' She bit her lip when she saw the look on Kath's face. 'Oh, what?'

Kath waved her hand. 'Nothing, it's fine. Lenny and I had a pretty disastrous evening there a few weeks back.'

An uncomfortable and short dinner date with Kath snapping at Lenny for an innocent comment and storming out. Then there was the incident on the way home that set off a whole new chain of events. A memorable night for all the wrong reasons.

'How are things on that front?' Shirl asked, hoping she wasn't going to regret it but curious to know any details.

'I've no idea,' Kath said. 'I was a bit of a bitch to him the last time we saw each other and I haven't heard from him since.'

Bitchy. Jealous. Guilty. Feeling unsettled because he'd had dinner with his soon-to-be ex-wife. Schoolgirl error 101, leaving him on the offensive and her very much in disgrace.

Kath glanced at Marvin, who looked away, not wishing to engage in any conversation that was to do with his boss's love life.

A text came through, and Kath took the phone from her jacket pocket. 'Talk of the devil,' she announced, reading Lenny's text.

I'd like us to talk. You up for that?

'Divine intervention,' said Shirl, getting up to make drinks.

Ruth groaned, tapping the whiteboard pen against her thigh. 'We've had enough of that, thanks very much.'

It was only a week ago they'd had to rescue a crazed vicar from the jaws of madness. There was very little divine about the whole experience.

Kath's fingers hovered; the reply not quite formed in her head. Maybe it was time to talk.

Yes. Mine about 8?

The reply was instant.

Great.

'Well, that's my night planned.' Kath put her phone down on her desk and picked up the file. 'So, this is a case that Shirl, Ruth and I worked on previously, when it happened,' she said as they all skimmed the pages.

'Nice to have some fresh eyes this time,' said Ruth.

Kath nodded and pulled herself up to her full five-foot-four. 'Quick run through, then. Jennifer Blunt was reported missing in April 2010. Seventeen years old, lived in Bridgnorth with her parents and a younger brother. Wanted to be a vet and was doing her A-levels. She went for a sleepover at a friend's house, or that's what she told her parents. The friend, Samantha, covered for her because she was meeting a "mystery man", as Samantha told us eventually.'

'Young girls love their secrets,' said Ruth.

'Indeed. According to Samantha, that night had been going to be a special night with the guy.'

'Sleeping with him for the first time?' Marvin offered.

'That was implied, yes.' Kath replied. 'She was supposed to get back to Samantha's house in the early morning. She never turned up. Samantha panicked, rang the parents and then the police got involved. Because no one knew who this guy was, we had no real starting point. Our colleagues suggested to the parents that Jennifer might have run off with this man. Parents vehemently denied this possible scenario, saying it was just not something Jennifer would have done.'

'Even though she kept this secret from them?' asked Byron.

Kath gave a half smile. 'They were adamant it wasn't like her, and friends agreed. Samantha eventually confessed they had been hanging out at a local pub, my local pub actually, in Restonfield.'

'The weird one or the regular one?' Ruth asked, grinning. She knew the answer but glanced at Marvin, knowing his interest would be on high alert.

'You have a weird pub?' Marvin sat forward, eager for more information.

'Yes, Marvin, we do. But we'll get to that later.' Kath pulled a face at Ruth. 'As I was saying, the girls had been in The Bell several times.'

'We were always in pubs when we shouldn't have been, back in the day.' Shirl leaned back in her chair and stretched, looking at the others. 'What, no? Oh, just me, then.'

Everyone laughed.

Kath cleared her throat. 'Anyway, all the regulars at the pub were interviewed, which gave us nothing.'

'When did you realise she hadn't run away? That she wasn't just a missing person?' Byron asked.

'When we found her body with the other two,' Ruth said. crisply.

Byron's cheeks reddened. 'Oh. Right.'

'Layla Mountford was our second missing girl, one year later,' Kath continued. 'Sixteen, left school. Worked three part-time jobs including glass clearing and odd jobs at The Bell.'

'She suddenly gave up her two day jobs but actually seemed to have more money available to her,' Shirl took over. 'Friends said she'd hinted at an older man she was seeing who liked to look after her.'

'That doesn't sound good.' said Marvin.

Shirl continued, 'We canvassed the pub again. Still nothing concrete. But this time there was no hint of her running off. She just vanished. Finished a shift at The Bell, went outside to wait for a taxi home.'

'But she never called one,' Ruth took up the story. 'No one saw or heard from her after she left the pub. Another year went by. Nothing more about Jennifer or Layla. Then Sophia Martin went missing.'

'And all hell broke loose,' said Shirl, sitting forward and leaning her arms on her thighs.

'Because...?' Marvin's impatience was growing.

'We had a suspect,' said Kath.

Marvin and Byron looked at each other.

'We liked him a lot, pulled him in for questioning and got nothing. We couldn't hold him or charge him.'

'Who was it?' Marvin asked.

'Rafferty Quartermaine.' Kath threw her file on the desk and sighed, the memory of the frustration seeping back into her body.

'Cool name,' Marvin muttered.

'Difficult to sign on your credit card, though,' said Shirl, trying to lighten the mood.

Kath raised an eyebrow and stared at her.

Shirl gave a forced smile. 'I can see our leader is as frustrated now as back on the original case.'

'So, fill us in.' Marvin grabbed a pen, tapping it lightly on his desk.

Ruth held up her hands. 'I'll pick this up. Rafferty Quartermaine is the only son of Clarissa and Farraday Quartermaine. Privileged, arrogant, money coming from all directions from hedge funds, oil interests and property development. A mummy's boy that really doesn't get on with his mummy but needs to keep her sweet if he's going to inherit the family fortune and the pile known as Quartermaine Manor.'

'So, was he protected by the family name?' Byron tucked his hair behind his shoulders, resisting the temptation to move his fingers over the keyboard to find out for himself.

Shirl and Ruth looked at each other and then at Kath.

'Not exactly,' Kath said. 'He wasn't given any special treatment. He was fully co-operative and, although I really liked him for the murders at first, he seemed genuinely shocked by what had happened to the girls and the fact that they had been found on the Quartermaine estate.'

'We just didn't really take to him as a human being,' Shirl clarified, getting up and moving to the kettle.

Kath gave a wry smile. 'We can't just arrest people because we don't like them.' She nodded at Shirl, who was holding up an empty mug.

'Was he the only real suspect, then?' Byron asked.

Kath nodded. 'One, he was at The Bell when all the girls were there.' She held up her fingers as she made her point. 'Two, the bodies were found, as you know, in the grounds of the estate, and three, and considered most important to us, he had a penchant for much younger girls.'

'You're not talking paedophile, are you?' Marvin screwed his face up in disgust.

Kath shook her head. 'No. His lady friends, for want of a better term, were all legal age, it's just that he was ten years or so older than them. In physical age anyway.' She reached for the mug of coffee that Shirl was holding out to her. 'Rafferty has an almost childlike naivety about him mixed with an arrogance that he can't quite pull off. He's a competent businessman but not very likeable.'

Marvin was flipping through pages in his file. 'So, the girls were discovered by four boys... Oh, bloody hell.' He looked up at Ruth, his face pale.

'Yeah,' said Ruth. 'Dead of night, they found a hole in the fence on the edge of the estate, thought they'd scare themselves with an adventure in the woods. Came to the folly—'

'Folly?'

'A stone tower, very old, built by one of the Quartermaine ancestors. They are usually just a stone tower with nothing inside, no roof, but this had a spiral of stone steps leading up to... I guess you'd call it a kind of mezzanine floor. That's where they found two skeletons and a decomposing corpse.' Ruth crossed her arms and looked down at the floor.

'That's quite an adventure,' said Byron quietly.

'The boys were all pretty traumatised,' Kath interjected. 'They couldn't tell us anything.'

Shirl sat down and took a sip of her tea as Kath continued.

'We'll look at re-interviewing the boys, or rather young men as they are now, but I'm not hopeful we'll get anything useful. I suggest we start at Quartermaine Manor. Rafferty still lives on the estate, and I don't think he'll be leaving any time soon. He has one of the cottages away from the main house. He'll probably be shocked that we're reopening the case, but it's Clarissa we may have problems with...again.' Kath let the sentence hang as Marvin and Byron sat up straight.

'To that end, I've asked Lane to join us on this one.'

Lane and her psychic abilities added an extra dimension to the team dynamic, mixing the ethereal with the nitty gritty of cold hard facts. When she had joined them for their first cold case only a few months previously, she had sensed that Byron had some sensibilities he had yet to explore.

'When is she coming? Is it today? Is she staying with you again?' Marvin straightened his tie, his eyes flicking from the window to the doorway.

'Calm down, wee boy,' said Ruth, grinning and using Lane's pet name for him.

Kath laced her fingers in front of her stomach. 'We haven't worked out the logistics yet.'

'Um, so...Clarissa?' Byron swayed in his seat, a sense of urgency threatening to overtake him.

Kath sighed and exchanged glances with Ruth and Shirl. 'You're an honorary detective; go do what it is that you do on your magic keyboard.' She waved her hand at him. He grinned back and began typing.

Ruth pursed her lips. 'Please don't say magic again.'

|3|

Kath coaxed her Audi quattro into a tight parking space, turned off the engine and removed herself from the car with ease. Ruth cursed under her breath as she tried to extricate her five-foot-nine frame without damaging the car next to them. The October sun was still doing its best to warm the early afternoon air.

'It is too nice a day to be doing this,' Kath remarked, pushing open the entrance door to The Mallard's Rest.

The old coaching house was now a popular pub with an established reputation for excellent food, and it was a place close enough to the addresses of the three sets of parents. Ruth had managed to secure the room at the rear of the pub for their meeting, calling the parents to explain that they were looking again at the investigation into their murdered children.

'Any day is a crap day for what we're about to inflict on these people,' Ruth replied, following Kath to the bar.

Kath spoke quietly to a woman behind the bar, who pointed to a door and nodded. A notice reading Private Meeting was secured to the centre of the door. Kath pushed it open. The French doors at the back of the room gave a view out onto the large gardens. Mismatched armchairs in tartan and tweed fabrics were dotted around the room. On a long green Chesterfield sofa sat two men and two women. The other couple sat in chairs close by. The three men and three women stared at Ruth and Kath as they entered. Everyone was nursing a glass. Kath guessed some of them were probably alcohol. She moved forward.

'Thank you all for meeting with us.'

Kath and Ruth sat down in two of the tartan wingback chairs facing the parents.

Ailsa Mountford sat forward, seemingly the spokesperson for the group. She wore a formal trouser suit, her blonde hair framing eyes that were steady and focused. 'I'm sure I speak for all of us'—she quickly glanced at the others, who remained silent—'we're a bit shaken by your phone call but glad that you're reopening the case.'

Ruth crossed her legs and gave a small smile that she hoped showed a good mix of consideration and determination. 'As I explained on the phone, now we have a dedicated cold case team, we can focus on devoting our time to finding out what happened to your girls, but we recognise that this cannot be easy for any of you.'

The six appeared stoic in their silence, but Kath knew all too well what was going on in their brains and their guts. Only a few weeks ago, she'd had that exact same awful realisation of her past inserting itself into her present, like a speeding train coming out of nowhere.

'So, how does this all work, then?' Dennis Mountford asked.

'Well, we look over all the statements and the evidence...'

John Blunt held up his hand, and Kath stopped speaking. 'Are you saying you missed something?'

There was an underlying aggression in his tone, and Kath knew she had to tread carefully. She crossed her legs slowly.

'No, not at all. But we have a new team now purely focused on cold cases and can dedicate all our resources to looking into what happened.' She wasn't ready to tell them that a psychic was joining them.

'You'll be seeing him though, won't you?' Angela Martin gripped her husband's hand. Kath knew Rafferty Quartermaine would crop up, but it was sooner than she had anticipated.

'If you're referring to Mr Quartermaine, then yes, we will be interviewing him.'

'That bastard knows something.' Angela's body trembled as the words tumbled out of her. 'He must still be your chief suspect.'

'Like I said, we will be looking at everything and everybody again and we will keep you informed of any developments.'

'Families like that always have the law in their pocket. Think they're above everyone else because they have money and live in a big—'

'Hush now.' Paul Martin stroked his wife's arm with his other hand. Angela shrugged him off and released her hand from his.

John Blunt looked over at Angela and then at Kath, sighing as he adjusted his sitting position. 'Why call us all together? Surely we could have done this over the phone and avoided this upset?'

The truth was that he hadn't wanted to come. The six parents had all met up before, during the original investigation, thinking it would be cathartic, a bonding exercise. Angela Martin had been the perfect hostess until her seventh glass of wine, when she had cornered John in the garden and tried to kiss him. His gentle but firm rejection had left spiteful words pouring from her mouth.

Kath had felt empathy and sorrow walking into the room; Now, her patience was wearing thin. She noticed Ruth's foot bobbing up and down, her face stern. She knew they were both thinking the same thing.

'It was a courtesy,' Kath said. 'Perhaps it was selfish of me to suggest this. I felt it was only right to look you all in the eye and assure you of our absolute resolve in finding out who did this. Gatherings like this can sometimes spark a memory that may have been overlooked at the time. I was trying to cover all the bases.'

Angela screwed up her face. 'We don't meet up every week like some sad club and talk about our murdered children. I mean, who does that?'

Kath gave what she hoped was an encouraging smile despite her fraying temper. 'People have to find their own path through tragedy. I apologise for the upset.'

Kath stood up abruptly, and Ruth followed.

'We will be investigating to our fullest capacity. Thank you all for your time.' Kath nodded in their general direction and turned to leave. As she pulled open the door, harder than she meant to, a male voice cut the silence.

'We really do appreciate your efforts. We're all a little raw, all the emotions coming down on top of us again. I am sure I speak for all of us in that respect.' Paul Martin was standing as Kath and Ruth turned around, an apologetic smile on his face.

'We will do our very best for you and your girls.'

Kath marched outside, sidestepping the tables of customers finishing their meals and drinks, then yanked the car door open as the lock beep sounded, narrowly missing the car next to hers. Ruth got in and secured her seat belt as Kath reversed quickly and then accelerated out of the parking area, swerving to avoid a pheasant as she pulled out onto the road.

'That went well,' Ruth muttered.

Kath gripped the steering wheel. 'Maybe I made the wrong call.'

'It's done now. Let's just get on with it.'

Kath pushed her foot farther down on the accelerator, and Ruth gripped the door handle.

| 4 |

Kath lifted the fox head knocker on the door of Lavender Cottage, wondering again why she'd volunteered to stop by and take details. Every light seemed to be on, every window illuminated.

He's going to be old and miserable and want to bend my ear for an hour.

She heard footsteps approach the door. She pulled her warrant card from her pocket as the door opened. They stared at each other, both seemingly surprised.

'Can I help you'—he peered at the card held up in front of him—'DCI Fortune?'

'Richard Bastion?'

All the saliva had drained from her mouth as she took in the man before her. Old and miserable? She could not have been more wrong. As he nodded, she felt a flutter deep in her belly. A head of white hair, wet and pulled back from his high forehead. Blue eyes that sparkled as he smiled. A neat salt-and-pepper beard revealed a set of perfect white teeth, and as he smiled, the small crow's feet wrinkled around his eyes.

If he wants to bend my ear all night, bring it on.

'You phoned... about men in the woods?'

He laughed—deep, throaty, sexy.

'Wow, does that warrant a visit from a DCI?'

Kath stared at him, focusing on the single bead of water just under his ear, unable to form a cohesive sentence.

He's fresh from the shower. Get a grip, Fortune.

'We're actually neighbours and you're on my way home, so I said I'd call in.'

'Oh, okay. Please come in.' He opened the door wide.

As she passed close to him, she breathed in his scent combined with sandalwood and citrus. The small lounge was homely, the fireplace wall stripped back to brick, several lamps dotted around the room giving a warm feel against the early evening.

'Are you renting?' She turned to look at him as he closed the door.

'Is this part of the interview?'

Stop smiling at me; I can't concentrate.

'Police officer's curiosity. We're bonding to make you more comfortable.'

Bonding? Where the hell did that come from?

'Ah, well, I'm very comfortable, thank you.' He moved closer to her. 'Yes, I've been here about three months. Thinking I might buy in the area if the right property comes up. And I like the look of the neighbours. That's a big plus.'

'It's a nice village, very friendly.'

What the hell are you waffling about? Get the statement and go home.

'Good to know.'

Silence fell between them. The bead of water was staying put, and she had the image of her licking it, then moving her lips across his beard.

'Would you like a drink? I was just going to put some coffee on.' He pointed at the kitchen through an archway, his black vest top revealing a smattering of grey chest hair.

'No, I have...no, not at the moment.'

He put his hands in his jeans pockets. 'So, shall I tell you what I think I know?'

'Yes.'

His face was serious. 'Started three nights ago. Noise woke me. I sleep at the back, where the woods are.' His cheeks flushed. 'But you probably already know the woods are over the back if you live near here anyway.'

She smiled. 'Go on.'

'I got up, didn't put any lights on. Heard voices, thought I saw a torchlight. Then it went quiet. The same on the next two nights. There were problems with poachers where I used to live, so it kind of feels the same, rather than just kids messing about.'

His soft Scottish lilt made the ordinary words seem like the telling of a fairytale to Kath's ears.

'Okay.' Kath nodded. 'I'll relay your information. There is a list of usual suspects, so they may get a visit.'

Silence again.

'So, you say we're neighbours?' He looked enquiringly at her, head at a slight tilt.

Kath didn't give out her home address on a whim, but she felt more than okay with this man knowing she was less than a mile away from him. 'I'm at Christina Cottage, just down the lane and off to the left.'

'Oh.' His eyes widened. 'Nice place. I was thinking of seeing if the owner wanted to sell. Just the kind of place I'm looking for. I often run past there. Good route.'

He runs. Of course he runs, hence the lean body.

'I'm not on the market.'

She pushed a strand of hair behind her ear. 'I mean, the house isn't up for sale. At the moment.'

'Well, I'm patient.' He grinned. 'Perhaps you'll get some action in the bedroom.'

She blushed and stared, open-mouthed.

His hands flew from his pockets, trying to wave away the faux pas. 'I mean, you might hear something yourself, in the woods, from your place.'

They both laughed at the same time, releasing the awkwardness but fighting for something more to say.

He has beautiful hands. Strong hands.

'As police interviews go, this is probably one of your weirdest, right?'

'In my job, I'm used to the weird and the wonderful.' She was afraid of making any further stupid comments. 'I'll let the station know what we've talked about and leave you to your evening.' She took the few steps to the door.

He moved to a small bureau in the window. 'Here's my card if you need to call, in the middle of the night or... not that I think you can't take care of yourself.'

She held onto the door handle, holding out her other hand for the card. 'I've done a few years in the Armed Response Unit; there's not much that scares me.'

Except for my emotional suitcase of unresolved issues.

'Oh. That's impressive. I wasn't trying to do the knight in shining armour thing, but...' He smiled apologetically.

But I think you were, and I'm okay with that, thank you very much.

'Even though I'm on my own, I can take care of myself.' She stopped, suddenly remembering Lenny was coming round. 'I really have to go.' She opened the door reluctantly and stepped onto the small driveway.

'Well...' Richard stood in the doorway. 'You may be handy with a gun, but what about a spade?' He gestured to the card in her hand. She looked at it.

'You're a landscape gardener.' She smiled, thinking about her wild back garden. 'Duly noted.' Kath waved the card at him. 'If you ever fancy a change of career, you have an interesting questioning technique.'

She turned and walked to her car, hoping he was watching her and fighting the urge to turn around. She tucked the card into her pocket and unlocked the car. As she got in and reached for the seatbelt, she couldn't help but look back at him still looking at her.

He stayed in the doorway until the car was out of sight.

It was past six when she got home in the gloom of the approaching evening light, but the weather couldn't dampen her mood as she set about putting lights on and changing into jeans and a low-neck sweatshirt. In the kitchen, she reached for her phone as the kettle boiled.

'Let's have a look at you, then, Richard Bastion.'

The kettle clicked off without her noticing as she passed over his Facebook, Instagram and Twitter feeds. She was so engrossed in reading about his development of a garden for a friend of Prince Charles that she jumped at the sound of car tyres on the gravel drive. She put her phone down on the table and got to the door before Lenny knocked.

'Hi.'

Lenny had got a funny little sketch all prepared, rehearsing it on the drive over. But he instinctively felt it was a bad idea now that she stood before him. He felt he couldn't be as natural and open as he used to be with her. The relationship had changed. Kath had changed. He waited on the doorstep, like a vampire.

'Come on in.'

Kath left the door open and walked back to the kitchen, Lenny closing the door behind himself and following.

She opened the fridge. 'Low-alcohol lager or coffee?' She grabbed a beer for herself and waited.

He'd thought about bringing chocolates or flowers and dismissed the idea, felt the attempt would be shot down, ridiculed. Is this where they were going? Afraid of making any kind of conciliatory gesture?

'Beer sounds good. Well, not good, but...' He spread his hands and smiled.

'I'm getting used to the taste.' She handed him a bottle.

'Given up wine?'

'Seem to have lost the taste for it.' She had imbibed far too much of it during the last few months and now it had connections to events she didn't want to remember. With her decreased appetite and letting go of the wine, the weight was continuing to drop.

They each twisted off the tops from the bottles and sipped, possible conversation topics racing through their heads but failing to reach their mouths. Kath moved to the back door, opened it and lit a cigarette. Lenny propped himself against the worktop, glancing at her upturned phone on the table.

'Richard Bastion? Who's he, then?'

Kath blew her smoke up into the sky.

I don't want to talk to you about him.

'He phoned in a situation in the woods at the back of his house. I called in on my way home to see what was what. Possible poacher activity.'

'He lives round here, then?'

'In the village.' She looked at him and indicated the direction with her bottle.

As a possible work opening had presented itself, he continued. Safe territory. 'How's the team after the events of the past few weeks?'

'You mean the case of the woman who's been silent for forty years and the crazy vicar? They're okay. We're all okay. Thanks for asking.' She turned her body back to face the garden.

He nodded. 'Good, good. You've wrapped up two cases in as many months. Not bad for a new team.'

'We'll be getting a reputation for efficiency if we don't watch it.'

'Your determination was never in question,' Lenny said, feeling the moment slipping away where he would have to voice his concerns about their own relationship. If they still had one. 'What's the next case?'

Kath blew a plume of smoke into the night, aimed the dwindling butt at the lawn and shut the door. 'Rapunzel murders.'

Lenny coughed and slammed his fist against his chest as his beer went down the wrong way. 'Clarissa Quartermaine? You'll need some luck with that.'

Kath put down her bottle and folded her arms defensively. 'I'm calling Lane in to help.'

She saw his body tighten at the mention of the psychic's name. Kath had asked Lenny for Lane's help on an active case four years ago and he'd reluctantly let her have her way. They got results, but it didn't sit well with Lenny's need for concrete facts. Kath had tried to explain about energies and resonance. He tried to be open-minded, but it only stretched so far. Now she was in charge of her relatively new cold case team and the first thing she had done was contact the psychic for help with the ten-year-old case of the murder of little Daisy Prospero. Lane's abilities had helped them close the case, albeit not the solution anyone would have anticipated.

Kath didn't want to fight, but unease was growing inside her. Their personal relationship might be rocky, but she didn't want any more of it spilling over into the job.

Lenny sipped his beer. 'I think that's a good call.'

The silence threatened to overwhelm them.

'How's Susan?'

'She's okay, thanks. We've put the house on the market. She's going to move to Bristol to be nearer her parents, something that we had talked about before we decided on the divorce.'

Kath nodded and took a deep breath. 'Where are we going, then?' She picked up her bottle and drained it, turning away from him, scared to see the look on his face.

'Nothing's changed for me, Kath. It's you that's different. I still feel the same about you as I did when we were fifteen. I think it has to be you that decides where we go from here.'

Her immediate response was to fight back, bite back, disagree. But she swallowed the words and knew he was right. Being defensive wasn't going to move them sideways or forward. 'I've let my past get in the way of our present,' she said carefully. 'I'm still working on that, so how about we just be nice, be friends and kind of pause things?' She didn't think it was the response he'd been hoping for, but it was all she could offer at present.

His body released the tension, and he sagged a little into an easy stance. He put down his bottle. 'I'm okay with that. Sounds like a plan.'

They smiled at each other, and he moved forward and kissed her lightly on the lips. She accepted the gesture and ran a hand down his arm.

'I'll be off, then. Thanks for the beer.'

'Good to see you.'

As Lenny closed the front door, Kath picked up her phone and stared at the face of Richard Bastion.

| 5 |

8th October 2019

'Morning, guys.' Kath yawned through the two words and put her bag down on her desk.

'I've just cleaned that,' Ruth pointed out as she handed Kath a mug of coffee.

'I'll be careful, Mum.' Kath saluted her and took the mug. 'So, who's the lucky gentleman we're interviewing?'

Byron had been tasked with tracking down the four boys, now in their twenties, who had found the three bodies in the folly. It was a long shot that they would have anything else to add to their statements of that night, but Kath felt it was worth a try.

'It's Dylan Paxton,' Byron said. 'He works at a local garden centre. Dhandi Samra is in Edinburgh studying medicine, Kaden Jones lives on the Isle of Wight helping out at a caravan park and Andrew Wallis moved to New Zealand with his dad after his mum died.'

Kath perched on the edge of her desk and sipped her coffee. 'One out of four. I guess we work with what we have.'

'Let's hope he's mentally strong enough for another interview,' said Ruth, sitting down and cradling her mug of tea.

They all took a moment to think about the impact. Kath had seen, all too often, the effects of a traumatic event on children and teenagers. Some were naturally resilient, others had suffered with mental health issues in trying to process what they had stumbled upon or witnessed. It was the worst part of this new role—raking up the past when people had tried valiantly to move forward.

'Looks like he's been pretty stable since he left school,' Byron offered. 'Worked at the garden centre cafe in the school holidays, worked his way up to cafe supervisor. Still lives at home.'

'So how did they come across the bodies?' Marvin asked. He'd skimmed the report, but it was always better for him to hear Kath, Ruth and Shirl elaborate.

Ruth signalled to Kath, who nodded for her to tell the story.

Ruth cleared her throat. 'They were just a group of good lads getting good grades. They went to Andrew's house one night to study, who lived closest to the Quartermaine estate. Basically, they were teenage lads. They snuck out on a dare, thought they'd scare each other.'

'All will become apparent about the Quartermaine estate,' Shirl butted in.

Ruth glared at her, and Shirl sank in her chair, waving her hand for Ruth to carry on.

'Anyway,' Ruth continued, 'they left a note in the summerhouse, which is where Andrew had his teenage hangout and study area, saying they had gone out to get some air—'

'When they could have just opened the bloody summerhouse door,' muttered Shirl. She pushed a hand through her blonde hair and sighed.

'Andrew's dad went out around ten to wind up the evening, found the note and set about looking for the boys.'

Kath picked up the story. 'As the house was close to the Quartermaine grounds, the boys cut across the fields and found a hole in the fence.'

Marvin shuddered, aware of what was coming next.

'They found the folly deep in the woods on the estate and went inside, in the pitch dark, lots of mucking about by all accounts and all fairly light-hearted until Dhandi, full of the bravado of youth, climbed up the stone staircase to the upper section. And suddenly it wasn't a game anymore.' Kath stopped and took a breath.

'Dhandi called them all up. Andrew had had the foresight to grab a torch. They could see the skeletons and the corpse lying beside them. One of them threw up, can't remember which one, and they all ran out.'

'Hell of an adventure,' said Marvin quietly.

'Indeed.' Kath drank the rest of her tepid coffee. 'Statements are all in the file. All pretty much the same, nothing that stands out.'

'I guess Dylan isn't really going to be able to add anything, is he?' Ruth asked as a question, but it seemed more like a statement of fact.

'Probably not, but it will put us back at the scene through his words,' Shirl said, not feeling quite so jovial anymore.

'I have a suggestion.' Byron had been so quiet they'd almost forgotten he was in the room.

'Happy to hear it,' said Kath, smiling at him to continue.

'My mum does regression hypnosis therapy, you know, taking people back to an event in a safe and controlled environment. Might be worth a shot.'

Everyone sat a little more upright, and Kath pushed herself up off the desk edge.

'As in maybe he saw something but doesn't exactly recall that it might be anything significant,' Kath ran through the idea out loud.

'Smells, sounds, tastes even. She's worked with victims of trauma. She's really good,' Byron added.

Byron's mum, Cassandra, had many strings to her bow with crystal healing, tarot card readings, massage therapy and life coaching to name but a few. She had a small shop in Much Wenlock that sold all manner of New Age items, with a room at the back for private consultations. She was tall, like Ruth, with dreadlocks, sparkling eyes and a svelte body that an Olympic athlete would be proud to have.

'I might be being a bit thick,' Marvin ventured, 'but why would you want to relive something so traumatic?'

Byron nodded his understanding. 'I get what you're saying, but Mum says we need to confront the things that frighten us, the things that make us afraid in the dead of night. Fear takes our power away. If we face it and deal with it, then it can't frighten us anymore.'

They all turned to look at Shirl who was about to confront one of her own fears. She and Cassandra had signed up to do a charity skydive in a matter of weeks, raising money for two charities close to their hearts.

'Yeah, yeah.' Shirl waved her hand dismissively. 'Don't look at me like that. It seemed like a good idea at the time.'

'I'm proud of you.' Ruth stood up and collected empty mugs from desks. 'It's a brave thing to do at your age.' She moved out of Shirl's way as Shirl searched on her desk for something to throw at her colleague.

'You're both doing really well raising the money.' Byron had set up the donation pages on the internet and was monitoring the amounts. 'You and Mum have raised over four thousand pounds between you.'

Shirl smiled, then pursed her lips and nodded. 'Maybe we can just give the charities the money and that'll be that.'

Kath laughed. 'I think you're actually supposed to go through with the challenge. That's the point.'

'The decision is genuine, but the reality, like the ground, is rushing to meet me. What a bloody crazy idea.' Shirl sighed.

'Mum said that you were the one that came up with it.'

Byron instantly regretted his words as Shirl stared at him.

'I think your dear mother plied me with wine until I didn't know what I was saying. And surely you can't go through with something if you're intoxicated?' Shirl's face brightened.

'I think that only applies to the event itself. Oh, hush my mouth.' Kath grabbed her cigarettes and lighter from her bag. 'Time for a sharp exit, I think.'

As Kath headed down the stairs, she heard Ruth trying to talk Shirl out of turning up to the skydive absolutely hammered and smiled to herself. She nodded to the PCSO coming into the station and headed round to the back of the building.

As she smoked her cigarette in the relative quiet of the cold morning, she couldn't help but grin as she thought about the previous evening and her meeting with Richard. An attractive, intelligent man who was stirring up all kinds of emotional responses. She'd had a few partners over the years, none of them lasting very long and usually other police officers. Ruth had often joked about setting her up with one of her husband's single dentist friends, but Kath usually didn't feel the need for a sexual connection. Relationships often got complicated after a couple of months and settled into abject complacency. But this? This was something altogether new and exciting.

'Are you singing?' Shirl rounded the side of the building, lit her cigarette and smiled enquiringly at Kath. 'Seriously, what gives?'

'Smoke your fag and shut up,' Kath replied, smiling back, not realising she'd been singing out loud.

'Had to get out of there.' Shirl signalled to the upstairs office. 'All this talk of flinging myself out of an aeroplane at stupid something feet is starting to really scare me.'

They smoked in silence, watching two young boys push their bikes through the dew-soaked grass.

'Maybe it'll be a bad weather day and they won't let us jump.'

'Will you stop? You're doing a great thing for charity and you'll be fine. People do it every day.' Kath ground her cigarette butt into the grass. 'C'mon, let's get back to the case.'

'I'm just saying, you never know what's going to happen,' Shirl mumbled, following her boss.

|6|

'By the way, how did last night go?'

'What?' Kath changed gear, Richard Bastion's face popping into her head.

'Lenny? He was going to yours last night?' Shirl moved the passenger seat forward.

Kath breathed a relieved sigh. 'Lenny, right. It was okay. Cordial.'

'Cordial? Mmm, not a word I would associate with the love of your life. So, what went down?'

'We chatted, we're friends. We're giving ourselves space. Satisfied?'

'I suppose it'll have to do,' Shirl muttered, knowing the subject was closed to further interrogation.

Kath lightly slapped Shirl's thigh. 'You're just in a bad mood because we're off to see Clarissa.'

'Naturally, because she's...'

Kath held her hand up quickly before moving it back to the gear stick. 'No excuses. You chose the case. You don't like it, tough.'

Shirl shut her mouth. It was true. When Kath had suggested she pick the next case, it hadn't been the first one that had sprung to mind from the multitude of A-Z files in the boxes. But as she had flicked towards the latter end of the alphabet, Clarissa's reedy voice had found its way into her head.

'She makes my buttocks clench.'

'Too much information,' said Kath, laughing and swerving to avoid a pothole.

Shirl huffed. 'She does this thing where she looks at me and I kind of want to confess stuff.'

'That's generally our job.'

The car seemed to be on autopilot, traversing the narrow lanes once they had turned off the main road. It had been seven years since Clarissa had declared the innocence of her only son. Kath was expecting a repeat performance. She had decided they would not announce their arrival; some people were better caught unaware in her experience.

The huge wrought iron gates looked as if they had received a lick of paint since the last visit, but the stone pillars they were attached to were crumbling and Kath guessed the gates were permanently open. The half-mile driveway was studded with deep holes and weeds and the wild gardens either side threatened to encroach on the earthen approach road. Brambles scrambled over tired camellias and clematis tendrils. Wildflower seed heads fought to be seen in their last autumn gasp amongst the knee-high grasses. Gnarled oaks and willow trees reached out to clasp each other as the house came into view.

'I'm still expecting Wednesday Addams to appear firing slingshots at us,' Shirl said quietly.

Kath stopped the car to the left of the house, the driveway continuing down to Rafferty Quartermaine's cottage—a less imposing structure with a semblance of order in the low-walled garden area.

They got out of the car and walked to the huge wooden front door.

'You'd think she'd fork out for a gardener for this. Hey, get it? Fork out?' Shirl tittered at her own joke.

'Maybe she likes it wild and untamed,' Kath replied, reaching for the bell pull. Richard Bastion's face came into her head again as she thought about how he would love to get his creative juices working on the landscape. Her own back garden was beginning to resemble what she could see around her, albeit in miniature form, and an idea began to fizz in her brain.

The door swung open almost as soon as the bell sounded. Kath suspected the owner had seen them arrive.

Clarissa Quartermaine was an imposing figure. Tall and thin, with a smile that said welcome and beware. Her skirt hem brushed the top of polished boots, the thigh-length blouse giving further impression of a spindly creature that would break in a high wind.

'Detective Inspector Fortune, how nice to see you again.'

Clarissa's voice was deep with a gravelly undertone. Shirl shuddered.

'Hello, Mrs Quartermaine. It's actually Detective *Chief* Inspector now. I hope we're not disturbing you.'

'Disturbance is a part of the natural order. Please come in.' She stood aside to admit them, giving Shirl a curt nod of acknowledgement as they passed each other.

'She's forgotten my bloody name,' Shirl growled under her breath as they stood in the hallway.

'Don't antagonise her before we've even started,' Kath whispered.

'I'll leave that til later, then, shall I?'

Clarissa closed the door and strode towards a sitting room, the double doors wide open and revealing the fireplace still cradling ashes from the night before.

'Please have a seat.' Clarissa gestured to a floral overstuffed sofa, and Shirl and Kath sank into it.

People were usually mildly alarmed when detectives showed up at their doors. Clarissa showed no signs of anxiety or agitation.

'Can I offer you something to drink?'

Kath knew Shirl was imagining pots of steaming herbal brews filled with hemlock and wolfsbane and jumped in first. 'Thank you, but we'll get straight to business.'

Clarissa sat in a wooden chair and folded her hands in her lap.

'I now lead a team working on cold cases, and our next investigation is going to be the murder of the three young girls found on your estate.'

Clarissa looked down, rubbing her thumbs together. 'I see.' She raised her head and looked at Kath. 'I will, of course, cooperate fully. Those poor parents still need answers.'

A silence fell between the three women.

'Don't look so surprised, detectives. I was happy to help seven years ago, as I am now, but I'm not sure I can add anything more to the investigation that you don't already know.'

'Why do you think the killer dumped the bodies on your land, in your folly?' Shirl went straight in.

Clarissa looked to the large window to her left framed by dark green velvet drapes and out to the woodland beyond. She pressed her lips together, taking her time to formulate an answer. 'My estate is over forty acres. As I said at the time, part of the old perimeter wall had collapsed and I had chain-link fencing erected as a temporary measure. You found the hole where the links had been cut. Objectively, it was a perfect hiding place. They may never have been discovered if it hadn't been for those boys trespassing.'

Kath had to admit her reasoning was sound, but she wasn't about to let it drop. 'Have you taken any steps to prevent anyone else straying onto your land?'

Clarissa smiled. 'The boys did not stray, they made a deliberate choice to trespass on my land. It was not accidental but a... happening that led to the discovery of the girls. The wall has been repaired and extra height added. It would be difficult to get in now apart from via the driveway, as you entered. I'm sure you saw that my gates need replacing—the next job on the list.'

Kath nodded. 'I see your son married at the end of 2012.'

Clarissa's face took on an amused expression at the mention of Rafferty. 'Yes. Fenella Williams-Mackie was always a sound choice. It just took a little while to get them together.' She brushed her hair from her face.

A sound choice? Pushed into the marriage to stop him picking up young girls, more like.

Kath sat forward. 'I would like to come back with another couple of members of my team to look around the folly again. Do we have your blessing?' She needed her permission to poke around the estate with Lane;

otherwise, it would be a whole mess of paperwork that would stall the investigation. She hoped her choice of words would elicit a favourable response.

'That would be acceptable, but I would appreciate some notice. I have various animals running wild through the estate. I wouldn't want you or your team to startle them and cause you any undue issues.'

Kath contained her relief and pushed herself up off the plush cushion. Shirl followed suit, glad to be leaving.

'Thank you for your assistance. We'll be looking at everyone again, plus all our evidence, with fresh eyes.'

Clarissa made a humming sound and stood up, brushing her long fingers down her skirt. They all moved into the hallway. Kath was about to bring up Rafferty again, but Shirl jumped in ahead of her.

'We'll be contacting your son, of course.'

'Of course, but try to contain your disappointment when you find as little as you did last time.' Clarissa opened the door and stood aside. 'They have a son, Brocken. A gifted and sensitive child. Please don't upset him.'

'We will do our very best,' Kath said and walked outside.

'Thank you for your time,' Shirl said as she passed by.

They stood at the car, looking across to Rafferty's cottage.

'Are we leaving him for another day?' Shirl asked.

Kath opened her door. 'Yes. Let Clarissa tell him we've been around.'

As they drove back towards the entrance gates, a black Porsche turned in off the road and moved slowly past them. Astonishment crossed Rafferty Quartermaine's face as the cars inched past each other.

'Guess we've lost the element of surprise,' said Shirl.

Rafferty burst through the door of the manor house. 'Mother? Mother!'

Clarissa appeared in the doorway of the drawing room. 'You were not born in a barn, Rafferty; close the door.'

Clarissa's eyes narrowed as he did as he was told.

'What did they want? Why are they here?' He gestured towards the driveway, then put his hands on his hips, waiting for a suitable answer.

'It seems they are reopening the case of the murdered girls.'

The colour drained from his face. 'Oh my god. What do we do? We can't—'

'Shut up. We do nothing. They know nothing, just as they did seven years ago.'

'Did they question you? What did you say?' Rafferty's hands fluttered between stroking his neck and pushing his fine hair back from his forehead.

Clarissa remained completely still. 'They came to inform me about the restart of the investigation. They will be back to look around and they'll want to interview you, obviously. Keep your head straight and your mouth shut and it will all be fine. Understood?'

Rafferty stared at the wood panelling, his hands moving as if unconnected to any other part of his body.

'*Rafferty.*'

He jumped and stared at his mother.

'I said, do you understand?'

He nodded.

'Good. There's nothing new for them to find. I'm sure they're just as ignorant and stupid as they were back then. I may just have to keep an eye on them when they decide they want to visit, steer them in the right direction. We are protected and that cannot be undone.' She turned and walked back into the drawing room.

'Are you really sure they won't find out?' Rafferty muttered softly to the empty hall.

|7|

'I'm just saying, Halloween is a big deal,' Byron said, ducking behind his monitors.

'Oh no. What have we just walked into?' Shirl asked as she entered the office and threw her bag on her desk.

Ruth was at the whiteboard, adding photos of the three girls to the wall space above. She pointed at Byron. 'Our internet wizard has been finding out about the stories surrounding Clarissa and the house.'

'Oh, the pagan sacrifices and blood rituals,' said Shirl, grinning.

'Stop with that nonsense; you'll frighten the poor lad to death,' said Kath as she took off her jacket.

'As if Clarissa dusting off her broomstick isn't scary enough,' Shirl muttered.

Kath glared at her, and Shirl hunkered down and fired up her computer.

Ruth turned to face Kath. 'He's just been telling me about pagan history and the estate. He's discovered all the tales and the local hearsay.'

Byron straightened up. 'Just because it's on the internet doesn't mean it's true.'

Ruth cocked her thumb in his direction. 'Wise beyond his years, that one.'

'But,' Byron continued, 'I can see why you want Lane in on this.'

'So, how was the lovely Clarissa?' Ruth asked.

'Scary as ever but apparently willing to cooperate,' said Shirl. 'Rafferty was just arriving as we left. The look on his face when he saw us was priceless.'

Kath cleared her throat. 'We start from the beginning. No preconceptions. The girls were found on the property. Whether they were killed there or elsewhere and then dumped is our starting point. We track back through what they did and who they saw prior to their disappearances. We have permission to go back and examine the folly. I didn't mention Lane would be with us. Byron, make a list or a spreadsheet or whatever of all the stories, rumours and myths surrounding the family and the estate. We can factor them in as we go along.'

Kath wandered over to look at the whiteboard. The photographs of the three girls sat attached to the wall above the board. Smiling, happy faces. Long hair cascading forward—the one thing they all had in common and that had ultimately been their downfall. When the story hit the tabloids and information was released about the manner of death, a journalist had dubbed them the Rapunzel Murders. Each girl had been strangled with their own long hair, neatly plaited to form a rope. Plus the fact they had been found in a tower. A fairy tale with no happy ending.

Ruth came up behind her. 'Booked the chat with Dylan Paxton for two o'clock at the garden centre.'

'Okay. I'll take Marvin with me. Where is he, by the way?'

As Kath spoke, they heard footsteps on the stairs, and Marvin appeared in the doorway.

'Sent him for supplies.'

'What did I miss?' Marvin entered the room with a large shopping bag that he deposited by his desk. In his other hand was a large bouquet of flowers. He walked over to Shirl. 'These are for you.'

Ruth laughed as Shirl, open-mouthed, slowly reached out to take the cellophane package.

'It's not often she's lost for words. Well done, Marvin.'

'Thank you, but why?' Shirl buried her nose into pink carnations and roses.

Marvin felt his cheeks grow warm. 'Because, despite all your jokes and bravado, I know that jumping out of a plane scares you. I realise it doesn't go any way to make you feel less anxious, but I just wanted to say I'm proud of what you're doing.'

Shirl smiled and laid the flowers on her desk. She stood up and hugged the young man. 'You're a good detective and a damn fine bloke.'

'Here, here.' Ruth clapped her hands.

Shirl let Marvin go. 'As we don't have a vase here, I'll take them home and—'

'Wait.' Marvin went to the shopping bag and pulled out a white ceramic vase. 'There you go, in case you wanted to keep them here.'

Shirl grinned, impressed. 'Kerry's a lucky girl. Thank you.' She took the vase and retrieved scissors from her desk drawer.

Marvin delved into his bag again and pulled out a shallow planter filled with miniature cacti. 'And this is for your mum, Byron.' He placed the pot on Byron's desk.

'Oh, mate, she'll love that. Cheers.' Byron turned the white pot round and smiled, imaging the look of joy on Cassandra's face.

'Erm, did you actually get the teabags and stuff that you went for?' Ruth asked.

Marvin gave her a resigned look, picked up the bag and began unloading it onto the table next to the kettle.

'That's all right, then,' she huffed.

Kath turned to address the room. 'Right. Marvin, you and I are going to see Dylan Paxton later. Shirl and Ruth, look at all the possible contacts with the girls, maybe we can see best friends again. Byron's going to check out all these weird stories floating about. Look at the family history in more detail as well.'

Byron nodded and went back to typing.

'And Lane?' Marvin smiled.

Kath smiled back. 'I'll keep you posted.'

She'd received a text from Lane earlier saying she would be at the office later that afternoon. Kath felt that Marvin didn't need to know that piece of information before an important interview. She needed him fully focused.

'That flower arranging course really paid off.' Ruth looked disparagingly at the flowers now in the vase as Shirl positioned it on the table in front of the window.

'My strengths lie in other areas,' Shirl quipped, unperturbed by Ruth's mockery.

'Maybe I'll ask Lane exactly what those strengths are, as it's a bloody mystery to the rest of us.'

A hum of laughter and conversation filled the room. Shirl grinned to herself and stroked the petals of a pink rose. Not even Ruth's annoying remarks could dampen her mood.

|8|

Clarissa walked through the woods, the woman next to her chewing on her bottom lip. Their coats were pulled tightly, scarves knotted.

'They said they'd give me notice of when they're coming to look around. They'll head for the folly.'

'There's nothing to find, you know that.'

'I know, but I'm uneasy. It feels different this time. She has a new team, this DCI Fortune.'

'But why the unease? There is nothing that leads them back to us.'

'They'll want to speak to Rafferty.'

'He'll be alright, won't he? He knows what's at stake now. He won't say anything.'

'I wish I had your confidence. His mouth has always been his biggest downfall. Maybe one of us should be with him.'

'Let's cross that bridge all in good time.'

'I can't lose what we have.'

They walked back the way they had come, the mantra echoing through the trees.

'I can't lose what we have.'

| 9 |

Cooper's Garden Centre sat back from the road, surrounded by open fields. Kath squeezed the car into the only space in the car park. It was busy for a weekday—people pushing trolleys laden with shrubs and bags of compost to their vehicles, toddlers running around in the sunshine.

'Nice place to work,' said Marvin, stretching as he closed the car door.

They headed towards a barn at the side of the main building that had been converted to house the Celandine Cafe. A young woman greeted them as they approached the counter.

'What can I get for you?'

'Dylan Paxton, please. He's expecting us.' Kath smiled back at the petite girl, who turned as a young man came up behind her.

'I'm Dylan. We'll sit over there in the corner.' He gestured to a table by the window, hands steady. A young man in control in his own environment. There were only three other tables occupied, and Kath felt okay with the location for their chat.

'Would you like drinks?'

Marvin looked at Kath expectantly. She took the hint.

'A couple of cappuccinos would be lovely, thank you.'
She pulled a ten-pound note from her trouser pocket, but
Dylan had already sent the girl to make the coffees and put
money in the till.

The young man, still only twenty-two, had a quiet
assuredness about him. His blond hair was pulled tight into
a bun on the top of his head and he wore black trousers and
shirt. Not a crease in sight. He moved over to the table, and
Kath and Marvin followed. He inspected the table as the
two detectives sat down and, satisfied with the cleanliness,
pulled a chair out and sat opposite them.

'Thanks for meeting with us, Dylan.' Kath pulled her
warrant card from her pocket, and Marvin did the same.
Dylan glanced at them and nodded.

'I don't know how much help I can be...' His voice
trailed off as the young girl approached with a tray of
drinks.

'Cheers, Sandy.'

She placed the tray down and left quickly.

'We don't want to take up too much of your time, and
I just need to ask that you're okay with going through
things again?' Kath didn't want to speak of the horror
Dylan and his friends had witnessed until it was necessary
and he was completely comfortable.

Marvin took a sip of his coffee and stared out of the
window. 'This is a nice place to work,' he said, echoing
his earlier comment.

Kath suddenly got it. Open fields. No trees, no
woodland pressing in on him. This lad before her who
was polite, switched on and efficient would always carry
the underlying fear of a wood in the dead of night.

Dylan took a sip of his espresso and waited.

Kath kicked Marvin gently and took a sip of her drink.

'So, Dylan, as my colleague said on the phone, we're looking again at the case of the three girls.' Marvin stopped short of words like murder and death.

Kath smiled to herself, knowing she'd made the right decision in having Marvin with her.

'We've gone over your original statement, which was really detailed and helpful,' Marvin continued, 'and we wondered if—'

'I couldn't stop looking at them.'

Dylan sat upright, his hands now clenched in his lap. His demeanour seemed calm, but Kath could almost hear the young man's pulse racing as the images came back into his mind. It felt all wrong to be sitting with the sun shining through the window, with people passing by enjoying their day out, all carrying on as normal. Before she could say anything, he spoke again.

'I'd never seen a dead body before or even a skeleton. Andrew dropped the torch and the other two ran outside. I think Dhandi fell down the steps. I picked up the torch and just stared at them.'

'It was a hell of a shock, for all of you. Something no-one should have to see,' said Marvin.

'You must see things like that all the time,' said Dylan.

Kath looked at Marvin, confident he would respond in the right way.

Marvin nodded and clasped his hands in front of him on the table. 'We're trained to cope with a variety of scenarios, but it still affects us. We have a support network if we feel overwhelmed, and I believe you were all directed to a professional counsellor to help you through what you'd experienced?'

Kath rubbed her foot gently against Marvin's leg. *Good lad. Keep going.*

Dylan nodded. 'Yes, we all saw her, nice lady. It was helpful talking it through.'

'Well...' Marvin continued, 'we have access to a professional hypnotherapist and wondered if you would see her? She deals with trauma and unlocking buried memories.' He paused, waiting for a dismissal of the idea. Dylan remained silent, but Kath could see he was mulling over the idea.

'You mean I might remember something that could help that I didn't recall at the time?'

'Exactly.' Marvin picked up his cup and took another gulp of coffee. 'If you think you could do that, it may just be that tiny bit of information we need to further our investigation.'

Kath sat back, proud of the young detective constable sitting next to her.

Marvin sensed Dylan was struggling with the idea. 'Why don't you think about it? No need to decide right now. Do your own research, see how it sits with you. We wouldn't have suggested it if we didn't think it would be beneficial all round.'

'Okay.' Dylan pushed back his chair and stood up. 'Thanks for not pressuring me. I appreciate it, and I know that this could be important.'

Marvin and Kath stood up, and they all shook hands. Dylan gathered the cups together and signalled to Sandy to come and collect them.

Marvin reached into his pocket and pulled out his card. 'Give me a call when you're ready.'

'Thank you for the coffees and your time.' Kath turned and walked to the exit.

Marvin gave one final nod of gratitude before rushing to catch up with Kath outside. 'I think he'll give it a try,' he said as they approached her car.

'You did really well.'

'Thanks.' He tried not to grin too hard, but he was pleased with the praise.

'Let's get back.' Kath reversed the car. 'There may be a little surprise waiting for you at the office.'

'Oh wow, you're here.'

Lane turned as Marvin launched himself at her from the office doorway.

'Hello, wee man.'

Ruth rolled her eyes at Kath as Marvin clung to Lane, his face beaming. Lane pushed him back.

'Let me look at you, handsome.'

Marvin's cheeks reddened. 'I'm so glad you're with us on this case.'

'Me too, honey. Now, Kath tells me there's a lady in your life.'

He gave a sheepish grin and bobbed his head. 'Yeah, well, it's early days but...oh.' He stepped further back from Lane, a look of genuine panic on his face. 'You didn't feel anything bad, did you? Please don't tell me... no, tell me if you—'

Lane held up her hands. 'Hold on there. You know it doesn't work like that. Now, catch yourself on and make me a coffee.'

Marvin's shoulders lowered to a more relaxed position as he turned to head for the kettle.

'So good to see you.' Kath moved in for a hug of her own, remembering their embrace at her cottage a few months previously when Lane had revealed that she knew about Kath's secret past, felt the tormented energy running through her body. The past Kath thought had been put to bed, forgotten about. Lane's revelation was only the beginning of the resurrection of old scars and old secrets that had finally been resolved. Kath hoped she was telling the truth to Marvin.

Lane took the proffered mug from Marvin and moved to the long a window, where the white Venetian blinds were pulled tightly to the top to allow views of the road framed by tall tree leading down into the Ironbridge Gorge.

'So, our chat with Dylan was good.' Kath's words brought the team back to the focus point. 'Marvin was really great with him. I barely said anything.'

'That's a first,' said Shirl.

Kath ignored the comment. 'We put the idea to him about the regression hypnosis issue. He didn't dismiss it. He doesn't think he has anything else to add, but I get the feeling he will be back in touch.'

'He wasn't spooked by the fact we're opening old wounds?' Ruth asked.

'No, he was pragmatic in a quiet way. He talked a little about finding the girls, but I get the impression he sees them in his dreams.'

'I've prepared some notes for Lane.' Byron stood up, his long hair swinging behind him.

'Thanks, hon. Bit of bedtime reading.' Lane took the file from him.

'Okay,' said Kath, 'we'll meet up in the morning when Lane is up to speed.'

'By the way, I've found Samantha, Jennifer's best friend. She works as a florist in Bridgnorth,' Shirl said.

'Good. You and Marvin go and see her first thing, get the ball rolling and people talking. Now, go home.'

'Where are you staying?' Marvin asked Lane as they walked out of the office and down the stairs.

'A hotel in Telford. Need some space, and I think Kath needs some too.'

Marvin nodded, unsure what to make of the comment. 'Do you want to get some food with me and Kerry? Pizza or something?'

Lane smiled and patted his arm. 'Thanks for the invitation, but I already made plans. And they don't include food.'

They went down the stairs. Lane pranced through the station doorway, her long dark curls swaying with the motion of her lithe body.

Shirl caught up to Marvin in the foyer. 'She looks like a woman on a mission.'

'Yeah,' said Marvin as they watched her car turn quickly onto the road. 'And apparently it doesn't involve pizza.'

| 10 |

Internet site – Folkus Pocus

DONAVANB

Magic is just another religion, a matter of faith. Scientists will tell us it cannot be proven. It is simply myth, story, invented nonsense to keep people in fear. But we have firsthand accounts across the centuries of the magic of Quartermaine Manor and the haunted woods. The spirit of the land lives on. The history was there before the trees were felled, the villagers cast out, the witches removed. So, are you saying the accounts from the 1600s that were passed down by mouth and later committed by the literate to paper were made up? Stories invented to frighten and subdue, terrify and amaze?

SILVERLIGHT72

No. There weren't stories, surely? They were accounts of what people saw – or thought they saw.

DOBBS

They're like religious hallucinations. Weeping statues of the Virgin Mary, apparitions of saints in crumbling walls. History is full of them.

DEMONBEARD

Drugs. All down to the drugs. Even back then they smoked all sorts of weird stuff growing in forests and woodland, and hallucinogenic mushrooms have always been around.

DONAVANB

We encourage healthy debate on this forum.

TRASHTALK

Rubbish. Utter fucking rubbish. All that shit about the land being cursed and wooden horses coming alive at night. Man, you people are so gullible.

DONAVANB

Everyone is entitled to their opinion, but it would be appreciated if you would temper your tone and language.

CONAN

It's a creepy place, though. My grandad said he and his mates used to sneak into those woods at night when the gates were left open. Scared themselves shitless... Sorry, but that's what he said!

WIREDOG

Even worse since those girls were found. That Clarissa Quartermaine is weird. We all think she's a witch and she cursed the girls.

SILVERLIGHT72

But they didn't strangle themselves, did they? No, some maniac did that for kicks.

WIREDOG

Maybe they were sacrifices to the old gods? Ah, see, didn't think of that, did you?

DONAVANB

I think we're getting a bit off topic here. This isn't a platform for ghoulish talk of those poor murdered girls. But there is substance to your earlier comment. Clarissa is indeed descended from Margaret Blackstock who was reported to be a witch and hunted down in the very woods of what is now the Quartermaine estate. Her daughters fled the village. Margaret was bound and her coat pockets filled with stones. She was thrown into a deep pool. Three days later, the body was pulled out, rent into pieces and left to rot.

SILVERLIGHT72

Wow! No shit!

DONAVANB

The rumour is that Clarissa married Farraday Quartermaine for access to the land.

SILVERLIGHT72

So, what about the horses story, then?

DONAVAN B

In 1896 Clarence Quartermaine, Farraday Quartermaine's great-grandfather, purchased a set of gallopers from a fairground that went out of business. He installed it in the grounds and held fetes throughout the year. The horses fell into disrepair over the years, but people say they have heard hooves racing through the woods at night.

TRASHTALK

Heard. Not seen.

DONAVANB

So if you don't see it for yourself, it can't be real? There have been a couple of accounts. In the early 1980s. It was after Theadora, Clarissa's sister, died.

CONAN

Oh yeah. I forgot about her. Hell of a lot of bad karma in that place.

'Can you stop reading that? We only have a few hours.'

Lane put down the folder and smiled at the man lying next to her. 'Ready for round two, then?'

He stroked her arm. 'I've been ready for ages.'

'Well, if anyone can take my mind off witches and curses and things that go bump in the night, it's gonna be you.'

She leant forward to kiss him as the file slid to the floor.

| 11 |
April 2010

Rafferty slowed the car as he passed the girl for the second time. The rain had been coming down steadily for half an hour and the girl looked as if she had been out in it at least that long. The bus stop had no man-made shelter. She was huddled under a tree, but it gave her little cover from the weather. She was dressed more for a warm summer day, in beige cotton trousers sitting low on her hips and a pink crop top, her thin brown cardigan stretched to capacity by the weight of rainwater.

Alone, cold and vulnerable. Just the way he liked them.

He stopped the car and pressed the button to lower the passenger window. 'Anyone call for a good Samaritan?' He smiled, leaning towards the open window.

The girl bent down, a puzzled look on her face. 'Sorry?'

'Can I offer you a lift? Buses can be so unreliable, especially out here.'

She shivered, wrestling with the idea of getting into a car with a strange man. She knew who he was though. His number plate, RAF 1, gave him away. Her long hair, wet like tropical vines, fell forward, and Rafferty felt a stirring in his body. He took a risk and guessed at her destination.

'Are you heading for Bridgnorth? I'm going that way anyway.'

She whipped her head round, looking both ways up and down the country road. There had only been one other car that had passed by and the bus was still twenty minutes away, if the old timetable was to be believed.

He sensed she was close to a decision. 'I'm Rafferty Quartermaine, by the way. Wouldn't want you getting into a car with a man you hadn't been introduced to.'

She wiped raindrops from her cheeks. The rain was coming even harder now, the sky showing no sign of relinquishing the heavy cloud cover. The town wasn't far away.

'Well, if you're sure...' She opened the door, then hesitated. 'I'll make your seat all wet.'

Rafferty grinned and gestured with his hand. 'It doesn't matter about that. C'mon. I'll put the heater on full blast and you'll dry off in no time.'

Uncertainty fluttered in her stomach. With a last look up the road, she got in and closed the door.

Rafferty pushed the button on his side and closed the window. He touched the console, and warm air instantly flooded the car. 'Weathermen and buses. Can't rely on either of them. Now, you'd better tell me your name so that we're properly acquainted.'

'Jennifer.' She smiled. The wet cotton of her trousers pressed into her thighs, but the warm air felt so good.

'That's a beautiful name. I believe it's of Welsh origin. It means fair and soft.'

He put the car into first gear, and they eased forward.

'So, Jennifer, tell me all about yourself.'

As the girl chatted amiably, Rafferty fought hard to control the vehicle and his emotions as they moved down the winding road.

Fair and soft. Oh yes. Fair and soft.

'Oh my god, Sam. He's *so* cool.'

Jennifer closed Samantha's bedroom door and flopped onto the bed, lying back and smiling. Samantha moved to give her friend more space and tucked her feet under her body. She leant back against the mountain of furry cushions stacked against the headboard.

'So are you actually going to tell me his name? I mean, it's been ten days and I am your best friend.' She punched Jennifer lightly on the arm.

Jennifer turned her head, her cheeks flushed, eyes sparkling. 'Can't. I'm sworn to secrecy.'

'What? Is he famous or something?' Samantha sat forward. 'Oh god, he is, isn't he?'

Jennifer laughed and pulled her knees up to her chest. 'No. He has his reasons and he trusts me completely, so I can't say anything. But... I think this is it. I think I love him.'

Samantha sighed and fell back to her furry support. 'You said that about Josh.'

'Huh, yeah, well, he dumped me, but that was the best thing that ever happened cos Josh is such a kid, but this guy...'

Jennifer paused, remembering Rafferty's lips on hers, his hands moving urgently across her body. She'd slowed things down to savour the experience, building up the event of their first night together in her head. She knew what she'd wear, how her hair would fall across his bare chest. She'd promised him it would be soon. She just needed to put her plan in place first. Then she would be all his. His eyes had closed in ecstasy at the thought.

'You said he was older,' Samantha pushed on, 'but, like, how much older? He's not a perv, is he?'

'Of course not,' Jennifer snapped. 'He's like twenty-six or something. And he's so into me, wants to know everything about me. I can *really* talk to him and he wants to hear what I have to say. He's so sophisticated as well.'

Jennifer was on a roll now. It was exhilarating to talk about Rafferty without actually revealing who he was.

'He took me to The Bell, and I really wanted vodka and coke, you know, but he was all like no, have wine, and he was telling me how to really taste it and enjoy the flavours and stuff.'

'Do you even like it, though?' Samantha wrinkled her nose.

Jennifer's face creased into mild dislike. 'Well, it's not great, but he really wants me to learn. He says I'll get the taste for it and really begin to appreciate it.' She flicked her hair back over her shoulder, the sleeve of her jumper riding up to reveal a bracelet that caught the light and glistened.

Samantha gasped. 'What the fuck is that?'

Jennifer held out her wrist for Samantha to admire the gift. 'Just a little something he gave me. Get this, it's white gold and real diamonds. *Real diamonds.*' She squealed. 'I can't wear it all the time though. Parents might start asking questions.'

Samantha felt an unease settle in her body as she watched her friend stroking the bracelet. 'He gave you that after only a week or so?'

'He's so loaded, Sam. I mean proper rich.' She was aching to tell her who the mystery man was, but Rafferty had been very insistent. It was cool having a secret, though. Cool and a little bit dangerous.

'So, I need a favour.' Jennifer sat up and looked at Samantha, hands pressed together as if in prayer. 'I'm going to tell my parents I'm sleeping over here tomorrow night. Can you cover for me?'

'And you'll be where exactly?' Sam grabbed a cushion and crushed it to her chest to try to quell the unease that just would not leave her. 'Oh. God. Really?' She saw the look on Jennifer's face and knew her guess had been correct. 'You'll be at his house?'

'Yep, but don't stress. I'll leave early in the morning, he'll bring me back to town. It'll be okay.'

Sam shook her head. 'Are you sure you can't tell me where you'll be? What if something goes wrong or you need... I don't know, I'd just really feel better if you tell me.'

Jennifer tilted her head. 'I'll phone you, won't I? But my phone will be off *all* night; he doesn't want us to be disturbed.'

Jennifer giggled and Sam joined in, but the mirth was half-hearted and tinged with a sense of unrest.

| 12 |

9th October 2019

'And that was the last time you saw her?'

Samantha Gordon lit her cigarette and sipped her coffee. Shirl felt the cold of the wrought-iron patio chair seeping into her buttocks, and she cradled her coffee mug for warmth, willing it to travel down to her other extremities. It was just after ten o'clock, but the October sun hadn't reached the courtyard of the Bridgnorth coffee house. She'd called ahead to Samantha to ask if she would meet with them, explaining that they were reopening the case. Samantha was at work at the florist's but agreed to meet them in the cafe across the road.

Marvin picked up his mug, wondering how he could move aside the froth on his cappuccino and drink it without leaving himself a milky moustache. 'We're very sorry for the distress this may cause,' he said, giving what he hoped was an encouraging smile, 'but we need to go over everything again.'

Samantha nodded. 'It's okay, I get it. It's just a shock, that's all. I still feel if I'd stopped her, then she'd still be alive.' She took a hard pull on the filter, the glowing ember fizzing into a long strand of ash that fell onto her thigh. She seemed not to notice and stared at the table.

Shirl patted her hand. 'I know it's little consolation, but there was nothing you could have done. It sounds like she was determined to meet this man. As close as you were, she wouldn't have listened, would she?'

Samantha stubbed out her cigarette end in the glass ashtray and immediately lit another. 'I don't get why you didn't arrest Rafferty Quartermaine. It's got to be him, right?'

Shirl sipped her coffee whilst she formulated a reply in her head. 'As you know, we did question him. He admitted to having a drink with Jennifer in The Bell. Other people in the pub said they'd seen them together. But they arrived separately, chatted at the bar like they'd just met. He bought her wine and they sat and talked. That was it.'

Samantha's eyes narrowed. 'Yeah, okay. But how many twenty-six-year-old blokes were there that could have done this?'

'Probably more than you think,' Marvin said, sensing the anxiety rising in the young woman. 'You're sure she didn't give anything away? A description of him? His car? Even the slightest thing might help.'

Sam shook her head. 'I thought it was weird because she was really rubbish at keeping secrets. But he must have had some power over her because, apart from being a really great kisser and the bracelet she showed me, she didn't give a thing away about him.'

'Bracelet?' Shirl sat forward.

'Yeah. You must have found it'—Sam swallowed—'with her.'

Shirl looked at Marvin, who shrugged.

'No, we didn't. Her clothes and shoes and bag but no bracelet.' Shirl reached into her bag and pulled out a notebook and pen. 'Can you describe it for me?'

Sam screwed up her face, remembering the glint in the light of her bedroom. 'She said it cost a fortune. Small diamonds set in white gold. Loose, you know? Not a solid bangle. She said she could only wear it when she was with him because he didn't want anyone asking questions.'

'So, when did you see it?'

'She'd been with him and then she came round to me and that was when she told me she was going to sleep with him the following night.'

'That's really useful, Samantha. Thank you.'

Samantha looked down at her hands. 'It's sort of strange. I actually wanted to be a florist because of her. The flowers at her funeral were so beautiful. It makes me feel close to her.' She shook off the memory. 'I really have to get back.'

'Of course,' said Shirl. 'Thanks again. It's never easy reliving something like that.'

'Just get him this time.'

Samantha rose quickly and hurried through the archway onto the side street.

'We didn't miss this bracelet the first time, did we?' Marvin asked, already knowing the answer.

'No, we didn't,' Shirl barked back. 'The clothes, shoes and bags of all three girls were piled up opposite them, neatly stacked. There was no jewellery.'

'So if we are looking at Rafferty as the killer, he's kept the bracelet as a trophy maybe?'

'It's possible. When we talk to the friends of Layla and Sophia, it's another angle for us.'

Marvin frowned. 'We'd need to search his house if we're definitely looking at him. Tell me again why he wasn't arrested at the time?'

Shirl turned to him. 'Kath. Her instinct. As much as we all don't like the guy, she said he was genuinely shocked when the girls were found. Shocked and upset.'

'Shocked or scared?' Marvin tilted his head.

Shirl stared at a robin hopping beneath the tables, searching for crumbs. 'Scared is interesting,' she muttered. 'Scared is very interesting.'

As Shirl and Marvin were sitting huddled in the café courtyard, Kath was getting ready to leave her house. She'd had a fitful night. Richard's talk of possible poachers in the woods had found her waking every hour, listening for voices. She'd found herself at the bedroom window several times, peering into the darkness. She'd tried to reason that it was all part of her job, acting on information he'd supplied. But when the image of his face flooded her brain, it wasn't with thoughts of poachers and wrongdoing, but accompanied by a strange and almost girlish flush running through her body. Her last foray into sleep had left her waking groggy and feeling unfit for the day ahead. She'd texted Ruth and Shirl saying she would be in at around nine-thirty. More coffee was needed before she stepped outside the front door. Shirl had told her that she and Marvin were off to see Samantha Gordon. A final blast of cold water at the end of her shower and a fifth coffee had encouraged her brain to full waking, and now she felt ready to face the day. She closed the front door behind her and unlocked her car. As she got in, she noticed a plant to the side of the front door.

'What the hell?'

She got out and went to the door, looking around to ascertain she was alone. A white envelope sat against the lilac plant pot. As she bent to retrieve it, she glanced around again. She pulled a card from the envelope, a pretty design of a cottage nestled in a sea of wildflowers. She opened it, puzzled.

Saw this and thought of you. It's called Christina—a rose for a cottage of the same name. If you'd like some advice on where to plant it, I'm happy to oblige... Richard

Kath smiled and bent forward to look at the label. The picture was of a perfect pink rose, blousy and glorious.

'Nice move, Mr Bastion.'

She pulled her phone from her jacket pocket and began to text him. She'd put his number straight into her directory when she'd arrived home Monday night.

Hi, Richard. It's DCI Kath

Bugger this.

With the braveness she was probably feeling due to tiredness not giving her the right brain tools to talk herself out of it, she deleted the text and called him. And with a speed that left her unable to question her decision, he answered

'Richard Bastion.'

'It's Kath... DCI Fortune. I just found your gift.'

She could almost hear him smiling.

'Flowers are so obvious.'

'It was a lovely gesture. Thank you.'

'The kind of gesture that would make you consider having a drink with me?'

Oh, you could have just asked. No flowers required.

'I'd like that. Tonight any good for you?'

Slow down, Fortune. Not too eager.

'Perfect. Any suggestions on location?'

Kath thought for a moment, and an idea formed quickly. 'How about I come to you and we take it from there?'

'Great. About seven?'

Kath grinned. 'Good for me. See you then.'

'I look forward to it. Bye.'

She got back in her car, feeling delighted and unable to remove the grin from her face. The Blasted Oak was the 'weird' pub in Restonfield. Strangers and drop-in visitors were actively discouraged but Kath wanted to keep Richard away from The Bell and its current connection to work. Kath had never had a problem going anywhere on her own, but she felt safer knowing that Richard would be with her. She yawned as she pulled out of the driveway. More coffee required.

| 13 |

'Oh my god, there's two of you.'

Ruth stood in the middle of the office with her arms crossed as Kath entered. Lane sat on the table next to the vase of flowers and smirked at Kath.

Kath smiled back at Lane. 'I probably don't want to know the answer, but two of what?'

'Lane walked in looking like Queen Smiley of the Smiley People and now here you are. Two smiley queens. It's unsettling.'

Kath went to put her bag on her clean desk, then thought better of it given Ruth's demeanour and dropped it onto her chair. 'So, smiling is a criminal offence now?' She winked at Lane. 'Why are you so grumpy anyway?'

Byron ducked behind his computer monitors and began typing as Ruth let out a long sigh.

'Roger traipsed in half the bloody garden just as I was about to leave the house.'

'Oh.' Kath nodded in understanding.

'And that made me late, cleaning all that up, and now we're off to see bloody Clarissa into the bargain. I'm just...' Ruth's words tailed off as Lane and Kath let out giggles.

'Two things that you hate—tardiness and mess. Not a good start to your day, then. Sorry.'

'Well, I had a night of unbridled passion and very little sleep, but why are you so smiley?' Lane tilted her head, a glint in her eye.

I'll just bet you already know, you damn psychic.

Kath yawned.

'So, no sleep for you either?'

Kath shook her head. 'Very little sleep is accurate, but not for the same reason as you.'

Ruth moved to the kettle, flicking the switch viciously, then proceeded to fill the room with the clattering of spoons and mugs.

Kath rolled her eyes and perched next to Lane. 'Who is he, then?'

Lane's eyes twinkled. 'Can't say. Secret.'

'Why don't you call another psychic? Then we'll all be suitably enlightened,' Ruth muttered as she squished a tea bag into hot water with more vigour than was necessary.

'That won't work,' Lane said, enjoying the banter. 'Us psychics have a code of honour. Anyway, you don't know any other psychics.'

'Yellow Pages is full of them.'

Kath looked up at the wall clock. 'Phone Clarissa and tell her we're on our way. You have twenty minutes to get the grumpiness out of your system. Byron, can I have a word in my office?'

At the mention of his name, he looked up. His face wore a confused expression. 'Er, this is your office.'

Kath shook her cigarette packet in his direction. 'My other office. Come on.'

They walked outside and onto the path underneath the trees. Byron pushed his hands into his jeans pockets and waited as Kath lit her cigarette.

'Don't look so scared. I wanted to ask if you would come along with us this morning to Clarissa's.'

'Oh. Why?'

Kath blew smoke away from him. 'You're an invaluable help as our internet wizard, but I thought you might appreciate a change of scenery.'

'Is that allowed?' he asked slowly, redness creeping across his cheeks. 'Well, I mean, you're the boss, so that's a stupid question. I mean, I'd love to, but why?'

'Because between you and Lane, I think you might pick up on things that the rest of us might dismiss or not even acknowledge.'

His face brightened as she continued.

'Forgive my terminology, but we all dismissed the weird stuff and things that go bump in the night back in the day. We didn't have Lane until recently. We deal in cold, hard evidence. Facts, not fanciful stories. Lane felt something in you a couple of months ago on our first case, and...' Kath paced and smoked for a moment, trying to find the right words. 'You mentioned something to me last week about going to Wales, remember?'

Byron nodded, recalling the moment.

'Your mum gave me a list of counsellors that might be able to help me come to terms with my personal problem. One of them is in Wales. And I'm guessing she never mentioned this to you?'

'No, she didn't. She wouldn't tell me anything about a client. Sorry, maybe that's the wrong word...'

Kath waved her hand, acknowledging what he was trying to say. 'It's fine. But somehow you knew. Picked up on something coming from me. Lane sensed something in you, and I think it would be useful to have you along when we go to Quartermaine Manor.'

Byron looked down at his feet. 'Mum always said she knew I had a talent. I could always find lost things as a kid, you know? Stuff like that. Things come into my head and I don't know where from.'

'You don't need to try and explain it.' Kath smiled and crushed her cigarette butt under her boot heel. 'Are you up for it, then?'

'Yeah, definitely.'

'Come on, then. Let's see if Queen Grumpy of the Grumpy People is in a better frame of mind.'

Lane reached out to put the radio on, then changed her mind, sensing that Byron wanted to talk.

'You okay with this, then?'

'Yeah,' Byron said slowly, 'but it's just that I'm kind of scared, like I might get all kinds of images in my head and get confused.'

Lane indicated and turned the car to follow Kath's Audi, where Ruth was a passenger, down the next road. 'Don't get ahead of yourself. You're in danger of overthinking this.'

Byron stared out of the side window. 'What if I don't get anything, though? What if Kath thinks I can do what you do and then I don't get anything?'

'There is no expectation. She's not like that.' Lane could feel the anxiety coming off him in waves.

They drove in silence for the remainder of the journey until she coaxed the car through the dilapidated gates and the house came into view.

'Holy mother.' She parked the car next to Kath's, and they got out. 'You don't disappoint, DCI Fortune.'

The house was a mixture of black and white timber frame and red brick, giving the impression of a medieval house but built much later in that style in the 1850s by the Quartermaine patriarch. It had a welcoming feel, much more so than the current resident. Rooks sat on top of the barley twist chimneys, enjoying the warmth of the October sun. Kath went to knock on the rounded oak door, but it swung open before she could reach it.

'Hang on to your hats,' Ruth muttered as Clarissa appeared in the doorway.

The lady of the house glared at the four people in front of her, jaw taut, hands clenched. 'I didn't realise there would be so many of you.'

Kath ignored the woman's obvious discomfort. 'DS Goodwin you probably remember. My other two colleagues are civilian members of my team.'

Lane moved past Kath and extended her hand. 'It's a pleasure to meet you, Mrs Quartermaine.'

Clarissa stared at the hand for a moment and then shook it, a light touch that was fleeting as if the proffered hand held an invisible disease. Kath watched Lane's face, eager for a sign. Lane gave nothing away as she dropped her hand. Clarissa brushed her hands down her skirt.

'We'll make our way to the folly and leave you to your day.' Kath gave a nod to Clarissa and strode off, hoping Ruth wouldn't make a crass remark that would make Clarissa change her mind about her level of co-operation.

'Stick to the path and keep together.' Clarissa's warning rang out as the door closed.

Kath waited until they were in the shelter of the trees away from the house before turning to Lane. 'I know I'm keen, but did you get anything?' Her eyes searched Lane's face for an affirmation.

'No, I didn't apart from the obvious fact that she doesn't want us here.'

'Byron, are you alright?'

He nodded and stared up at the green canopy.

'Okay, then,' said Kath. 'Let's go.'

The four walked two abreast, Kath and Ruth in the lead, both hoping they could remember the way. The beaten earth pathway was sandwiched between untamed undergrowth spilling across the bare earth and fallen branches lying rotting, their twig limbs reaching skyward like discarded shop mannequins. They walked in silence, each lost in their own thoughts until they came to a fork in the pathway. Ruth and Kath looked at each other.

'Forgot the way?' Lane asked.

'No,' said Kath, turning to face Ruth. 'We forgot about Clemency. She lives down there in the other cottage.' She pointed to the right-hand pathway through more tangled undergrowth. In her haste to relay information to Marvin and Byron about the original investigation, she'd forgotten about Clemency Craven. A mousy woman who had lived on the estate as long as Clarissa.

'What did Clarissa describe her as?'

'That funny name...' Ruth looked up at the trees, struggling to remember the term that Clarissa had used. She snapped her fingers. 'That's it. Clarissa called her a henwife. All bloody strange, but no surprise there.'

'It's an old term,' said Byron. 'A henwife is another name for a wise woman in the community, a herbalist and counsellor and known for keeping chickens, hence the name.'

'Not more bloody chickens,' Ruth muttered.

'Presumably, she was interviewed at the time the bodies were found?' Lane raised her eyebrows.

'She was,' Ruth replied. 'Got nothing out of her. She was unremarkable, as I recall, but one of those people that just seem insignificant.'

'Yes, so insignificant that we forgot about her. Maybe we'll drop in on the way back. Let's get to the main attraction.'

They moved on down the left-hand path. After a few minutes, the path began to narrow, shafts of autumn sunlight trying desperately to pierce the tree umbrellas. The clearing before them seemed an oasis of calm, the stone folly standing proud amongst the vegetation. Lichen crept across the bottom stones and wildflower seed heads stood erect in the stillness.

'Didn't there used to be a door?' Ruth stood at the open archway, peering into the gloomy interior.

'Can't remember.'

Byron suddenly brought his hands to his chest, clutching at his multicoloured wool jumper, his face pale.

'Can you feel it too?' Lane put a hand on his arm.

Ruth and Kath turned to look at him.

'Horses,' he blurted out.

'Can you explain?' Concern flooded Ruth's face as Byron's breathing became heavier.

'It feels...there's a thundering. I can feel it in my chest.'

Lane nodded. 'I feel it as well. I got a flash... horses running through these woods.'

'It's been heard before by a few people,' said Kath, 'but there are no horses on the estate.'

Lane closed her eyes, still holding onto Byron. She took a deep breath. 'Bright horses.'

The air seemed to close in around them, and Kath looked around, aware that she too felt unsettled. A noise in the trees startled her, and she looked up to see a crow staring at her.

'Lane?' Ruth reached out her hand but withdrew it.

Lane opened her eyes. 'Gone.'

'Dizzy,' Byron said, then threw up. He put his hands on his knees and wiped his mouth with the back of his hand as he waited for the feeling to pass, staring at the patch of bile.

Ruth moved next to him. 'Just stay like that for a minute. Kath, I don't think he should go inside.'

Byron stood up slowly. 'I'm okay. I can do this.'

'No,' said Kath. 'Lane and I will go in. Ruth, stay with him.'

Lane nodded. 'I think that's a good call.'

Kath pulled a small torch from her jacket pocket and switched it on. Lane followed her into the folly. The cloying smell of damp earth was overwhelming. There were two narrow vertical slits in the stones, but they barely let in any light. The stone steps curled upward to the next level. Kath led the way with Lane close behind her. Three slightly larger slits on the upper level gave a little more illumination.

Lane's breathing changed. 'Absolute despair.' Her Northern Irish accent gave the words a soft sadness. She moved past Kath to the wall where the chains, thick and rusting, coiled on the floor.

'They saw a glimpse of the world they'd been taken from, a cruel taunt.'

Kath reached out and laid her hand on the stone wall. The cold seemed to snake its way up her arm. She snatched it away.

'You feel something?'

Kath shook her head. 'You're the one for that. I'm the facts gal. They were naked, all three of them.' Her voice dropped. 'The clothes were found over there, opposite. Piled up. Neat and tidy.'

'Significant?'

'Again, don't know. If you're not getting anything, let's get out of here.'

Lane took the lead down the steps. Kath took a last look around the bare, sombre interior and walked away from the entrance. She stopped and turned slowly 360 degrees. Ruth watched her, knowing that something was brewing in her brain

'Why here?'

'We asked that question at the time,' said Ruth.

'Yes, well, I'm asking it again.'

'Who even knows this is here if you don't live on the estate? It's huge and we're quite a way from the fence where the boys came through when they had their night adventure.'

Byron cleared his throat, not wishing to embarrass his boss but feeling the need to answer her question. 'Actually, there's a lot of information about this place on the internet.'

Kath felt a little foolish but smiled encouragingly. 'I guess. I forget sometimes that everything is on the internet now. But still, it's a hell of a way to carry, drag or whatever a body from the areas outside of the estate.' She waved her hands. 'It's surrounded by fields and other woodland. You can't get a car anywhere near here, unload a body and bring it to this spot. The only way with a vehicle is to drive through the main gates and up the driveway, and that's right outside the house. I can't see that happening.'

'Is that why you thought it was the son, Rafferty?' Lane asked.

Ruth nodded. 'That and the fact we don't like him.'

Lane smiled. 'Don't hold back now.'

'We can't just go with convenience,' Kath continued, 'but if anyone else can tell me how you get a body in here from so far away from the perimeter...'

'What if they weren't bodies? What if they were still alive and came here willingly?' The colour was coming back into Byron's cheeks.

Kath raised her eyebrows. 'I guess we didn't properly explore that option.'

There were a lot of the case details that she'd been able to recall and reading the files had jogged even more memories, but were there discussions and details that she couldn't remember?

'Ruth?'

'Well, I'm willing to concede that we may have overlooked that. We couldn't absolutely convince ourselves of a motive, could we? Certainly the team that took the case over from us didn't explore that angle.'

That spring and summer had kept all active teams busy with seven different murders. Some blamed the moon and astral alignments. Officers just knew it was people doing more bad stuff to people and they had their job to do.

'So there's a chance you focused on Rafferty because he was convenient, as he had an attachment to the location where the girls were found?' Lane raised her eyebrows.

Kath nodded.

'That seems a fair point.'

'So you're not getting anything?' Ruth asked. Like Kath, she knew her expectations were impossibly high, but it never did any harm to have hope.

'Sorry, honey, it doesn't work like that. All I felt was the essence of hope draining away. A sadness washed through me, but if you're referring to clues, then no. Not here.'

Ruth tried to hide her frustration, but her face betrayed her.

Lane continued, trying to infuse some enthusiasm. 'Sometimes things just come. I don't even have to be in the place where something happened. You remember Daisy's case?'

She was referring to the first investigation that Kath's team had tackled a few months previously. Lane had been key in picking up on the murderer of five-year-old Daisy Prospero. She saw Kath looking at her, and a knowing smile passed between them. Lane had also picked up on the dark secret Kath had been harbouring for many years, but they had never spoken about it.

Kath held up her hands. 'Lane, sorry. Please don't feel pressured. We do know that what you do can't be conjured out of thin air. Byron, if you're okay, we'll head back.'

Lane linked arms with Byron, and they fell in behind Ruth and Kath. Amongst the dark overtones of the location, they could not dismiss the beauty that surrounded them even as nature was in the process of dying down for a restful winter sleep.

They came to the fork in the path, and Kath stopped.

'Do you think we're pushing our luck if we swing by Clemency's cottage?'

'I'm up for it.' Ruth rubbed her hands together, as much in anticipation as keeping her fingers warm. 'The element of surprise and all that.'

'But I don't want to piss off Clarissa. We are reliant on her compliance to a certain extent.'

'I'll go, then,' said Ruth. 'Pissing off old women is what I do best.'

They all laughed.

'We could say we got lost?' said Byron, grinning.

Kath looked at the expectant faces before her. 'Okay, okay. Off we go.'

| 14 |

The stone cottage sat cocooned within the woodland.

Lane ducked under a low branch and signalled for the others to halt. 'We're being watched.'

'You feel it?' Kath removed her hands from her jacket pockets.

'Movement. Upstairs window.'

Before any of them could step onto the zigzag pathway that led to the front of the cottage, the pale blue front door opened.

'Ruth, with me.'

Kath pushed past Lane and made her way across the mismatched coloured stones, towards the woman in the doorway, who was brushing flour from her hands.

'Oh, it's DI Fortune, isn't it?'

'Ms Craven. I hope we're not disturbing you.' Kath didn't bother correcting the woman regarding her promotion and new title. The timid close confidante of Clarissa seemed open and affable and Kath wanted co-operation.

Clemency held up her hands. 'Bread day. I won't offer to shake hands. What brings you here?' She peered behind Kath and Ruth at the two other people who were almost enveloped by the huge buddleia plants either side of the path.

As if Clarissa hasn't already told you.

'I'm heading up a new cold case team and we're revisiting the case of the girls found in the folly.'

'Oh, I see.' Clemency tucked a strand of pale brown hair behind her ear, leaving a floury smudge on her cheek. Her fingers played with the wooden clip holding the rest of her hair at the nape of her neck.

Ruth stepped forward. 'DS Goodwin. Clarissa has been informed of our investigation. She's given us permission to look at the folly.' She gestured behind her. 'We have two extra civilian members on the team. We're just going over everything again.'

'Mmm, yes. I see. Well, I can't really tell you anything different to what I said in my official statement.'

Kath caught a movement in an upstairs window. 'I'm sorry, you seem to have guests.'

Clemency turned her head back to the door. 'Yes, I have a friend over. I really should be putting the bread in the oven.'

'Oh bloody hell,' Ruth muttered, stepping back as six chickens rounded the side of the cottage and made a beeline for her.

'They won't hurt you.' Clemency made a clicking noise with her tongue and bent down, holding out her hand.

Kath stifled a laugh and cleared her throat. 'I'm afraid DS Goodwin has an unhealthy relationship with fowl unless they're freshly prepared by an American colonel in a white suit.'

Lane and Byron snuffled softly behind her as Ruth glared at her and then turned her attention quickly back to the advancing birds.

'We've taken up enough of your time,' said Kath as Ruth moved nearer to her for protection.

Clemency stood upright, glancing quickly back at the cottage. 'Well then, I wish you all the best in your investigation.'

'We'll be going over your statement again and may want another chat.'

'Really? As I said, I'm not sure I can add anything.' She gave what she hoped was a smile of finality.

'And as we said, we're going over everything again.'

Kath turned and walked back to the others as the door closed. Some considered it a flaw in her character that she liked to have the last word, but she simply found it a useful tool to unsettle those who thought they had the upper hand. The chickens had given up the idea that the four humans had anything interesting for them and returned to pecking at the gravel in between the flower beds. Lane and Byron were facing the cottage, whereas Ruth and Kath had their backs to it.

Lane gave a big grin and put on a ventriloquist-type voice, her lips barely moving. 'Don't turn around. Just laugh at what I'm about to say. We're still being watched.'

Their forced laughter echoed through the trees as Clemency appeared at the bedroom window.

'They'll be back.'

'Maybe,' Clemency replied. 'I'll go and see Clarissa later.'

'The one with the long dark hair is the one to watch.'

'There's nothing to see and nothing to find. We'll be fine.'

The two women watched the foursome walk back along the path.

'The one to watch. Mark my words.'

| 15 |

April 2011

Layla swore as she stubbed her toe on a table leg. The tray of glasses wobbled in her hand, and she steadied it with her other hand as she stood upright. A couple of the regular drinkers at the bar cheered and held up their glasses to toast her near-accident.

'Not cool, morons.' She flashed a mean stare at the men as she deposited the tray on the bar and set about putting them in the grey plastic box to transport to the kitchen.

Rafferty watched her from the corner table, his wine glass almost empty. When she emerged from the kitchen, she glanced around at the pub tables. Rafferty held up his hand, smiled and beckoned her over. Her long hair was threatening to escape from its scrunchie as she pushed tendrils back from her face and pulled the scrunchie tighter as she walked over to Rafferty's table.

'You work hard for your money.' He held up his nearly empty wine bottle. 'Care to get me another of these?'

She sighed and looked across at the bar to see if Paul, the landlord, was watching. She saw him disappear into the kitchen and wiped her hands down her thighs. 'I'm not supposed to serve drinks. I told you that last time.'

She'd seen Rafferty in the pub before, always alone and always drinking the most expensive wine they had.

He discreetly turned his palm over to reveal two folded twenty-pound notes.

'Where's the harm, just this once?'

He grinned and patted her hand, passing the notes to her. She looked around again. It was a quiet night and no-one was taking any notice of her now there was no impending accident on offer. She took the notes and put them into her jeans pocket. She wasn't supposed to serve; her job was merely glass collection and wiping tables.

'There's a bonus for you on your return.' He downed the rest of his wine and smiled at her.

At the mention of more money, her eyes lit up. This was her third job along with working in a cafe serving breakfast several mornings a week and looking after a local gift shop. Rafferty had overheard snatches of conversation with her friends one evening about how she was gathering all the money she could to go travelling across Spain and Portugal, mentioning her parents, their fights, needing to get away from the family drama.

'I'll be back.'

He watched her walk to the bar with his empty wine bottle, imagining how he would release her hair from its prison. She had attitude, and he liked that. He still missed Jennifer. Missed how she'd looked at him with those adoring eyes, lips slightly parted with expectation. But she was gone now, and here was the lovely Layla. He pushed his wallet back into his pocket as Layla returned with a new bottle.

'Show me the money.' She waved the bottle in front of him, aware of the way he was looking at her. He leaned forward and gestured for her to come closer. She looked at the notes he pressed into her hand and nearly dropped the bottle. He grabbed it and grinned.

'There's two hundred quid here.'

He slowly poured the red liquid into his glass. 'Plenty more where that came from.'

Ten minutes ago, he'd been just Rafferty Quartermaine, rich, a bit arrogant, sort of cute with the way his hair flopped over his eye and he continually pushed it back. Now he was a meal ticket to get her the hell away from this town and her screaming parents. She was only eighteen, but she was smart.

'Doing what?' She pushed her hands into her pockets and looked defiantly at him.

He sat further back in his chair, crossing one leg slowly over the other. 'Nothing illegal.'

She smiled. 'More information.'

'I have a couple of events to go to, out of town. I think you'd look perfect on my arm smiling, drinking vintage champagne and letting that fabulous hair down to frame that beautiful face.'

She removed her hands from her pockets and gestured down her body. 'Not gonna be posh enough in charity shop jeans.'

He laughed and flicked his hair back. 'Of course, you'd be wearing a gorgeous designer dress and shoes, which I will pay for and you can keep.'

'And the money?' Her stern face hid the excitement coursing through her body. This could be a very good deal.

'Straight to the point. I love that about you...Layla, isn't it?'

'Tell me.'

'Two evenings, possibly three. A grand for each night.'

If she'd had the tray of glasses in her hands, that would have been the point at which they would have cascaded to the floor. She pushed her weight onto one leg and brushed stray hair from her cheek. Her brain was racing with possibilities. *Why me? Why not me? Easy money. Out of here sooner than expected. Sleazeball? Genuine? Three fucking grand.*

'You don't even know me. How d'you know I'll be up to the job?'

'I know what I see and I like it. And I think you like this idea.'

A couple near the door got up and left.

'Layla?' Paul Barton pointed to the glasses on the empty table.

She waved at him. 'On it.'

She gave Rafferty a smile and left to gather the glasses. On her way back, she stopped at his table.

'Why me?'

'Maybe I just feel the need to spend a little more quality time with you. Look, think about it. I'll be here tomorrow night. Tell me your decision then.'

She nodded and went to the bar, already planning to quit her other jobs. Was it too good to be true? Maybe. But she could look after herself. It was going to be fun and she was going to be away very soon.

| 16 |

'Productive?' Kath nodded towards the phone as she entered the office, the rest of the team who'd gone to the Quartermaine estate behind her.

Shirl replaced the receiver. 'Not bad. You?'

'Ditto, although Ruth came up against another poultry situation.'

'Not eggs-actly what you were expecting, then?'

Ruth glared at Shirl. 'Have a biscuit and shut up,' she muttered, sitting at her desk.

'Okay, let's all sit and share.' Kath went to the window and perched on the edge of the table, looking at the eager faces before her.

'We've been to the folly. Nothing from Lane, but Byron had an interesting reaction.'

All eyes turned to him.

'I'm alright. Just felt really dizzy, disoriented. And I threw up,' he added.

'And you got nothing?' Shirl looked at Lane.

'Like I said, it doesn't always happen the way I want it to, but we had an interesting development—'

Kath held up her hand. 'Hang on, Lane. We'll get to that.' She wanted to reveal the information in order. 'It occurred to us that the folly really is inaccessible except through the main gates to the house and grounds and the pathway through the woods. We have to ask again how anyone got a body up there, let alone doing it three times.'

Marvin tapped his pen against his forehead. 'I guess if someone was strong enough, they could have carried each girl. They were all quite slim.'

Byron lifted a finger. 'But it would have to have been at night, and how would they see with no torch or light of any description?' He leant forward, elbows on his knees, hands clasped between his open legs. 'I can see why you looked at Rafferty, not just because of the other stuff, but did you ever consider Clarissa or Clemency?'

'It was briefly considered,' Ruth admitted, 'but I think I see what you're getting at. One or all of the three are still possible for the killer because of the location of the bodies, but, practically speaking, we're looking at neither of the two women being physically strong enough to carry even a slim body.'

'I suppose the girls could have got there on their own,' Marvin said, setting down his pen. 'I mean, maybe they were told to meet someone, maybe Rafferty, at the folly?'

Byron grinned as Kath nodded.

'Byron already brought up the possibility they could have been alive when entering the folly. But we don't want to back ourselves into a corner in narrowing the suspect list down to just those three.'

'Tell them about Clemency,' said Ruth, itching to move things forward.

'So, after the folly visit, we went to Clemency's cottage. She came out to see us, got the feeling she wasn't keen on inviting us inside.'

'I got more from being outside her place than I did at the folly,' said Lane, 'and I was not expecting that. We were being watched by someone from an upstairs window.'

'And you were feeling it was more than curiosity?' Marvin asked.

Lane nodded, her fingers picking at the air. 'I'm trying to think of a way to describe it. Like… it was like a psychic curtain being pulled across so I couldn't see.'

'Like a Klingon cloaking device?'

Ruth sighed. 'If I've said it once, I've said it a million times. You really do need to get out more.'

Everyone laughed, and Marvin stuck his tongue out at her.

Byron's face lost all expression, and he tilted his head to the side, as if to line up his thoughts. 'I felt it too. It was weird, but I can't explain it.'

'I said the boy has a gift.' Lane shared a smile with him.

'Shirl and Marvin, what did you get?' Kath asked, taking eyes away from Byron and Lane's tender moment.

Marvin gestured to Shirl. 'You go.'

'We spoke to Jennifer's best friend, Samantha. Still no clue as to Jennifer's mystery man, but she did mention something that might help.' Shirl paused.

'Cut the dramatics and get on with it,' Ruth barked.

Let me have my moment.' She smiled sarcastically at Ruth. 'The clothing of all three girls was found in neat piles directly opposite the bodies where they were chained up, right? It's in the original reports and we all remember. But Samantha told us that the mystery guy had given Jennifer a really expensive bracelet—diamonds and white gold, no less. There was no mention of this being found.'

'Maybe she just wasn't wearing it?' said Kath.

'We considered that, but then Samantha said that Jennifer told her that her man insisted she wear it when they were together. Stands to reason she would have been wearing it that night, given the significance of what was presumably going to happen.'

'And there's no mention of it at all?'

Kath was fighting to remember. There had been too many murders, too many cases in the intervening years. Like with all detectives on major incident teams, some details stuck like glue in the memory. Every so often, something insignificant would bring the memory to the forefront, fresh as if it had just been discovered. A song on the radio, a snatch of conversation, a line from a comedy TV show. Things you wanted to forget but couldn't. She quickly combed through the image of the team arriving at the folly, seeing the horror, seeing the clothes piled up. There was nothing.

'I did a rough sketch.' Marvin stood up, flourishing his notebook. 'Just to try and get as much detail as possible.' He walked round to each member of the team to reveal the sketch.

Kath looked over at Byron. 'Can you do some of your magic with this? See if we can track down where it was made or bought?'

He nodded, the image already etched in his mind as he typed. 'I can do a colour mock-up, search for similar items. Would he have got it locally, do you think?'

Kath stood up and paced between the desks. 'Possibly. Given the timescale of his meeting up with Jennifer, I doubt he would have had time to commission something bespoke. Birmingham's jewellery quarter could be a start.'

'He does have business in London as well, though. Could have got it there.' Shirl tapped her chin. 'That'll make it harder if that's the case. Do we ask him about it?'

Ruth shook her head. 'I would say no. Let's see if Byron can do anything first.'

Marvin sat back in his chair, toying with his pen on the desk. 'Maybe he gave the other two girls something similar, so the killer may have taken them all, possible trophies?'

Kath smiled to herself. The young man was growing in confidence within the team before her eyes and she felt something akin to maternal pride. 'That's really good, Marvin. Why don't you and Shirl carry on talking to the friends of Layla and Sophia, test your theory.'

Shirl winked at Marvin and waved him towards her desk.

Lane reached out and halted Kath's pacing. The two women huddled, voices low. 'Your wee man will be after your job soon. 'Her eyes twinkled, but her tone was serious.

'That's what I'm training him for. He's got a good head on him but still happy to be guided by us veterans.'

Marvin was bent down at Shirl's desk but suddenly looked up, as if he was aware he was being talked about. He blushed and avoided eye contact, returning to Shirl's scribbling on her notepad.

'Me and Ruth and Shirl have years of experience under our belts, but he brings fresh perspective and insight, good ideas, good instincts. He and Byron balance us.'

'The force is with you.' Lane winked and tossed her curls over her shoulders. 'My bedtime reading was interesting, courtesy of Byron.'

'Then I guess it's time to share thoughts with the group.'

Kath cleared her throat and waited for the team members to look over before nodding to Lane to take the floor.

'I took a look at some of the background around Clarissa and Quartermaine Manor.' Lane's accent had the ability to command a room, and now she had everyone's attention. 'I don't want to freak you guys out, but I felt the energy as soon as I saw Clarissa. I think she felt it too.'

Ruth opened her mouth to speak, but Kath caught her eye and shook her head.

'I didn't say anything,' Lane went on, and Ruth nodded, her question answered, 'because I know the focus here is the girls and getting justice for them and their families, but I think we need to factor in the stories, the folklore, the tales that people have told over the years.'

'Are we talking about, and I don't want to be dramatic here, but dark forces or something?' Ruth was expecting a jokey comment from Shirl at her remark, but the look on Shirl's face made it clear it was not a subject for levity.

Lane frowned and looked down at her hands. 'I wouldn't say that exactly.' She was trying to weigh her words, not wanting to scare the team but needing them to know the gravity of the situation. 'Like I keep saying, it's difficult to put into words what I feel.' Her fingers danced in the air before her. 'When you sand wood, you go with the grain. If you go against it, it doesn't feel right. I kinda feel there's an emery board being scraped across my knuckles. That's the best way I can put it to help you understand. Friction. Disturbance.'

The room was silent, the outside noise of traffic and passing conversation muted.

'The land has always had power. I feel Clarissa and probably Clemency know how to harness that power. They wear it around them like an invisible cloak, and it should not be underestimated.'

The team looked from one face to another, eyes relaying concern and anxiety.

'Do you think this invisible cloak could be hiding a killer?' Kath's question echoed the thoughts of everyone in the room.

'I'm saying it's a possibility.'

Clarissa gripped the crystal tumbler and drank deeply, the smoky amber liquid warming her thin body. 'There was power in her touch, Clemency. You saw her. Did you feel it?'

Clemency turned her back to the fireplace, where a large pile of logs succumbed slowly to flames. 'It was coming off her like a tidal wave. I had to pick a spot on the path to shield myself.'

'Fortune seems different this time, more focused. We need to be even more careful.'

Clemency crossed her arms. 'She said she'll be back. I fully expect her to bring the woman with her. They're not done with us.'

Clarissa walked to the window and looked out to the woods. 'We require a strong banishment spell for the woman. You need to get closer to her, gather what we need.'

'She'll have her guard up.'

'Then we'll have to make sure we peel it away. She will never see it coming. I'll make sure of that.'

| 17 |

The contents of Kath's wardrobe lay strewn across the bed like a table at a 1950s jumble sale. Drawers were half open, spilling their contents. She stood in the middle of her bedroom in her bra and knickers, fresh from a hot shower.

'It's a drink, silly mare,' she spoke to her reflection on the inside of the wardrobe door. 'Just pick something.'

On the drive home, the butterflies in her stomach had begun to awaken and she'd felt ridiculous and excited. Now the excitement was turning into anxiety.

She took a deep breath. 'It's not a date, it's not a date.'

She picked up a maroon V-neck sweater, then put it back on the bed and gasped as she noticed the hands of the wall clock creeping past six-thirty. She held up a green blouse by the sleeve, shook her head and let it fall.

'It's work,' she shouted at the bed. 'A recce for work, that's all.'

The Blasted Oak pub had its own spooky stories and myths attached to it and was known for its eclectic clientele. She felt safer combining work with what she hoped would be a pleasurable evening.

Too cold to care anymore, she pulled on black jeans and grabbed the maroon sweater. A touch of eyeliner, mascara and lip gloss made her feel as if she'd made just enough of an effort for her non-date. As she turned in the doorway and looked back at the mess on the bed, she realised she'd come back to a night of tidying up before sleep was on the cards.

'Sleep is overrated anyway,' she muttered as she turned out the light.

There was still daylight clinging to the horizon as Richard and Kath walked to the other end of the village towards The Blasted Oak.

We look like a couple from an advert for supermarket clothing. That over-fifties couple who like to be casual in their matching black jeans and our waterproof jackets that say we're trendy and outdoorsy. We like hiking in the hills on a weekend, retiring to our new kitchen with the hip marble-topped island. We make our own organic soup and like to have friends over for wine and cheese.

Kath snapped back from her fantasy as their arms brushed against each other.

'...and I saw the rose and thought of you.'

'Hmm? Oh right, yes.'

'Distracted by work?' Richard's pace was even and the closeness comfortable.

'Little bit. Sorry. Comes with the territory.'

'Well, I promise not to ramble on about potentillas and sandy soil.' He grinned at her.

'You're a nice distraction... I mean flowers, gardening...'

Why does my mouth run off when I'm with him?

He ignored her embarrassment and stopped outside The Bell, stepping in front of her to push open the door.

'No, we're not going in there.'

'Oh.' Richard's hand dropped to his side.

'Further on.' Kath pointed. 'The other pub.'

'The Blasted Oak?'

'Yep. You haven't been in yet, have you?'

He shook his head. 'The Bell is closest and they do food. Been in a couple of times.'

They walked on.

'I have a confession to make,' Kath pushed her hands into her pockets then took them out again.

'Shouldn't that be my line?'

She laughed. 'I'm kind of combining a social evening with a little work thrown in.'

Richard nodded. 'Okay. Can you talk about it?'

'Actually, I can share some of it.'

'I'd like that. Guess we're here.'

The cottage stood within its own walled garden. The pub sign hung straight down in the still evening air, depicting a blackened oak tree with a bright fork of lightning against an orange and purple sunset sky. The curtains were drawn against the two downstairs windows. Richard peered through the two small panes of glass in the top of the door.

'Ladies first.'

He pushed the door open and stepped back for her to enter. The pub interior was the opposite of The Doctor's TARDIS. Wall and table lamps gave a muted glow. The stone open fireplace on the right-hand wall was flanked by empty tables and skeletal wooden chairs. Where most rustic pubs embellished their hearths with dried flower displays and horse brasses, this one was completely bare. Three men were at the bar, another two at a table near the door and a lone man sat at a table at the back of the room. They all turned and stared at the visitors.

Kath forced a smile. 'Have you seen the film *An American Werewolf in London*?' she muttered under her breath.

'I have indeed,' Richard replied softly. 'You still want to do this?'

'We're here now.' Still smiling, Kath walked to the bar. She nodded to the man behind the bar, his meaty hands holding a ragged towel and polishing a glass. 'Evening.'

'You locals? Haven't seen you in here before.'

'Yes, we are, and no, you haven't.' She was waiting for a reciprocal smile, but she immediately felt that it wouldn't be forthcoming any time soon. Another approach was required.

'What can you recommend for a woman who can't hold her drink?'

'Another pub.'

Everyone in the bar laughed, including Richard. He rested his arms on the bar and looked at the pumps.

'What's the real ale like?'

'Real,' said the barman.

'In that case, in the probable absence of an espresso martini, I'll have a pint of Sheep Dip. Kath?'

She guessed that low-alcohol lager had never passed across the bar. 'Dry cider. Half, thanks.'

Richard placed a ten-pound note on the bar before Kath could protest.

Change and glasses picked up, they sat at a table by the fireplace, chair backs digging into their spines. Richard took a sip of his ale.

'How is it?'

'Sheepy.'

They shared a smile, and Kath took a sip of her cider. The strength of the liquid took her by surprise, and she coughed. The other drinkers resumed conversations, and she started to feel more comfortable about talking.

'So, how was your day?'

I'll bet you went for a run and had a cold shower. Then you squeezed organic apples with your bare hands and let the juice dribble into your mouth...

'Not very exciting.' Richard sipped his drink and began to appreciate the taste more with every mouthful. 'Started off with a run, then I squeezed some oranges I got from that farm shop up the... What? You're blushing.'

Kath managed a controlled smile. 'Nothing. Just hot, that's all.'

He grinned. 'Whatever you say. So I'm guessing your day was a bit more interesting.'

In a low tone, between careful sips of cider, she told him about the investigation, revealing only pertinent details that were already known and reported on, how they were looking at everything fresh and how Lane was helping them.

His face was serious, but there was a sparkle in his eyes as he listened intently. 'A psychic? That is interesting. It's not generally known that psychics help the police, is it?'

'We like to keep it under the radar, but Lane is so gifted. She picks up on things that we miss or dismiss.'

And I'm never going to introduce you to her because she is too gorgeous.

'I get it. Everything is energy, everything resonates.' He shifted in his chair, trying to get more comfortable than the wood would allow. 'When I started out gardening, I used to explain to the tree or shrub that I was planning to prune or move it. Must sound a bit weird.' He looked at her, waiting for a joke or a laugh.

'Actually no. Go on.'

He stretched out his legs and crossed his ankles. 'We take the land for granted. I feel I need to acknowledge the beauty, the steadfast nature of...nature. It sleeps, decays, then comes back and starts a new cycle. I'm perpetually in awe, I guess.'

'I'm looking at gardening in a whole new light now.' She smiled at him sincerely. She understood. Knowing Lane had helped her understand so many things she had previously shrugged off.

'You certainly have the knack of making me confess what's in my soul. That's a gift.' He raised his glass to her. 'I think your job is awful and fascinating in equal measure.'

'That's a fairly accurate description.'

'How do you deal with the monsters that aren't actually under the bed but walking amongst us?'

Kath avoided his eyes and looked past him at the photographs in frames on the wall. There were some landscape shots, presumably local, mixed with images of stern-faced farmers with tractors and a couple of photographs of smiling women. 'Each case is different. That great grey path between the light and the dark can be messy and frustrating, but we just have to stay curious and focused.'

'Don't stray from the path.'

She looked at him, puzzled.

'*American Werewolf in London*?'

Kath grimaced. 'That's the second time today someone's said that to me. Ironic.'

Her eyes kept flicking back to one of the photographs.

Richard turned around to see what held her attention. 'Do you know them?'

'I don't know...' Kath stood up and moved closer to Richard's chair, staring at the image of two smiling young women with their arms around each other. Her brain was rapidly trying to process the myriad of faces she had seen in her career.

'Oh my god, it's Clarissa Quartermaine.'

'Blackstock.'

The voice behind her made her jump, and she turned to face the barman, who was staring at her.

'Before she married Farraday. That's her and her sister, Theadora.' He moved away and picked up the two empty glasses from the table by the door, nodding to the two men leaving.

'I forgot all about her sister.'

'Want to fill me in?' Richard stroked her arm, and she shuddered with delight at his touch, as if her arm were free of the jumper sleeve and he had connected with her bare skin.

She sat down. 'Not much else I can say. The girls were found on her land. She's allowing us to visit. We need to play nice to get the result we want.'

'The result being finding the killer?'

'That's the job.'

Richard felt her energy drop and changed the subject. 'How do you switch off, then? What do you do in the dark of the night?'

She picked up her glass. 'I do this. Make new friends.'

'I like that I'm a new friend.' He raised his glass to her and drank. 'What about gentleman friends...other than me?'

She didn't want to lie and found that she didn't need to, as the words formed naturally. 'There's someone, but like they said on *Friends*, we're on a break.'

'Oh.' He struggled with the kernel of disappointment but kept his face even, interested to learn more.

'Known each other since school,' Kath continued, 'and we've recently reconnected. He's going through an amicable divorce. I'm working out what I want.'

Richard stroked the side of his glass. 'Didn't mean to pry.'

'It's alright. My work tends to get in the way of relationships.'

Well, that was a stupendously stupid thing to say, Fortune.

Lenny's face came into her mind, and she waited for a response in her body that didn't come.

'I get that. I'm guessing you can't help but take your work home with you.'

She gave a small laugh. 'I try not to, but it happens. What about you?'

Don't share with me the stories of a host of women with broken hearts scattered across the country.

'Ah, well, recently out of a long-term relationship. Hence my relocation.'

Please tell me there won't be rabbits bubbling on your cooker hob when you get home.

'On a break?' She grinned at him.

'A permanent one. She found someone else.'

'Oh, I'm sorry.'

I'm really not, though.

'Don't be. It was dead in the water. We both knew it. One of us had to make the move to bury the corpse of our relationship... Sorry, I'm talking shop in your world.' He paused. 'She moved in with an estate agent who is compact and bijou, with an exterior that needs some attention.'

The mouthful of cider threatened to cascade from Kath's lips. She swallowed quickly, coughing and laughing at the same time. 'I shouldn't laugh at your pain.'

'Actually, it really wasn't that painful, which was a good indication. He has red hair.'

'She gave up Scottish beef for a short guy with red hair...'

His lips paused at the rim of his glass, and his eyes dared her to continue.

Her cheeks reddened. 'Oh dear god, I just compared you to meat. I can only blame the alcohol.'

What the fuck, Fortune.

'Scottish beef? Hmm,' he teased. 'Anyway, are we having another?'

She wanted to stay but was almost afraid her mouth would run off again and maybe ruin the evening.

'Yes, but a soft drink.'

He stood up and picked up their glasses. 'Any preferences?'

'Surprise me.'

'I think I might be able to do that.'

She resisted the temptation to watch him walk to the bar. She caught the eye of the man at the corner table at the back of the room, handling a deck of cards. He smiled at her. She looked away and focused her attention back on the photograph of Clarissa and Theadora. Smiling, happy young women. Kath found it hard to reconcile the image of Clarissa with the woman she knew now.

'It's a great photograph, isn't it?'

Kath turned her head to the man, one of those men with naturally curly and unruly hair that women would always be jealous of and spend a lot of money forcing hairdressers to emulate.

'Yes, it is. Do you know Clarissa?'

'I do, yes.'

Kath's senses were alert now. She saw the cards in his hands and realised they were Tarot cards. He saw her eyes flicker to the deck.

'Would you like a reading?'

She laughed. 'No, you're okay.'

Richard returned and placed a glass in front of her. 'You look underwhelmed by my choice.' He sat down and sipped his orange juice as she stared at the pink fizzy liquid.

'I'm just trying to work out what it is.' She picked up the glass and tentatively took a mouthful.

'You're the detective. If you guess correctly, I'll spring for a bar of chocolate from the garage on the way back.'

'You know how to show a girl a good time.'

'It has been said. Well?'

She took another swallow. 'Soda water with blackcurrant.'

'Chocolate it is.'

The man with the Tarot cards stood up and headed for the door. He stopped at Kath's chair and spread the cards in a fan. 'Pick a card.'

She raised an eyebrow but decided to humour him. He knew Clarissa and therefore he might be of some use in the future. Her fingers teased a card out, and she found that she had pulled two.

'Let's see what you have,' the man said.

She turned over the first card. Two figures, a male and female. They stood in woodland dressed in clothes of autumn shades, the girl with flowers and leaves entwined in her long hair. They were smiling, each offering a chalice.

'The Two of Cups. A meeting of two minds and two hearts. The promise of a new soul partnership. Also, a decision to be made.'

Kath could feel Richard's eyes on her and willed herself not to look at him. The artwork on the card was beautiful, but she focused on trying to push the card and its companion back into the man's hands.

'What about the other card?' Richard inched forward like a meercat, trying not to smile.

Oh shit. This needs to be over.

'I suppose I ought to see.' Kath turned over the second card and wished there was something stronger than soda water in her glass

'The Devil. An interesting combination.'

The man accepted the cards into the pack as Kath picked up her glass.

'Thanks. Very interesting, yes…' she muttered, hoping her tone would elicit a swift exit.

'Why is it interesting?' Richard asked.

Oh shut up, please shut up.

The man tilted his head. 'Each card has meaning, but it can change the whole perspective according to other cards around it.'

Kath was looking at the table, but she felt both pairs of eyes on her. She mentally gritted her teeth and looked up. 'I know you're dying to tell me.' She gave a fixed smile.

The man smiled back. 'I feel this speaks of a choice in matters of the heart. The Devil wants to tempt us back into old ways, where we feel stuck but safe. Explore the new path. You might surprise yourself. I have a shop in Bridgnorth if you'd like a more comprehensive reading. The Bright Stone.'

The man pushed his cards into his oversized jacket pocket and went out into the night.

'What a very interesting evening this is turning out to be.'

'And it's not over yet,' Kath replied. 'You still owe me a bar of chocolate.'

| 18 |

10th October 2019

Ruth had just flicked the kettle on as Kath entered the office.

'Yes, I'll have one of those.' Kath placed her bag under her desk and sat down.

'You look bright-eyed and bushy-tailed,' Ruth said with surprise, wondering if Kath had been up all night drinking coffee or had actually had some decent sleep. She poured water onto her tea bag and Kath's coffee granules.

'Six hours of blissful sleep, for a change.'

Ruth handed her a mug and sat down at her desk. 'So, how are you feeling about the case?'

Kath thought for a moment. 'Like I've been given three jigsaw puzzles where all the pieces have got mixed up in the three boxes. I know what each picture looks like, but it's taking a long time to sift through all the pieces to make them fit.'

'Good analogy.' Ruth sipped her tea. 'But you could look at it this way. All the pieces of all the puzzles are there, so it's just matching colours and patterns. Maybe we shouldn't be starting at the straight edges. We should just jump in and get all the pink bits out, all the sky, all the boats... whatever. Build from the middle.'

'Okay. That's positive.'

Kath looked at the clock and wondered what Richard was doing, debating whether to text him. When they'd reached his cottage last night, he had invited her in. Although she'd wanted to prolong the evening, her brain had been buzzing with thoughts of Clarissa, Theadora and the incident with the Tarot cards. She'd politely refused and avoided the awkwardness of a possible kiss by standing well away from him and then getting quickly into her car for the very short drive home. She'd thought he might watch her drive away, but he'd shut the front door immediately. Maybe she'd played it all wrong.

'What do we focus on next, then?' Ruth asked.

'What do we know about Clarissa's sister, Theadora?'

Ruth frowned. 'She's dead, isn't she? And where did that come from?'

Kath wasn't ready to tell her about the photograph she'd seen, wanting to keep her outing to the pub a secret along with her new companion. 'Humour me. What happened to her?'

Ruth started typing. 'Theadora Quartermaine...'

'No, Blackstock was her name,' Kath interjected.

'Oh yes. I've got bloody Quartermaine on the brain.' Ruth continued typing. She read through a report that her search had found. 'She died in 1988 in a fire at a psychiatric facility in Derbyshire.'

Kath swivelled her chair to face Ruth. 'Do we know why she was there?'

'Hang on, seems she had a recreational drug habit. Went to a party, took some bad pills. Induced a psychotic episode... Okay, long story short, she never recovered, mad as a box of frogs, and Clarissa shipped her off out of the way, I guess.'

Kath thought Ruth's tone was unfairly harsh. 'Maybe we should look at it as Clarissa and Farraday had a small child, maybe Theadora was deemed a risk and her sister put her in a place of safety where she could be looked after properly.'

'You're trying to say that's why Clarissa is a cranky old mare?'

Kath grinned at her friend. 'Maybe she just did what she thought was right for everyone. Give the woman a break.'

Ruth grunted. 'Says here she actually set the fire, got caught in it and that's how she came to her end.'

'Anyone else injured?'

'Nope. Just her. Twenty-nine. A life cut short.'

'Sad story.'

'Mmm. So, back to the plan.'

Kath stood up and went to the whiteboard. She stared at the smiling faces beaming down at her. 'Why these three, Ruth?'

Before Ruth could offer a suggestion, Kath continued. 'Why three years apart?'

They heard footsteps coming up the stairs.

'If I'm killing girls with long hair, there's plenty of them out there.'

Marvin stopped in the doorway and looked at Kath. 'Career change?' He gave a half-smile.

'You're alright. I'm just thinking out loud.'

'Good to know.'

'So, continuing my thought process, why every three years? And then I just stop.'

'You died or you're in prison for something else,' said Ruth.

'Okay, but if none of those parameters apply, why don't I just keep doing it after Jennifer? Why don't I escalate? I've got away with it. People think she's run off, I haven't been questioned. I can keep doing it. But I wait. And then Layla happens. Again, I can carry on. Another runaway, missing girl, no clues, no questions. I think I'm safe after Sophia and then the boys find the bodies and it's all over.'

'I don't think it's about the urge,' Marvin said. 'The need to do it isn't there.' He joined her at the whiteboard. He looked thoughtful, and Kath waited, knowing there was more for him to vocalise.

'He doesn't need to do it, so that isn't what drives him.'

'It's personal,' said Ruth. 'Maybe we have been looking at this all wrong.'

Kath nodded and turned, pointing at Ruth. 'You, Marvin and Byron, when he gets here, cross-reference the three girls again. I want to know everything they possibly had in common.'

'Got it.' Ruth started typing, and Marvin was just about to speak when a text came through on Kath's phone. She resisted the temptation to look at it.

'Before you get started, ring Rafferty...no, ring Clarissa. Tell her we're coming to see Rafferty this morning at eleven.'

Ruth picked up the receiver. 'She'll say it's not convenient, I'll bet.'

Kath grinned. 'Doesn't matter. We'll be there at nine-thirty.'

'Sneaky,' said Ruth, punching in Clarissa's number.

'So, did Rafferty admit to knowing any of the girls?' Marvin lowered his voice as Ruth spoke to Clarissa.

'He said he knew *of* them,' Kath replied. 'He'd seen Layla at The Bell. Witnesses confirmed conversation between them. When we showed him the picture of Jennifer, he said he might have seen her in Restonfield as he drove through. She had friends in the village, so that was reasonable. Sophia... I can't remember what he said about her.'

'What's your approach going to be?'

The eyes of the girls gazed down at her, and she reached up and grabbed the photographs. 'I'm going to make them real again, not skeletons in a tower. Not tissue and sinew left to rot, but young girls, vibrant, their lives ahead of them.'

Ruth replaced the receiver. 'All done. She said we shouldn't upset Brocken. He's home-schooled and the tutors will be at the house.'

'She's very protective of him,' Kath muttered as she sat down and placed the photos on her desk.

'He's her only grandchild. I get that,' said Marvin.

'I wonder why they haven't had any more children?' Ruth pondered.

'It's an interesting question, but I don't think it's something we need to concern ourselves with.' Kath was focused on Jennifer's photo, and she tapped it slowly with her fingers. 'Jennifer was the first. It all started with her. Why?'

Before Marvin or Ruth could respond, more footsteps were heard on the stairs, and Shirl and Byron appeared.

'Morning, team.' Shirl was carrying a cardboard container tray housing takeaway cups. 'Pumpkin spice lattes for you all.'

As she passed them round, Ruth grimaced at the thought of the milky froth but took the proffered cup and muttered thanks.

'What gives, then?' Shirl looked round to see Marvin frowning as he lifted the lid from his cup.

'You and I are going to see Rafferty in half an hour,' Kath replied.

'Oh right.' She crushed the cardboard container and stuffed it deep into the waste bin.

Byron sat down, shrugging off his jacket. 'What do you want me to do?'

Ruth turned to him. 'We need to dig around for more information on Clarissa's sister, Theodora, and chase up friends of Layla and Sophia. We're also looking at anything and everything that the girls might have had in common.'

'Okay.' He sipped his latte and turned on his computer.

Marvin picked up his phone as a text came through, and Kath remembered the unread message on her own phone.

'Dylan's agreed to the regression session.'

Kath smiled. 'That's good news. Liaise with Byron about Cassandra's availability.'

Kath wondered if Cassandra would allow her to sit in on the meeting. She wouldn't admit it out loud, but her expectations were high. TV shows played up the drama of the practice, but she'd read reports about instances where people had remembered tiny details, a sound or a smell, that had led to incredible results. She felt safe in the knowledge that Dylan would be in excellent hands. Cassandra had an easy way with herself that radiated out to others. She was comfortable in her tattooed skin with her dreadlocks snaking down her back. Kath had no doubt she would be a fearsome and strong opponent if crossed, but her manner put clients and customers at ease.

She picked up her mobile and smiled. She opened the text message.

I had an interesting evening with an interesting woman. Hoping for a repeat...

I'd like that. Your choice this time.

I was thinking dinner, maybe tonight?

Sounds good

Happy for me to choose the venue?

Certainly

I'll let you know details when I've booked.

Look forward to it

'Hey, smiley face. Is that Lenny, then?' Shirl grinned at Kath, a pale foamy moustache adorning her top lip.

Kath put her phone down. 'No,' she said slowly. 'A friend.'

Ruth and Shirl looked at each other. Ruth was going to indicate the foam lip but then decided against it.

'Want to share?'

'No.' She stood up. 'Let's go and surprise Rafferty.'

Shirl moved to the door, holding her cup.

'That stays here.'

'But I haven't finished it.'

'You're not having that in my car and that's why microwaves were invented.'

Kath pushed past her and headed down the stairs, grinning. She could hear Shirl muttering behind her, but even the grumblings of her colleague couldn't dampen her mood as Richard's face came into her mind.

The windscreen wipers were on their highest speed as torrential rain lashed the car, and Kath was regretting not grabbing her waterproof jacket as the weatherman had suggested on the morning radio forecast. Kath parked as close to Rafferty's cottage as she could and frowned as she peered through the windscreen, seeing the front door open and a woman looking at the car, holding a cardboard box.

'That's Rafferty's wife, isn't it?' Shirl asked, and Kath nodded.

They got out of the car and hurried up the path, trying to avoid the water from the sky and the gathering raindrops from the foliage that tried to cling to their knees. Fenella stepped back so they could enter the hallway. She clutched the box to her chest, eyes wide.

'Hello. Who are you?'

'DCI Fortune, DS Thompson. We'd like to see Rafferty.'

'Oh, he's at the house.' Fenella gestured towards the manor with one finger, her other digits still gripping the bottom edges of the cardboard box.

Shirl glanced behind Fenella at the stack of boxes. 'Moving out?'

'Yes actually. We're moving into the manor house. Clarissa thought it best.'

Kath could feel the anxiety coming off the drab woman before her.

'Why is that?'

Fenella looked down into the box, then looked past Kath out into the grounds. 'It's for Brocken's benefit, he's our son, as he has all his schooling over there. The tutors come every day and there's more space.'

'I see,' Kath said, stepping to one side. 'Lead the way, then.'

Fenella hesitated. 'I was waiting for a break in the rain. Don't want the boxes to get wet.'

'As you wish. We'll go over on our own.' Kath nodded a goodbye, and they stepped back out into the rain to walk the short distance to the manor house.

The door to the manor house was ajar, and Kath went straight in. Shirl followed, shaking raindrops from her coat. The doors to the drawing room on the right were open. Kath peered inside from the doorway. The room was empty.

'Should we announce ourselves?' Shirl didn't know why she felt the need to whisper.

To their left was a long hallway, an intricately patterned runner covering the wooden floor. Voices could be heard in the distance.

'Let's surprise them.'

Kath strode down the hallway with Shirl at her heels. They rounded the corner and found Clarissa and Rafferty.

'What are you doing here?' Clarissa crossed her arms and stared at Kath.

Shirl stood open-mouthed at the scale of the galleried room. She'd never ventured into this part of the house before, Clarissa always holding court in the drawing room, as close to the exit as possible. The mock-medieval vaulted ceiling seemed unfeasibly high. Plush sofas and small antique tables were scattered around the room, the wood-panelled walls resplendent with paintings and tapestries. A huge stag's head adorned the space above the stone fireplace, where a fire was pushing out welcome warmth. Rafferty stood next to his mother, surprised by their early arrival but trying to mask it by emulating her stance.

'I've had to call an emergency team meeting for later this morning. This was our only available window. Shall we do the interview in here, or is there another room more appropriate?' Kath felt dwarfed by the size of the room but was determined to stay in charge of the situation.

Rafferty looked at his mother, her mouth set in a line of disapproval. A flicker of movement caught Kath's eye, and she looked up at the galleried landing at the end of the room. Between the wooden rails stood a dark-haired boy. Clarissa followed Kath's gaze and brought up her right hand. Her fingers moved quickly. Rafferty looked up to see the boy signalling back. Before he could speak, the boy turned and walked into the room behind him.

'Rafferty, take the detectives to the study. I'll see what's keeping your wife and then join you.'

'That won't be necessary,' Kath said quickly. 'We need to speak to Rafferty on his own.'

Rafferty looked from Kath back to Clarissa, as if unable to move without permission.

'Go to the study,' Clarissa barked and walked away to disappear down a side passage.

Rafferty cleared his throat and led them back down the hallway to the room next to the drawing room. He waited whilst Shirl shut the door behind her. The room, like the others, was wood-panelled, with more paintings and sketches jostling for space on the walls between laden bookshelves. A desk nestled in the bay window. Rafferty perched against the edge, a half-stance between sitting and standing, seemingly uneasy in the closed environment with the two women.

'Is this really required?' His eyes darted between Kath and Shirl.

Kath was pleased at his discomfort and moved closer to him. 'We could always do this down at the station.'

His cheeks flushed, and Kath wasn't sure if it was the threat or her proximity.

'No, no...th-that's fine,' he stammered.

'But, depending on how this goes, we might end up there anyway.'

He pulled himself up from his slouch. 'So what do you want to ask me?'

'DS Thompson?'

Kath moved back, still holding Rafferty's gaze. Shirl picked up her cue. She was playing good cop. As usual. She pulled a file from her bag and stepped forward to the desk. Rafferty looked at his watch despite there being three clocks in the room and watched as Shirl set out the photographs of the three girls.

'Would you like to sit down?' She lightly touched Rafferty's arm, and he pulled it away as if burned. He knew he was expected to look at the smiling faces. His breath quickened. The two women remained silent.

Rafferty brushed his hair from his eyes. 'I'm fine. Ask your questions, then.'

'I'm sorry if this is distressing,' Shirl began, 'but we're hoping you remember something, anything, that perhaps you didn't tell us seven years ago.'

Kath watched him as he stared at the photos for a moment and then then looked away, wiping his hands down the sides of his trousers.

Kath pulled a small notebook from her pocket and opened it. 'Just to clarify, within a day or so of each of the girls being reported as missing, you said you had seen them.' She waited, her eyes searching the blank pages. 'Jennifer in the village, Layla at The Bell and Sophia—'

'Golf club,' said Rafferty quietly. 'She was waitressing. It was the club's anniversary.'

Now it came back to Kath. Sophia's father was a member of Brushten Golf Club, a few miles outside of Restonfield. They'd had a series of events over a three-week period.

Kath flicked through more empty pages. 'So you were working in London at that point.' She frowned and looked up at Rafferty. 'How did you happen to be here... April 2010, 2011 and 2012? The same time. Three years running.'

'I think I said at the time, if you look at your notes.' He nodded to the notebook.

Kath smiled. 'Just for clarification, if you wouldn't mind.'

Rafferty focused his attention on Shirl, away from Kath's stare and the smiling faces of Jennifer, Layla and Sophia. 'My godfather was mentoring me, grooming me to take over his business.' A little bit of swagger came back now. 'He always spent April and May at his house in the Caribbean, so I would come back here.'

'And miss all that partying in London? Or didn't he trust you while he was away?'

'No, that's not it at all, 'he snapped at Kath. 'I just didn't see a lot of my mother, so it was natural for me to come back here and spend time with her.'

'Of course,' said Shirl, 'only natural to want to spend time with family.'

'Your family extended when you married in 2012,' Kath said, flicking over a couple of pages. 'Must have been difficult to sustain a long-distance relationship.'

'My family and Fenella's have known each other for years. We were deemed a good match.'

'She seems lovely,' said Shirl, smiling.

'You've seen her?' There was panic in his eyes now.

'Briefly,' said Kath. 'She told us you're all moving in here.'

The door burst open, and Clarissa stood glaring at Kath. 'There's a lot to be done, detectives. Rafferty, Fenella needs you.'

Kath gave a controlled sigh. She wasn't going to get anything further, so she nodded. 'Of course. We'll go. Thank you for your time and information.'

At the last word, Clarissa turned her glare on her son. Rafferty swallowed hard and shook his head.

Clarissa escorted them to the door. Kath had purposefully left the photographs on the desk, but Rafferty rushed towards her and pushed them into her hands.

'You forgot these.'

Kath held his hands as he tried to pass the photographs. 'No, not forgotten at all.'

She snatched her hands away and walked quickly to the car. The rain had eased, but a stiff breeze had awakened.

Rafferty and Clarissa watched them drive away.

'This is bad, Mother. Really bad.'

'I hope you kept your mouth in order. Now go and get the rest of the boxes. I need to tend to Brocken.'

| 19 |

Back at the office, the mood was charged with anticipation. Kath filled the rest of the team in on the Rafferty interview and was excited to hear that Dylan had agreed to meet with Cassandra that afternoon.

'Mum says you can sit in on the session,' said Byron.

'He's a bit nervous,' Marvin added, 'but he just wants to help.'

'That's great news, Marvin. Go and pick him up when he's ready and you can take him home afterwards. I don't know much about what Cassandra has planned, but I don't want him driving afterwards.'

Marvin relayed the information to Dylan in a text.

'So Rafferty is moving in under Mummy's protection?' Ruth raised an eyebrow.

'Hmm. I'm suspicious about the timing,' Kath said. 'Rafferty was definitely different. Can't put my finger on it. It's got me wondering what's changed and if he knows something now that he didn't know then.'

'What about the wife?'

'Looked like she was just doing as instructed,' said Shirl.

Ruth nodded. They'd interviewed Fenella briefly seven years ago, but she seemed almost insignificant, as if overawed by the family. 'Might be worth getting her on her own, giving her a grilling.'

'Steady on, Ruth,' Shirl snorted. 'Keep your mean streak in your handbag.'

'She wouldn't take much breaking. You know I can't be doing with namby-pamby women.'

Marvin and Byron looked at each other.

'What's a namby-wotsit woman?'

Ruth gave Marvin an admonishing look. 'Sorry. I lapsed into old-person speak.'

'I think what my learned colleague is trying to say is that she's just a bit wet.'

'It's a thought, though,' said Kath. 'I think Shirl should talk to her. Clarissa and Rafferty have both said that Fenella is a good match for him.'

'Marrying an arrogant mummy's boy with an overbearing mother. Poor girl never stood a chance.'

Kath looked full of thoughts as Ruth spoke. 'Exactly. Rafferty had a thing for younger girls. Clarissa seems to have engineered the most unlikely partner for him.'

'So I guess I'm playing good cop again, then?'

'Actually, maybe take Lane with you...Byron, what have you dug up?'

Byron's head popped up above his monitors. 'Theadora Blackstock. Younger sister to Clarissa. Party girl, known for disappearing for months on end. In 1987, there was a police report. She went on a rampage through Restonfield, trampled some gardens. Police took her in, just a caution. Clarissa put her in the home in Glossop soon after.'

'Where's she buried?' Kath asked.

'Restonfield. Apparently, there's a small gate at the back of the cemetery. It's a walled enclosure. All the Blackstocks are buried there.'

'Interesting again.'

'Clarissa paid handsomely for repairs to the church, put in heating etc in exchange for enclosing the rear area of the church. She had all the headstones remade. It had been overgrown, forgotten about. The church basically reconsecrated the ground, agreed on the upkeep. Having the dichotomy of witches buried in sight of the church had its challenges.'

'But money set it all right again?' Ruth huffed.

'Pretty much.'

Kath exhaled loudly. 'Ruth, anything to report?'

Ruth shuffled papers on her desk. 'I spoke to Kenny, Layla's best friend. Described her as feisty but secretive. Even he didn't know where she was suddenly going to find the cash she needed to go travelling after she quit two of her jobs. They had a big row. He made a joke about her basically prostituting herself. She went ballistic. He knew he'd crossed a line and that she would never do anything like that. It was meant as a joke. But she really took offence. Then she disappeared and he still feels horrible about how they left things. Their last conversation held what he thought was a harmless remark, but that's the last thing they rowed about. I wasn't going to press him. Poor chap sounded wounded.'

'That's sad,' Marvin sighed as he thought about Kerry. They hadn't really had any cross words. He meant to keep it that way.

Kath went to the whiteboard and tacked up the photographs into their original spots. She acknowledged that although there were many physical objects in the world that could kill, words were often the most destructive weapon.

'Sophia?' She turned round to Ruth.

Ruth looked at her notes. 'Mild-mannered. Liked by everyone. Wanted to go to uni to study art history. Dad's an architect. Mum runs an art gallery in Shrewsbury. Sophia did some waitressing at the golf club in Brushten and helped her mum out in the gallery.'

The mood in the office was now sombre, everyone reflecting on the fate of each girl, lives cut short, potential snuffed out.

Kath stretched, rotating her shoulders, trying to shrug off the weight of the case. 'Shirl, take Lane with you and go and talk to Fenella, get her on her own. Then go and see Clemency. Lane knows the way.'

'Bloody hell. Clarissa's not going to be happy with that,' said Ruth.

Shirl was loathe to admit it, but she thought Ruth had a point.

'Yes, she might not like it but, as I told her, I'm happy to go down the paper trail of search warrants and hauling them all into Malinsgate for further interviews.'

Malinsgate Police Station and its dour interview rooms had seen many people break down in confession. All of them were wondering how Clarissa would fare in that environment.

'I'll play nice,' said Shirl.

Ruth was about to comment, but Lane appeared in the doorway, dressed for the weather but still looking as if she'd stepped off a magazine cover.

'Hi, Lane. Let me bring you up to speed.'

Lane smiled at everyone and went to Kath's side.

Byron had been busy typing and motioned to Shirl to join him. 'Clemency is a bit of a mystery. There's nothing about her at all. I can't even find a birth certificate.'

Shirl leant against his desk. 'Maybe it's not her real name?'

'Maybe.' He nodded. 'Just thought I'd let you know. Lane might prove your best resource.'

She patted him on the arm. 'Thank you, internet guru.'

Marvin went to Ruth's desk. She narrowed her eyes.

'What's troubling you, then?'

Marvin pulled Kath's chair closer and sat down. 'I don't want to question where this case is going...'

'But?'

'Well, Kath said we were starting from scratch, looking at other possible suspects for the murders, but we still seem to be focusing on Clarissa and Rafferty. I'm not calling Kath out or anything.'

Ruth held up her hand. 'It's fine. You're right to ask. You are the fresh eyes and ears. But I've been looking at all the possible crossovers. All the girls had been in The Bell, Sophia with her parents, the other two, well, we know Layla worked there and Jennifer had been in with friends. People in the pub were interviewed, as were the guests at the golf club after Sophia disappeared. We were always curious about the location of the bodies, and it's still leading us back to the occupants of the manor.'

Marvin sighed. 'Okay, just wanted to say it out loud, that's all.'

'Keep questioning us,' Ruth encouraged. 'Just because we've been doing this a long time doesn't mean we don't get blinkered.'

'I'm not saying that Rafferty is guilty or innocent, just that I'm struggling for a motive.'

'Some people kill just because they can.'

'But Kath was sure seven years ago that he wasn't responsible.'

'I've known Kath a long time,' said Ruth, looking over at her friend and boss. 'She feels that something is different, something's shifted. She just needs us to help her work out what that is. Anyway, what time are you collecting Dylan?'

'Two o'clock. We're going to Cassandra's shop in Much Wenlock. Byron says she's got a room at the back where she does readings and stuff.'

'Stuff?'

'Sorry. Is that disrespectful?'

'I'm teasing,' said Ruth. 'Stuff is a good word.'

Lane and Kath separated, Lane heading for the kettle and Kath homing in on Shirl's desk. Shirl took the hint and left Byron typing. Marvin sauntered over to join Lane.

Shirl nudged Kath with her elbow as they watched his attempt at nonchalance. 'I think Lane's a witch because she's sure cast a spell on our Marvin.'

Another text alert came through on Kath's phone. She calmed herself and focused on Shirl. 'Well, he can take care of himself. I want you to watch yourself and Lane when you go up to the manor.'

Shirl pulled a face. 'Maybe Fenella won't treat me like I just stepped out of the 1960s police-typing pool.'

Ruth was listening in and sniggered as she typed.

'You've been cast as the affable, unassuming detective. Deal with it,' Kath said, adopting a stern demeanour but laughing inside. 'Lane is the unknown quantity. She unsettles people, and that's exactly what we want. Let's see how she responds to the house when you get in there. Then go and see Clemency. Another unknown quantity.'

'Okay.' Shirl looked over at Lane. 'My car in half an hour?'

Lane nodded.

Kath went to her phone and read her text.

Pick you up at seven?

I'll be ready.

See you then

Her finger hovered over the x key. No. Too soon.

Ruth saw the smile on Kath's lips and stood up. 'Pub lunch. I'm buying.'

Everyone murmured agreement.

Shirl pouted. 'That's not fair, we have to leave.'

'My heart would bleed, but it's made of stone, as you well know.' Ruth grinned at her. 'Get a Greggs on the way to the manor. Just make sure there's no pastry stuck in your teeth.'

Ruth walked past Kath's desk. 'Busy afternoon ahead.' She pointed at the whiteboard. As Kath looked towards the board, Ruth looked down at Kath's message. Richard? That was new. Kath was keeping something very quiet, but Ruth was a good detective. She'd find out. She liked a challenge.

| 20 |
April 2012

'Thank you all for coming to celebrate our club's sixtieth anniversary.' James Lewis smiled at the assembled crowd of club members, wives and friends.

'Golf is one of life's greatest joys, as I'm sure all of you here will attest to, and we therefore laugh in the faces of those that turn their noses up at our rugged determination to climb the mountain of the scorecard.'

Laughter filled the room and several cheers went up.

'I know for all of us here, our club is a sanctuary from the stresses of daily life, so enjoy the free food and drink, and here's to the next sixty years.'

The guests broke away into small groups. Sophia moved easily through the guests with her tray of pulled pork and goat's cheese canapés. Rafferty sipped his champagne and smiled as Sophia threaded her way through the bodies. He caught her eye and beckoned her over. She stifled a yawn as she proffered the tray.

'And what delights do we have here?'

The yawn made its way out of her mouth as she started to speak. She covered her mouth with her free hand. 'So sorry. Goat's cheese and pulled pork.'

He took one and grinned. 'Don't apologise. Busy day?'

She turned her head quickly to see if the head waitress was watching. She'd been told to keep moving and smiling, no chatting to the guests. Her ponytail was pulled tight from her make-up-free face and her hair swung like the arc of a golf club as she looked back at him.

'I've been helping my mum in her gallery all day, then quick shower and change and now I'm here. Not that I mind,' she added quickly.

Rafferty admired her slim frame encased in the tight black pencil skirt and white blouse buttoned to the neck. 'Which gallery?'

'My mum runs the Whiston Fine Art Gallery in Shrewsbury.'

'Interesting. Do you enjoy being there?'

'Oh, I love it. I want to go to uni to do art history.'

'Fascinating. Good for you. I'm Rafferty Quartermaine, by the way. I live up at the manor.' He pointed in the general direction of the estate. 'We have some wonderful paintings, particularly Pre-Raphaelite works.'

Sophia's eyes lit up. She knew who he was and where he lived. Her mother had often spoken of the collection of paintings at the manor. She sighed dreamily. 'How lovely to be surrounded by all that beauty.'

'I'm sure your family feel the same way.' He tipped his glass at her as she blushed.

She saw James Lewis give her an inquiring glance.

'Look, I have to go, but I'd love to hear more about the paintings.'

'Why don't you pass by with your next tray of goodies and we can talk about your visit to my house. You really need to see them in their glory to appreciate them.'

Her heart quickened. A look inside the manor. Her mother would be so envious. She nodded and moved to a group of people nearby.

Half an hour later, Rafferty was explaining about a night time visit for her as he plucked an avocado and venison pastry case from her tray. He lowered his voice, telling her it would have to be a secret.

Sophia's father looked over at the arrogant and obnoxious lord of the manor in waiting and felt uneasy about his daughter's animated face as she nodded and spoke to him. He would have words with her. The likes of Rafferty Quartermaine were not for Sophia.

| 21 |

10th October 2019

'That's a stroke of luck.'

Shirl pulled up close to the cottage and saw Fenella pass by a window. 'Hopefully she's on her own.'

Fenella raised a hand and went to open the front door. 'Hello again.'

'Mrs Quartermaine, this is one of our colleagues on the case with us. Can we have a word?'

Fenella's eyes flickered towards the manor house and nodded. She led them through to a comfortable lounge and indicated to a two-seater leather sofa. 'Can I get you a drink?'

'No, we're fine. Thank you.'

Shirl and Lane sat down. Lane had an international reputation, but she hoped Fenella might not know who she was and hence why she hadn't introduced Lane by name. Fenella showed no signs of recognition towards the brunette beauty sitting on her sofa.

'Just packing up the last few bits,' Fenella said to fill the silence.

'I bet it will be strange going from this to the manor house. You'll be rattling around in there.'

Fenella clasped her hands in her lap. 'I'm very lucky to live in such a lovely place.'

The sentence sounded rehearsed.

'Yes, you are,' said Shirl. 'You've been married seven years now, is it?'

Fenella seemed puzzled by the question. 'That's correct. The thirty-first of May 2012.'

Barely three weeks after the bodies had been discovered.

'Brocken was born in the December. He was premature.'

'Children are a gift,' said Shirl, smiling.

'Do you have any?'

'Four boys, two sets of twins.'

Fenella's eyes widened. 'Gosh, that must have been quite a handful.'

'It was a challenge,' Shirl admitted, 'but worth it. I always knew I wanted a large family.'

Sadness settled on Fenella's face. 'I was advised not to have any more. The pregnancy was difficult, along with the birth.'

'That's a hard thing to come to terms with, but you have a super little boy, don't you?'

Fenella looked at the mantelpiece, then remembered she'd packed the photograph of Brocken, taken last year, standing next to his grandmother, Clarissa's hand firmly placed on his shoulder.

'He's my greatest achievement,' she said, then lowered her eyes. 'I was pregnant when we got married.' She blushed in her shame, and her hands went to her face. 'Sorry.' She looked up. 'I'm one of those people that feel the need to confess when confronted by the police.'

If you could confess to the murders of three young girls, that would make my day. But, looking at the vaguely pathetic woman sitting in front of her, Shirl was absolutely convinced that Fenella was not the perpetrator.

'That's okay. We're not here to interrogate you, honestly.'

Shirl was wondering whether Lane was also pitying the woman. She had been chosen like a piece of prime beef for the feast. There had been no discussion on thoughts and wishes and desires for Fenella. Her fate had been decided and she'd accepted it. If there was any love in her marriage, it was engineered, forced like fruit out of season.

Lane remained silent, and Shirl wondered why Kath had suggested she come along. Then she remembered they were to go on to Clemency's cottage. She sat forward a little.

'It must have been quite a challenge organising a wedding with everything that was going on here with the investigation team around the folly.'

'Oh, not really. I was still at home with my parents. Clarissa and my father organised everything. Clarissa even picked out my dress for me. All I had to do was turn up at St Saviour's Church and... that was that.'

Fenella's words were matter-of-fact, straightforward, emotionless. Shirl felt a desire to give the woman a hug. There was nothing Fenella could give them, and she was ready to leave.

Fenella picked at the cuff of her cardigan sleeve and then stopped as if hearing a parental voice admonishing her.

'You didn't even get to pick out the flowers for the church?' Lane spoke for the first time.

Fenella's head snapped up. 'Oh, there weren't any flowers. Clarissa doesn't approve of cutting flowers for unnecessary decoration. She says they belong in the land.'

'You didn't have a bouquet, then?' Shirl was suddenly feeling an almost ghoulish fascination for more details.

'Clemency gave me herbs tied with string. It was pretty. They smelt nice.'

'Who was Rafferty's best man?' Lane asked.

'Clemency, actually.'

'What?' Shirl's voice flew up an octave as Fenella nodded.

'Rafferty doesn't really have any close male friends, so Clarissa decided Clemency would step in. It was fine.'

Clarissa decided. Clarissa arranged. Clarissa the wedding planner from hell.

Shirl took the cue and stood up. 'We're on our way to see Clemency next.'

'Oh… right.'

Fenella stood up and led Lane and Shirl to the front door. As she opened it, Lane held out her hand. Fenella stared at it for a second, then shook it, a limp touch. Lane kept hold of Fenella's hand, and she made no attempt to pull away.

'Are you lonely, Mrs Quartermaine?' Lane's expression was impassive.

Fenella let her head drop slightly. 'Call me Fenella, please. Do you know the way to Clemency's cottage?'

Lane nodded. 'We've been there before. Thank you for your time today.' Lane released Fenella's hand and ran her fingers softly and comfortingly down Fenella's arm. 'You didn't answer my question.'

Fenella gestured to the manor house. 'I'm cared for. Watch your step through the woods; the rain has made the ground soft.'

Shirl and Lane walked past the manor house, heading for the woodland path.

'I do not feel good about that,' Shirl said, looking up at the grey clouds threatening more rain. 'What do you think?'

Lane plunged her hands into her jacket pockets. 'When she said call me Fenella, that was telling. It's all she has left of herself.'

Cassandra's shop was on the main street, sandwiched between a dress shop and a jewellery shop. Her double-fronted windows displayed an array of crystals, Tarot cards, books and coloured scarves. A bell tinkled as Marvin nervously pushed open the door, a quiet Dylan behind him.

Cassandra smiled and looked up from her seat behind the counter. 'Hey, Marvin. How's it going?'

'Good, thanks.' He closed the door. 'This is Dylan.'

She moved forward, towering over Dylan as she shook his hand. 'Are you worried?'

Dylan's brow creased. 'Not exactly.'

'It's okay. I'm not going to hypnotise you. You'll be in a relaxed state in a safe environment and we'll just talk.' She looked at Marvin. 'Kath on her way?'

'Yep, should be close behind me.'

Dylan was looking at a shelf of beads and crystals.

'Help yourself.' Cassandra gestured. 'Pick up anything you feel drawn to.'

Dylan wandered over to some larger crystals and picked up a brown one with a black stripe.

'Tiger's eye. For protection.'

'Do I need it?' Dylan gave a weak grin.

'You picked it for a reason. Keep it.'

'Let me pay you.' He reached into his back pocket for his wallet.

'No need.'

'Thank you.' He rolled the stone around in his hand, then pushed it into his jeans pocket.

The shop door opened, and Kath entered.

'Hi. Good to see you.' Cassandra smiled.

'Likewise,' Kath replied. She moved towards Dylan. 'You okay?'

'Yes,' he said, now sounding more confident.

Cassandra turned the OPEN sign to CLOSED and reached across each window, releasing the purple and green voile panels from their swags.

'Right. Let's go through to the back room.'

Cassandra led them through an archway on the left-hand side, holding back a curtain of beads to allow the others to pass. Two wooden chairs with cushions sat against the back wall, angled towards each other with a small table in between.

'Marvin, there's a café across the street. Would you mind waiting in there?'

'No problem,' he said and left quickly.

Cassandra gestured to another chair by the arch. 'Kath, if you'd sit here. Dylan, pick a chair by the wall.'

He dutifully sat in the right-hand chair. Three wall lights gave off a dim glow. Cassandra pushed a button on a CD player on the floor, and a haunting orchestral melody filled the room.

'Now, Dylan...' She sat opposite him. 'I want you to close your eyes...'

'She's here. Clemency. *Clemency*.'

'I know. It's fine.' Clemency ushered the woman back into the bedroom. 'You just need to stay quiet.' She guided the woman towards the bed and sat her down, the patchwork quilt barely registering the impression of her body.

'Now is your chance.'

'Yes, it's all in hand.'

Clemency turned her head at the sound of the knock at the front door. 'I have to go. Be still.' She kissed the woman on the cheek and closed the bedroom door behind her before running down the stairs and opening the front door.

'Hello.'

Shirl produced her warrant card. 'DS Thompson. This is my colleague...Diana. May we have a word?'

Clemency brushed the creases from her apron. 'Certainly. Come in.'

Clemency led them into a small sitting room. Shirl tried to mask her surprise at the interior. There was no electrical equipment, no television or radio, and not even any plug sockets in the stone walls. The wooden floorboards were polished to a high sheen and a small rug sat in front of the open fire. The alcoves either side of the fireplace held a variety of old books and hurricane lamps, wooden boxes and opaque glass bottles. A large spider appeared on top of the logs in the basket alongside the fireplace, and Shirl made a mental note to keep an eye on it.

Clemency pointed to a two-seater sofa with flat wooden arms and even flatter seat cushions. Two stark wooden chairs were positioned opposite, and Clemency sat down. Shirl caught her foot against a basket filled with multi-coloured material, and she bent to reposition it as she sat down, the coloured squares spilling out over the sides, the brightest things in the room. As she sat down, she glanced at the log basket. The spider was gone.

Clemency brushed hair from her cheek, avoiding Lane's gaze. 'I take it you're here about the dead girls.' Her tone was even, her gaze directed at Shirl.

'We are, yes.'

'My original statement still stands, as I told your colleague. I knew nothing until the police arrived.'

'You obviously live closest to the folly where the girls were found, so we are...' Shirl fought for the best word without raising hostility. 'We are interested in anything that you may have heard or seen.'

'That's true. But there's nothing else I can tell you.' Her voice softened. 'Such a tragedy. We were all very shocked.'

The words seemed polite enough with just the right amount of sympathy, but Lane sensed the invisible barrier rising, shutting her out.

'So you can't offer any suggestion as to how the bodies came to be there or why?' Shirl pressed.

'Suggestion? It is surely not in the remit to offer conjecture or suggestion. I rather think that's down to you and your colleagues.' Clemency looked at Lane on the last word, then gave a light laugh. 'Otherwise, I would have gone into police work.'

'Talking of jobs, what do you do?' Shirl had been wondering this all day. It wasn't watching *Bargain Hunt*.

'I don't have what you would know as a conventional job and certainly not for money.'

'Oh?'

'It's not really relevant to your investigation, is it?'

Shirl sat upright. 'No, just plain curious.'

'I grow our own food, make clothes and quilts and tend the woodland.' She glanced out of the window then returned her gaze to Shirl.

'Not with a chainsaw,' Shirl joked.

Lane stifled a laugh as Clemency's eyes narrowed.

'Your humour is delightful but—'

All the women looked up as footsteps were heard overhead.

Lane's heart was beating faster, her mouth dry. 'Someone else lives with you?' Her vision blurred, and she shook her head.

Clemency smiled. 'I have a sick friend staying with me. I really should get back to her if we're done here?' She rose and went to the front door, signifying the end of the interview.

'Are you okay?' Shirl said quietly as Lane pressed her fingers into her forehead as they made their way to the door.

'We should go,' Lane said. As she went to brush past Clemency, she felt a sharp pain, and her hand went to the nape of her neck.

'Sorry, you had a leaf in your hair.' Clemency closed her hand and pushed it into her apron pocket.

Lane said nothing and strode off down the path, head lowered.

'Thank you for your time,' Shirl said. 'We'll leave you to your day.' She started down the path, then turned suddenly. 'Does your friend need a doctor or anything?'

'No. She'll be fine.' Clemency closed the door, and Shirl looked up at the window as movement caught her eye.

Lane had walked quite a way down the woodland path, and Shirl had to jog to catch up to her. The ground was indeed soft from the heavy rain, and she had to veer into brown ferns at the side of the path to avoid her boots becoming even muddier.

'Lane. Wait.'

The overhanging branches had no other job than depositing their drops of rain down the neck of Shirl's jacket, and she wiped away the moisture as Lane stopped and turned to her. Shirl pulled her cigarettes and lighter from her pocket and lit one, blowing the smoke angrily up into the offending branches.

'Are you really okay?'

Lane's face was stern, her cheeks even paler against the dark of her hair framing her face. 'Something's wrong in that house,' she said carefully. 'I got more sensation from being in there than from the folly, which has my defences on high alert.'

'Let's walk back.'

Shirl smoked quietly as they picked their way through leaves and soft earth.

'Do you think we should be focusing more attention on Clemency?'

Lane folded her arms around her torso. 'Yes. I think we should.'

'So where are you now, Dylan?'

The young man's eyes flickered beneath his closed lids. 'We're at the fence. Dhandi's found the...' He twitched, kicking the chair leg.

'It's okay. What was that?'

Kath leaned forward in her chair.

'I think it was a fox, that sound they make at night. Scared me.'

'Can you get through the fence?'

Dylan wiggled his shoulders. 'Tight.' He reached across to his shoulder. 'Jacket's caught. Mum will go mad.' His hand fell back to his lap.

'You're in the woods now.' Cassandra's voice was low and smooth.

'I'm a bit scared. A lot scared really... Oh.' Dylan smiled. 'Andrew tickles the back of Dhandi's neck and he jumps. Funny.'

'You see the folly now. What do you do?'

'Wow. It's cool. Creepy. Andrew shines the torch up.'

'Move forward, Dylan.'

'I'm at the back. I don't know whether I want to go in.' Dylan's hands trembled in his lap.

Although the mood in the room was calm and relaxed, Kath was feeling anxious for the young man.

Cassandra's eyes were locked on Dylan.

'Oh.' Dylan's hand went to his toes.

'What's that?'

'Kicked something. Metal. Leaves are sticky. A ring. Big. Metal.' His brow creased.

Kath was breathing hard. She was sure he hadn't mentioned this in his original statement.

'Can you clear the leaves away?'

Dylan's fingers scraped against the carpet. 'All metal. Weird. They're going inside the tower.' His hand came up to his chest, pressing into his jumper. 'I'm following them.'

Kath signalled to Cassandra to stop. She didn't want him going inside to play out the scene at the top of the folly. His memory of a metal ring was enough for now. They didn't have that before.

Cassandra nodded to Kath and held up her hand. 'Alright, Dylan. That's really good. Now, I'm going to count back from five. When I get to one, your eyes will open and you'll be awake and relaxed. Five...four...three...'

Shirl watched as Fenella struggled at the door to the manor house and sprinted forward to help her. Fenella smiled at her, trying to reposition the box in her arms.

'Someone's shut the door. Would you mind?'

Shirl grabbed the big metal ring and turned it. 'There you go.' She pushed the door ajar.

Fenella's arm slid across the box as she moved, and Shirl saw a glint on her wrist as the cuff of her cardigan rode up. Shirl's mouth filled with saliva, and she swallowed quickly and smiled.

'That's a lovely bracelet. Present from someone?'

Fenella looked at the diamonds set in white gold. 'Yes, actually, Rafferty gave me this as a wedding present. Such a beautiful gift. Thanks again.' She pushed the door further open with her foot and went inside.

Shirl signalled to Lane to get in the car, and she pulled away before Lane had a chance to fasten her seatbelt.

'I'm not one for clichés, but you look like you've seen a ghost.'

Shirl accelerated down the driveway and then slammed on the brakes, causing Lane to lurch forward. Shirl turned to Lane, her hands gripping the steering wheel.

'The bracelet on Fenella's wrist. I need to check when we get back, but I think it looks exactly like the one that Jennifer's mystery man gave her.'

| 22 |

Kath paced in front of the lounge window, watching for Richard. She'd texted everyone earlier and told them to leave for the day as Dylan walked across to the cafe to meet Marvin. She was pumped from the information that Dylan had revealed. Cassandra had made Dylan sit quietly with a glass of water as she assured Kath that Dylan would be fine. Kath was torn between wanting to share the information with the team but also knowing she couldn't do anything about it until the next day. Shirl's text reply had revealed she may have further news but needed to double-check back at the office. The light was fading fast, the afternoon trying to push its way further into early evening. There was nothing to be gained from a hyped-up team meeting only to encroach on everyone's downtime when they left for the day. They would all start fresh tomorrow.

Kath's clothing decision had been swifter this time, thanks to her rearrangement of her wardrobe after her previous date with Richard, and she found herself dressed and ready far earlier than anticipated.

Her mobile rang, and she left her lookout spot at the window to walk quickly to the kitchen table.

'Hi, Lane. What's up?'

'Nothing, sweet. Just wondered if you fancied getting some dinner with me.'

Kath grinned .'Ah. I have plans. Any other night...'

'Okay, no worries. Plans with someone else?'

'Yes, just dinner with a friend.'

'So, not Lenny?'

'Stop fishing.' Kath felt her cheeks redden and was glad Lane couldn't see her. 'Anyway, you're the psychic.'

'Yeah, talking of which, we need to talk in the morning, maybe before the others get there?'

'Seven-thirty and bring coffee.' Kath turned as she heard tyres on her gravel driveway and saw headlights sweeping across the window. 'Gotta go. Catch you in the morning.'

Kath walked to the window and waved at Richard as he got out of the car.

'Sure. Have a good night.'

'I think I just might. Night.'

Kath put her mobile into her bag, drew the curtains and grabbed her jacket from the back of the sofa. Richard smiled at her as she closed the front door. In the beam of the outside security light, she could see he'd opted for black jeans again with a three-quarter length wool coat. As she had no idea of where they were going, she'd chosen smart black trousers and a green silk blouse, praying there would be heating.

'Hi. Everything alright?' Richard mimed holding a phone to his ear. 'Thought that call might be you about to rush off.'

She walked to the passenger side of his SUV, pulling on her jacket. 'Actually, it was another dinner invitation.'

They got in and he started the car.

'It was Lane,' she added.

Richard grinned and placed his arm across the back of her seat, angling himself as he reversed the car out of the driveway. 'I wasn't going to ask.' His fingers brushed her shoulder.

'So, where are we going?'

'Still a surprise. Hope I've made a good choice. It's a lovely little place, somewhere I found just after I moved here. It's not far.'

They chatted easily about gardening and weather, and she hadn't realised exactly where they were until Richard swung his vehicle into the car park of The Mallard's Rest.

'Your face is telling me you're not happy with my choice.' He turned the engine off and unclipped his seat belt.

'Sorry. No, it's fine. I have been here before. Not a great night.'

'We can go somewhere else.' He was still clutching his seat belt.

'No,' she said. 'Anyway, I didn't actually get to eat last time.'

As they got out of the car, her mind replayed the memory of the scenario with Lenny. His innocent comment and her stupid reaction. Storming out. And then there was the unbidden excitement that had followed on the way home.

Kath pushed open the door. Tables were already starting to fill up with diners. A young man greeted them with menus as Richard explained his booking. The young man guided them to a table, the same one where she and Lenny had been seated.

'Give me a break,' she muttered. She shrugged off her jacket and the bad memory and sat down.

'Any drinks while you decide?'

Richard slipped off his coat and placed it over the back of his chair. 'Sparkling mineral water for me. Kath?'

She thought for a moment and then realised that she didn't have to drive. She didn't drink to excess any more, but it was nice to have the option. 'Gin and tonic, thank you.'

The waiter disappeared, and Richard studied the menu. 'So, are you a starter and main, main and dessert or all three kind of girl?'

'Well, I've lost some weight recently and my appetite isn't what it used to be, so I'm a cheap date.' She looked up from her menu to see him grinning.

'So this is a date, is it?'

She looked down, trying not to smile. The waiter appeared with their drinks, and Kath poured all her tonic into her glass and took a big mouthful.

'The starters are small and the mains generous, if that helps.' Richard sipped his water and watched her over the top of his menu.

Her mind was in turmoil, food the farthest thing from her focus. She didn't want to rush into anything, but she didn't want to push him away. Was it a date? Wasn't that exactly what she wanted? She'd told enough lies in her lifetime, so she took a deep breath.

'You seem to have the ability to make me open up to you, a strange experience for me, particularly as we've just met. Let's call this dinner as friends... for the moment.'

I do want more. Thank god you can't hear me screaming this in my head. I need to get my shit together. Do not blow this. Order food.

She signalled to the waiter, who came immediately. He edged his way around more customers, and a flurry of waiting staff appeared like penguins.

'Ladies first.' Richard gestured to her.

'Salmon mousse, then the Dover sole. Thank you.'

'Same for me.' Richard took her menu from her and handed them to the waiter.

He pushed them under his arm and keyed their order into his tablet. 'Any wine with your meal? We have a lovely Chardonnay that would complement the fish perfectly.'

Kath shook her head. 'Thanks, but we're fine for now.'

The waiter moved away, and Kath grimaced. 'Sorry, just realised I didn't ask you.'

Richard waved his hand. 'You're used to being in charge. I like that.' His eyes sparkled. 'Anyway, I'm out with a police officer and I am the designated driver.' He picked up his glass. 'To fish with friends.'

Kath laughed and sipped her gin and tonic. 'Continuing the fishy theme, are you angling for clients?'

Richard groaned, and Kath slumped in her seat. 'Christ, I'm really bad at this. Shirl's the funny one in the office. I can't really pull it off.'

'You're doing okay.' Richard smiled. 'Funnily enough, the meal I had here was with a prospective client. Big house in Tettenhall. She wants a swimming pool. He wants topiary. I think he'll talk her round.'

'Do you swim?'

'I do. Like a fish.'

'We need to stop the fish analogies now.' Kath wiggled her open hand back and forth, smiling.

Richard sat back, opening his napkin and spreading it across his lap. 'I grew up on the banks of a loch, so I do the wild swimming that's becoming popular now.'

Naked muscle combing through clear water. I could get on board with watching you do that.

'You?'

She shook her head, playing with her napkin. 'No. Something I've never really wanted to do. Forced lessons at school. Mouthfuls of chlorine. Not my bag, but I admire people that can do it.'

'It's a wonderful feeling.' He leaned forward, his face animated. 'There's this incredible power in a large body of water. Something that looks so calm. You don't fight it. You harness it. Respect it. Because deep down, it has the strength to consume.'

'Wow. That's beautiful and terrifying at the same time.'

'I haven't sold you on the idea, then?'

Kath snorted. 'No, but I appreciate the effort.'

'I'm all about the effort.' His hand snaked towards hers, and he touched her thumb with one finger. He stared at her with an intensity that shut out the hum of conversation around them.

The waiter appeared with their plates, and they both sat back. The ramekins of mousse, accompanied by a small salad and a slice of bread, looked lost on the large oval plate.

'My niece would call this mouse,' Richard said, picking up a fork.

'That's cute. How old is she?'

'Ten. My sister's girl.'

'Any brothers?'

'No, just me and Morag.'

Kath took a forkful of creamy mousse. 'Good Scottish name. Yet you're Richard.'

'It's not my first name.'

'Which is?'

'I'm not telling you, Detective.'

She smiled and stabbed a cherry tomato. 'You know I can find out.'

'Do your worst.'

Kath relaxed as she ate, the memory of her previous encounters in the building subsiding although the meeting with the parents of the murdered girls popped into her head and she mentally brushed it away. She'd get back to the case in the morning.

Richard cleared most of the food on his plate and set his cutlery down in a neat formation. 'Anything new on the case that you can share, or should we not be talking about it tonight?'

She laid down her fork, giving up on the onion strands and lettuce. She picked up her glass and told him sparse details of the regression with Dylan.

'But I…' Mid-sentence, she suddenly had the feeling that she was being watched, and she turned to her left. Standing next to a table near the bar was Lenny. The look on his face mirrored her own shock.

'Shit,' she muttered. Her hand shook, and she set down the glass.

Richard followed her gaze. 'Someone you know?' As he spoke, realisation flooded his face.

'Would that be your "on a break" friend?'

Kath looked at him. 'It would.'

'Is this awkward?'

'Little bit.'

From her peripheral vision, she saw Lenny sit down. She desperately wanted to turn again to see who he was with, but she fought to keep looking at Richard.

The waiter approached them and cleared their plates. 'Your main courses will be a few minutes.'

Richard noted the distress on Kath's face and took his cue. 'I'm afraid something's come up and we have to leave. I'll pay for the food now, of course.'

Kath exhaled noisily and nodded at him.

'Okay, sir, no problem. I'll just arrange the bill.'

'Thank you. I'm sorry.' Kath stood up and pulled on her coat. Richard did the same.

'It really is fine.' He watched for the waiter, taking the opportunity to look at the man who had caused such a reaction in Kath.

You couldn't hold it together, could you?

Kath turned her body, making her own meal of doing up her coat, head down but eyes firmly fixed on Lenny and his companion. She didn't recognise the woman with the red hair piled on top of her head. She wore a long skirt and fluffy jumper, her rings catching the light as she waved her hand towards Lenny and laughed.

Richard produced his card for the waiter.

'Shame you missed out on the Dover sole.' The waiter handed Richard a receipt.

'Give it to that man in the red shirt sitting with the redhead. It's his favourite.' Kath turned and marched her way through the tables, aware of Richard following and hating herself just a little bit.

Richard pulled the car up three feet from her front door and got out as Kath, keys in hand, got to the door. The bright security light caused him to squint, and he shielded his eyes with his hand. Their drive back had been punctuated with polite but uneasy conversation.

'You didn't need to get out.' Kath played with her keys, not knowing what else to say, aware that she had allowed a great night to be ruined.

'Only right that I see you to your door. My father would insist.'

'He sounds like a good man. You're a good man. Look...' The light was too intense, and she pulled Richard round to the side of the cottage where semi-darkness afforded her a little more dignity. 'I'm really sorry.' She looked up at him.

He stared at her, not moving. 'I really want to kiss you.'
I really want you to, but it's all wrong. Shitty and wrong.

'But I'm not going to, not tonight. We'll catch up again if that's okay with you.'

He stroked her arm, and she felt tears pricking her eyes. She nodded, not trusting her mouth to say anything other than repeated meaningless apologies.

He walked quickly to his car, and she watched him drive away.

***

'Hi, it's Kath. Can you talk?'

Lane swapped the phone to her other ear. 'Hey, Kath. Yeah, I can talk. What's up?'

The man in Lane's bed gestured to the bathroom and mimed washing himself. Lane nodded and mouthed *thank you*. The bathroom door closed, and she heard the shower turn on.

'I'm a bloody stupid woman,' Kath blurted out, then proceeded to tell Lane about Richard and the experience at the restaurant.

'This new man sounds lush, honey, and by the way you're talking about him, I think you think so too.'

'Me and Lenny are in such a weird place. I was okay with it, the break thing, leaving us both to work out what we wanted. Then Richard appeared in my life. It's messed up.' Kath paced across her small patio, smoking and sighing.

'Okay, so how do you feel about seeing him with this woman?'

Kath considered the question. 'I guess I have to admit I felt jealous, but I don't know who she is or what their relationship is. She could be his bloody cleaning lady.'

Lane heard the water turn off. 'He obviously saw you with Richard. You saw him with a woman. Maybe you just need to speak to him and clear the air.'

'Maybe,' Kath replied, dropping her cigarette into the pottery ashtray on the patio table, watching the ember suddenly snuffed out by the rainwater that threatened to cascade over the rim. 'Where are you, anyway?'

The bathroom door opened, and the man stood in the doorway, a towel draped around his waist.

'I had something to eat and now I'm in bed. Bit of a headache, so an early night.'

'Thanks for the chat. By the way, no-one else knows about Richard. I guess I'm trying to keep him under the radar for the moment, seeing how things go. If they go anywhere. See you at seven-thirty. Don't forget that coffee.'

'Okay, hon. Sleep tight.'

Lane ended the call, placing her mobile on the bedside table. The man let the towel drop from his waist, and Lane forgot all about her headache.

Kath went into the house. It wasn't even eight-thirty and Lane was having an early night? Her stomach growled, and she opened the fridge. Three forkfuls of salmon mousse and a couple of tomatoes had not really worked, even for her small appetite. She suddenly had a craving for chips. She donned a cardigan, grabbed her coat and headed out to Bridgnorth.

The three women sat around Clemency's roaring fire, candles and hurricane lamps giving muted illumination.

'I bind thee to the North. You shall not come forth.'

Clemency's fingers clutched the poppet, Lane's strand of hair firmly attached to the head.

'I bind thee to the South. Silence for your mouth.'

She wound string around the figure, starting at the head, covering the face and moving down to cover the shoulders and arms.

'I bind thee to the East. You shall not feast.'

The string tightened around the torso and down to the legs.

'I bind thee to the West. Put thee to rest.'

Clemency laid the poppet on her lap, and the women linked hands, Clarissa's grip as tight as her lips. They muttered quietly, normal words tinged with mystery and magic, then they broke their circle.

Clemency stood up and placed the bound figure on the shelf. 'The secret is safe. She shall not see.'

'The horses will run tonight.'

Clarissa and Clemency looked at the woman staring into the fire. Clemency nodded and went to get their coats.

Kath drove up to High Town and parked in the street by the library. As she approached the chip shop, she groaned. There were no lights on. She read the sign on the door: Closed due to family bereavement.

'I don't believe this.'

The Chinese takeaway three doors down had closed down over a year ago.

'Sainsbury's it is, then.'

She turned to walk back to the car but heard a door slam and crying. A woman stood outside a shop further up the street. There was light coming from the shop's small window, illuminating the woman who had a large scarf wrapped around her heaving shoulders. She blew her nose and stared at Kath.

'Are you okay?' Kath moved towards her.

'I'm fine, but do not go in there. He's a bastard.' The woman walked off, and Kath stared up at the sign above the door. The Bright Stone.

'Could my night get any fucking weirder?'

Kath saw the man from The Blasted Oak emerge from the rear of the shop and rest his hands on the counter, shaking his head. Her curiosity, coupled with professional interest, decided her next move. She was about to push open the front door of the shop when the man saw her and beckoned her inside.

'Hello again.'

Kath shut the door behind her. 'I can't believe I'm saying this, but I really was just passing.'

He laughed. 'Maybe you were directed here for a reason.'

'That in your Tarot cards, was it? No, I'm afraid the truth is much more ordinary. I came out for chips.' She gestured to the shop.

'Ah. So you didn't come for your reading?' He pointed to his bookcase holding the multiple decks of Tarot and oracle cards.

'No, but I would like to know why there was a woman crying on your doorstep.'

'Before I tell you, let me introduce myself. Donovan Brightstone.' He came from behind the counter, and they shook hands.

'Detective Chief Inspector Fortune.'

He gave a resigned smile. 'I did hear you discussing your case with the gentleman in the pub.'

Kath looked around. The shop was a cosy and much smaller space than Cassandra's shop, and she wondered about the significance of being in two very similar places on the same day.

'Difficult not to be overheard in that place,' she replied. 'So, please tell me about the woman outside.'

'She came for a reading, her third actually. I basically told her that unless she went away and put some metaphysical elbow grease into her shadow work, nothing about her situation would change. She didn't like it.'

'That's it?'

'That's it.'

Kath moved to a small display of tumbled crystals, resisting the temptation to pick them up.' So she paid you money and got a bollocking.'

'I told her the truth and she's not ready to acknowledge it.'

Definitely not having a reading, thank you very much.

'I thought these readings were supposed to help people.' Kath picked up a pack of Tarot cards and turned it over in her hands.

'People are responsible for themselves, their thoughts, their actions. Some want to shift that responsibility onto the reader.' Donovan leant against the counter, crossing his arms. 'We don't offer a quick fix, although there are people out there who have no problem with feeding on the emotional vulnerability of a troubled psyche.'

'Thanks for the insight, but I only came out for a bag of chips.'

He held up his hands in surrender. 'Sorry. I tend to get on my soapbox. Look, I welcome sceptics and naysayers. An open mind is a gift.'

Kath's gaze drifted towards a cork noticeboard on the wall. Business cards and leaflets for yoga classes, psychic groups and a range of complementary therapies jostled for attention. One notice caught her eye.

'Folkus Pocus. You're Donavan B.'

He was the moderator and creator of the forum regarding the myths and legends that Byron had dug up about the Quartermaine estate.

'Guilty as charged, Officer. You've seen the forum?'

'Yes. One of my team alerted us to your site. It's been helpful.'

'The Quartermaine estate still holds the power of the past, from centuries ago. It's in the DNA of everything that grows there.'

Kath smiled at him. 'I don't doubt it, but it would really make my night if you could tell me who murdered the three girls.'

'I can only say it was via human power. The myths of the land and the power of nature played no part. In my opinion,' he added.

Kath replaced the pack of cards. 'On that we're agreed.'

She moved to the door, then stopped and turned. 'You said in the pub that you knew Clarissa. Mind telling me how?'

'Hold that thought.' Donovan disappeared into the back room, grabbed his coat and keys and turned off the lights, leaving only the streetlight illuminating Kath. He peered at his watch as he joined her at the door.

'Fancy grabbing those chips in the pub round the corner? They should still be serving.'

Kath gave a relieved sigh as her stomach growled again. 'That's the best idea I've heard tonight.'

Lane woke suddenly to find a warm but empty space in the bed. Her mouth felt dry and her limbs heavy. She propped herself up on one elbow and switched on the bedside light. She picked up her phone and read the text message.

Sorry to leave. You were dreaming and muttering. Thought you needed the bed to yourself. Call me. X

She replaced the phone and fell back onto the pillow. Her arms felt leaden and not quite attached to her body. She reached for the glass of water next to her and made to take a sip as the glass fell from her hand.

| 23 |

The look of astonishment on Kath's face told Lane that her efforts at hair and make-up fell very short of disguising how dreadful she felt.

'Are you ill?' Kath took the cardboard tray holding two cups of coffee from Lane's drooping hand.

'I don't get sick, but I have to confess I feel rough.'

'Sit down before you fall down.' Kath guided her to Ruth's chair.

'Is it something you ate?'

Lane managed a smile. 'I don't know. I'll be fine. So, are you going to speak to Lenny soon?'

'I guess I have to, but I don't know what to say. Sometimes my mouth has a mind of its own and words come out that seem to make situations worse.'

'Can't help with that. You'll find a way through it. Do you see this going anywhere with Richard?'

'We nearly kissed last night,' Kath admitted. 'Probably would have done if Lenny hadn't been in my head. Anyway, enough of my failed love life. Tell me what happened yesterday.'

Lane sat back in the chair. 'Fenella seems like a lost soul. She told me about her marriage. Clarissa organised everything, even picked out her wedding dress.'

Kath raised an eyebrow. 'Doesn't surprise me. I think when Clarissa wants something to happen, nothing gets in her way. So, nothing relevant to the case from Fenella?'

Lane tried to cross her legs, but they wouldn't seem to obey her brain. She gave up and sat forward. 'Actually, Shirl has something to share on that score, but I'll let her tell you. Don't want to steal her giraffe.'

Lane reached for her cup and took a mouthful of coffee, grimacing at the taste of the warm milk. She swallowed quickly when she saw Kath's bemused expression.

'What?'

Kath laughed. 'You said giraffe. Steal her giraffe. Did you mean thunder?'

'Did I say that? Huh. Yeah, well, ignore me. Not much sleep. Brain's foggy.'

Kath brushed off the remark. She didn't want to draw any more attention to the fact that Lane looked like crap and energy seemed to be leeching from her body before Kath's eyes.

'Did you see Clemency?'

Lane nodded with effort. 'She didn't say a river. People with the candlestick shot the arrow.'

Kath put her cup on the desk, giving her full attention to Lane. 'Okay, what is happening here?'

Lane screwed up her face. 'I don't understand.'

It wasn't just the hit of caffeine that awakened Kath's senses. 'Did you not hear the words that just came out of your mouth?' Her apprehension had sharpened her tone, and Lane looked genuinely upset.

'What did I say? I was just telling you about the celandine smell of the shark hammer and...' Lane stopped, realisation flooding her face. 'Okay, I heard that. Did I say hammer?'

'You're frightening me.' Kath stood up and felt for Lane's pulse. Her wrist was clammy and limp in Kath's hand. 'Your pulse is really slow. I think I need to take you to A&E.'

Lane, with great effort, pulled her hand away. 'Don't be crazy. I just didn't sleep well. 'I'm really okay.'

'Tell your face that.' Kath said abruptly, feeling Lane's forehead, which had the same clamminess as her wrist.

'Tell me I'm hot stuff, Doctor Fortune.'

Kath managed a smile, but it wasn't convincing enough to hide her worry. She was wondering if Lane had had some kind of mini stroke. Her face looked even, no temperature, but she had the feeling something was going on in Lane's head.

'When's my birthday?'

'December twenty-fourth.'

'What's Shirl's last name?'

'Thompson.'

'Those three girls on the board.' Kath pointed. 'Tell me their names.'

'Layla. Jennifer. Sophia.'

'Seventeen plus four.'

'Twenty-one. Satisfied?'

'Marginally,' Kath replied, sitting down. 'How was your drive here? And don't lie to me.'

Lane looked at her hands resting limply in her lap. It had been a challenge, her lethargy making it difficult to depress the brake as she'd cut up a van and got a long blast on the horn for her trouble.

'Not easy,' she said.

They both turned to the door as they heard footsteps on the stairs. Byron stopped in the doorway.

'Morning.'

'Hello, early bird.'

'Mum had an early client at the shop, so she dropped me off. Sorry, are you having a private meeting? I can go... Lane, are you okay?'

He moved quickly to her side, and Lane pushed back tears.

'Apparently not.'

'Is there anything I can do?' Byron moved to his desk and threw his canvas bag onto his chair and went back to Lane, touching her arm. He jumped back as if receiving an electric shock.

'Byron, what is it?'

He tentatively touched her again and got the same reaction. 'This doesn't feel good.'

He stood back and looked at both women. 'This is gonna sound weird...'

'Hah, weird's written all over this,' said Kath. 'Tell us.'

'There's nothing coming from you.' He stared at Lane intently. 'I usually feel your energy. But there's nothing there. It's like a darkness.'

'Right. Enough of this. When the others get here, we'll debrief, then I'm driving you to your hotel to get your stuff. You're staying at my house.' Kath folded her arms.

Lane nodded. 'Okay. Just don't cook for me. I feel bad enough already.'

More footsteps on the stairs heralded the arrival of Shirl, Ruth and Marvin. After expressions of concern over Lane and Kath explaining, as best she could, about the situation, she motioned for everyone to sit down.

'Shirl, take us through your visits yesterday.'

Shirl nodded, flicking through the papers on her desk. She held up a piece of paper with the image of the bracelet that had been described as being the gift given to Jennifer by her mystery man. 'Has Lane mentioned that we didn't really get anything from Fenella?'

Lane looked at Kath, then over at Byron.

'She hasn't said much,' said Kath carefully. 'You go on.'

Shirl explained about meeting Fenella at the door to the manor. She waved the paper. 'I think the bracelet is identical. Rafferty gave it to her as a wedding present.'

Ruth, leaning against the table by the window, crossed her legs and arms. 'I don't want to get too excited, but this could point to Rafferty being Jennifer's man.'

Marvin nodded. 'It all fits.'

'It's a bloody big coincidence and we don't like those,' said Kath. 'We'll go back and confront him with this. I think he'll break. He's itching to tell us something, I just don't know what it is.'

'What about Clemency? How did that go down?'

Shirl looked at Ruth. 'House is tidy. No TV, radio, electric lamps. She was committed to her original statement, with nothing to add. She wasn't overly friendly, but she wasn't hostile. She didn't take to Lane though.'

Lane nodded, not trusting herself to speak.

'Oh, we heard footsteps upstairs. She said her friend was still there. I offered her assistance, but she said it was all in hand.'

'So nothing unusual or out of the ordinary? As much as this case is anything but ordinary,' Kath pressed, desperate for any sniff of a clue.

'No, although Lane left pretty quickly, didn't you?'

Lane nodded again. Shirl stared at her, confused by the lack of verbal interaction.

'Lane's feeling a little nauseated,' Kath said quickly.

'Did Clemency touch her?' Byron said suddenly.

'Er, yes actually. As we were leaving, she pulled a leaf out of Lane's hair.'

Lane's eyes widened.

Byron was typing. He stood up and moved to Lane's chair. 'Did she take anything from you?'

Lane stared at him.

Shirl pointed. 'Lane gave a sort of yelp, like Clemency had caught her with a fingernail or something.'

Lane moved her hand to her neck and pulled out a couple of strands of hair. She held them out to Byron. His face was pale, and Kath felt a sense of dread flood her body.

'Byron, what's going on?'

'I think I know what's wrong with Lane,' he said quietly.

Rafferty stared moodily out of the window.

'*Rafferty.*'

He jumped as Clarissa slammed her hand on the table.

'Eat your eggs.'

He scowled at his mother but averted his eyes when he saw her face harden. 'I'm not hungry,' he muttered.

'Brocken, go to the study. Resume your reading. I will join you shortly.'

The boy left the table and made his way down the hallway as instructed.

Fenella tried to hide her disappointment. 'I thought I might take him for a walk in the woods, see the carousel.' She placed her cutlery carefully on her plate and dabbed at her mouth with a napkin.

'He needs to study,' Clarissa said sharply. 'I will take him out later. Stay away from the gallopers.'

'Alright. If you think that's best.'

Fenella looked at her husband, but he was staring out of the window again.

'I think you should go back to London now, Rafferty.' Clarissa stood and began to gather the breakfast plates together.

'I think I should be here.'

Clarissa snorted. 'Thinking isn't really your forte. Fenella, take these plates to the kitchen.'

It wasn't a request, and Fenella complied quickly, glad to be away from the impending conflict. Once she was out of earshot, Clarissa stood over Rafferty, pinching his cheeks between a bony finger and thumb and forcing his head to look up at her.

'Clemency and I are handling everything. You're a liability.'

'Is that all I am? A liability?' His voice was small, childlike.

Clarissa sighed and walked away. 'It's all you've ever been,' she muttered quietly.

***

'Byron, you're scaring us all just a little bit,' said Ruth. 'Tell us what you think.'

He brushed his long hair back over his shoulders and took a deep breath. 'I think Clemency has put a binding spell on Lane.'

'A what?' Marvin was confused, but Lane's eyes confirmed recognition.

'Like all spells, they can be used for good and evil,' Byron continued. 'There are many ways of performing it as there are incantations.'

Ruth pulled the face of a healthy sceptic. Kath saw it and weighed in.

'It makes sense, as much as any of this makes sense, and I think Lane agrees.'

Kath ran through Lane's symptoms in detail, and Byron nodded.

'In order to perform the ritual, you need something either belonging to the person or something from their body... fingernail, blood—'

'Hair,' said Shirl.

'Yep. That's what clinched it. I think she's used your hair, possibly with some kind of poppet or maybe in a fire ritual.'

Ruth held up her hands, her face an open book of disbelief. 'Poppet?'

'It's a type of doll figure. It can be made of anything: wool, material, wood. The figure is made and assigned to that person who needs to be bound for whatever reason and then the fluid or item or object belonging to the person is integrated into the figure, which is then bound with twine, wool or something like that.'

'So, what's the purpose? What do you use it for?' Marvin sat forward, his elbows resting on his thighs.

'I'm no expert, but I know a bit about it. People ask my mum for them, but she won't do them.'

'Can you give us an example?' Shirl looked at Lane's inert body slumped in Ruth's chair. Ruth followed her gaze, amazed that they were talking witchcraft and spells but feeling a genuine concern for the usually vibrant psychic now resembling a marionette with the strings cut.

'Well, years ago, they would have been used to silence a village gossip or banish an evil spirit. Now, you might wish to use one to get rid of an abusive spouse or lessen the impact of their behaviour or for someone bullying people at work. Spells are all about intention. The person requesting the binding needs to believe that it will work.'

'So, what do you think Clemency's done to Lane?' Kath asked. 'I have a thought, but I'd like to hear what you think now we have more information.'

Byron knelt by Lane's chair and held her hand. 'I think this has been done to keep you away from the manor and the woods. You're lethargic, heavy limbs, fuzzy head?'

Lane forced herself to speak. 'Yes. Stops me seeing...in here.' She tapped her head.

'Lane can't seem to speak about Clemency. That's why I wanted Shirl's account. Lane is basically talking rubbish.'

'That's not new,' Ruth joked, and everyone gave a light laugh.

'Lane, tell me about when you went to Clemency's cottage, like you did earlier.'

Lane swallowed and screwed up her face in concentration. 'She said the soft water lies inside tree smiles and feather.'

Byron stroked Lane's arm. 'Did you hear that?'

'Yep.' Lane pulled herself upright. 'Can't talk about her.'

Kath chewed her bottom lip. 'You said the power lies within Clemency's cottage, with Clemency, didn't you?'

'Yes,' said Lane slowly. 'That is correct.'

'Well, this is all a bit "when shall we three meet again?", isn't it?' Ruth said, moving to the kettle for something to do.

'The question is, what do we do about it? Byron, suggestions, please.' Kath searched his face for an answer.

Byron stood up. 'If it is a poppet, and I think it is, it must be captured and destroyed. That's the way to break the hold. The only way to release Lane from this state.'

'Is she in danger?' Marvin asked.

Byron pushed his hands into his pockets. 'I think that's the wrong word. They obviously see Lane as a threat. We need to get that poppet somehow. That's my opinion, for what it's worth.' He went and sat down at his desk.

'Well, that's great.' Ruth mashed her tea bag. 'We don't know what we're looking for, we think we know where it is and we probably won't be allowed access to get it back. Brilliant.'

'I'm printing off some images now,' said Byron. 'Rough ideas.'

'Will it be hidden somewhere or in plain view?' Shirl asked, feeling Ruth's mood cover them like a cloud.

'Can't say,' Byron replied.

'You're quiet.' Ruth sipped her tea and looked at Kath. 'And you've got your "big idea" face on.'

Kath grinned, feeling a little more optimistic. 'We need to get Clemency to the manor, get them all away from her cottage and stage a break-in.'

'Do you want a volunteer?' Marvin held up his hand. 'Because I'm up for it.'

Kath shook her head. 'I'm not having you compromised by doing anything illegal, but I appreciate the offer. No, I think I have a plan. Leave it with me. Now, on to Dylan. Was he okay when you dropped him off?'

Marvin nodded. 'He said he felt tired but was really pleased he could help.'

Kath had explained to Dylan what he'd remembered in his relaxed state. He admitted to remembering the metal ring now that Cassandra had guided him back through the experience.

'We need to go back and check that out,' Ruth said, smiling. 'Clarissa is going to be seriously pissed off with us.'

'Catching a murderer is supposed to piss people off,' Kath said harshly. 'Now, I'm going to take Lane back to the hotel to get her things and then take her to my house. Marvin, would you follow us in Lane's car and then stay with her until I get home?'

'Happy to.' Marvin beamed, and Lane mouthed a thank you with a weak smile.

Kath looked at the clock. 'Actually, scratch that. Ruth, would you take Lane? I'll give you my spare key.' She began searching in her bag.

'What are you going to do?' Ruth asked, accepting the key.

'I'm going to arrange a break-in.'

| 24 |

'Fuckin' hell, copper. You better have a good reason for dragging me outta bed.' Mikey wrapped his hands around his mug of coffee as he stood with Kath in the carport attached to his grandmother's house.

'You should be at school, not in bed.' Kath lit two cigarettes and passed one to the young lad, then picked up her own mug from the workbench.

'You knew where to find me though.' Mikey drew heavily on his cigarette and shivered in his thin dressing gown.

'I always know where to find you. Remember that.'

Mikey had been Kath's unofficial informant for eighteen months. He knew what was what and who was who, and if he didn't, his grandmother did.

'What d'you want, then?'

Kath had struggled with her idea on the short drive up to Broseley, but Lane's situation took priority and she was prepared to do what was necessary to release her from whatever psychic bonds were holding her.

'I want you to do something illegal for me.'

Mikey's mug stopped before it connected with his lips. 'You wearin' a wire?'

Kath laughed. 'You watch too much TV. No, I'm not.'

'Maybe you should strip off so I can tell you're not lyin'.'

'Too cold. You'll have to take my word for it.'

'Maybe I should frisk ya. Worth it now you've lost the weight.'

She smiled at his teenage bravado and sipped her coffee. It was thin brown liquid, the water barely acknowledging a coffee granule. She took a very small mouthful.

'New hair as well. You got a bloke?'

Kath couldn't stop the flush rising in her cheeks. 'None of your business. So, are you interested or not?'

He shrugged. 'Tell me.'

'It's a potential breaking and entering or trespass if the door's open and you walk in.'

'You serious?' He looked like a boy who'd been told Santa does exist and the moon is made of cheese.

'I am, and this is important. Someone's wellbeing rests on you pulling this off.'

Mikey stubbed out his cigarette under his slipper. 'Okay. More info.'

'I need you to find something and bring it to me.'

'You want me to nick somethin'?' Mikey narrowed his eyes a little as he looked at Kath, unsure of how much more this would involve.

'I'll describe it as best I can, although, and here's the problem, I can't say for sure what you're looking for or where it might be in the house.'

'Christ, this gets better. Give us another fag.'

She pulled two fresh packets from her pockets and handed them to him. He pushed them into the pockets of his dressing gown and snapped his fingers at her. Kath sighed and got out her existing packet. He took one and lit it with his lighter from the workbench.

'Is it worth somethin'?'

'Not in money terms. As I said, someone's life may be on the line. It's a big deal, Mikey. Think you can handle it?'

He grinned. 'You know I can, or you wouldn't be here.'

She threw her dwindling cigarette into the garden. 'I can pay you and fix you up with something more productive to society than a continued life of crime.'

'Cash is fine.' Mikey drained his mug. 'How much?'

'Let's negotiate.'

'It's not the TV, copper.' He paused. 'Is it dangerous?' A flicker of fear sparked in his eyes. Kath chewed on her bottom lip. He caught her look.

'Really?'

'You know the Quartermaine estate?'

He snorted and flicked his ash repeatedly onto the floor. 'You want me to break into the manor?'

'Not quite as grand. Cottage in the woods.'

'Empty?'

'No, but I'm working on a plan to get the occupant out of the way. They shouldn't need to lock the door, hence hopefully easier access for you.'

'When?'

'Very soon. I'm finalising details. Keep tomorrow night free.'

Kath shivered as she watched Mikey turning over the idea in his head, the carport affording little shelter from the cold morning air.

'You're not gonna use this against me, like, in the future?'

Kath shook her head and wondered for the millionth time if she was really doing the right thing. 'No. You have my word. And you obviously can't tell anyone. That goes without saying.'

'But you said it anyway.'

They shared a smile.

'I want a grand.'

'The offer is three hundred and a job.'

Mikey's eyes widened. 'A what?'

Kath knew he struggled at school, hated it and played truant most weeks. He wasn't academically bright, but he had a gift for mechanics. She looked at the motorbike next to him, almost finished, rebuilt from scraps of metal. She'd phoned Roy, her garage mechanic in the village, who had looked after all her vehicles for many years. She'd told him about Mikey's skill with engines and asked if he'd take Mikey on as an apprentice when he officially left school. Roy had agreed to meet with the lad.

'Apprentice mechanic. Taking things apart, putting them back together, all the stuff you're good at.' She knew he was interested but trying not to show it.

'Why are you doin' this?'

'Don't make this hard. I don't see you stacking supermarket shelves or going on to further education. I'm keeping you from a life of crime.'

He grinned. 'And yet you want to pay me to break into a house and steal something.'

'Don't rain on my parade.' Kath handed him one of Roy's cards. 'Talk to him. Visit. See what you think.'

He turned the card over in his hand. 'Kay. Ta. What's this number on the back?'

'My mobile. Text me so I have yours. I'll be in touch about our other arrangement. I need to go. Thank your grandmother for the coffee.' She smiled at him and turned to go.

'You've got me back, right? If something goes wrong?'

'It won't go wrong.'

'How do you know?'

'Because you're not going to get caught.'

He pushed down his moment of weakness.

'And you can call me Kath.' She walked to her car and opened the door.

'Oi, Kath.'

She turned to look at him.

'I'm still gonna call you copper.'

He went into the house, and Kath started the engine, hoping she wasn't going to regret her decision.

Lenny picked up his mobile for the fourth time, then replaced it on the desk. Each attempt at texting Kath had resulted in him deleting each one. He'd been shocked to see her at The Mallard's Rest, unable to get the image of her with another man out of his head. He'd cut dinner short, his companion sensing that his head and heart were not committed to an evening of laughter and good conversation.

He sighed at the knock at the door. 'Come in.'

The door slowly opened, and he stood quickly, his eyes widening as Kath walked into his office.

'Hi.'

'Is this a good time?'

'Of course.' He went to kiss her on the cheek but stopped himself.

Kath had not planned to see him, but as she was signalling to turn into the Madeley station, she suddenly changed her mind and headed towards Malinsgate in the centre of Telford. Now she was here, she felt awkward. The workplace wasn't the ideal setting for a personal confrontation, but she needed to clear the air, taking Lane's advice. For the first time, she felt real tension between their professional ranks. They had always flirted and traded jokey and insulting banter, but now it was different. They had reconnected—physically, emotionally and mentally—and she felt she'd blown it.

'I'm not disturbing you?'

'No, no. Sit down.'

He waited for her to sit before lowering himself into his desk chair.

'I like the new hair.'

'Thanks.' She touched the side of her neck with her hand. 'Felt like a change.'

'Suits you.'

The silence made her want to run for the door, but she swallowed quickly.

'I thought I should explain about last night.'

Lenny held up his hands. 'Hey, we're Ross and Rachel. You're free to sleep with whoever you want.'

Her cheeks coloured. 'I was having dinner with a friend. That's a cheap shot.'

He flexed his fingers, feeling she was about to blow like a volcano. Again. 'We agreed to give each other space while you figured out what you wanted.'

Kath opened her mouth to berate him but realised he was right. The process had now been muddled by Richard's arrival into her life. 'Well, if we're interrogating on dinner companions, who were you having dinner with?'.

'Are you jealous, Kathleen?'

'Don't full-name me.' She managed a smile, and he reciprocated.

'It was Louise, Susan's best friend. She's been very supportive to both of us through the divorce. I wanted to buy her dinner as a thank you. There's nothing more to it.'

Another silence stretched like cling film, threatening to suppress words that wanted to come out but would not lead to a solution. Kath sent up a silent prayer for a text or phone call to get her out of the room without another argument. As if by divine intervention, her mobile heralded a text message.

'I need to check this.'

She read the message quickly. Marvin. Lane was safely at Kath's cottage.

'Friend?' Lenny pointed to her phone, concern and jealousy threatening to dislodge his breakfast.

'Work,' she said sharply.

Work. Neutral territory. Safe ground.

Lenny nodded. 'How's it going?'

'It's throwing up some interesting challenges,' she said evasively.

Her phone sounded again. Another message. Richard.

My horoscope says good Fortune is coming my way...

She tried not to smile, but Lenny saw it hovering around her lips. She looked up at him as she pocketed the phone and stood up.

'I need to go.'

'What do we do, about us?' he asked, rising but not moving to the door after her.

Kath turned. 'I don't know. I can't think about it right now.'

'So we just keep avoiding this?'

She felt guilty at the pain she knew she was causing by her indecision. 'I said I can't do this now.'

She opened the door, the only sound in the outer office being fingers on keyboards.

'Obviously.' He fought to keep his frustration in check, but it reared inside him like a wild stallion. 'Thanks for the Dover sole last night. It was delicious. Even better as it was paid for by your *friend*.'

The emphasis on the last word cut deep. 'We're not in school anymore, Lenny. Grow up.'

She slammed the door, and he slumped back into his chair, tears pricking his eyes.

| 25 |

Shirl was smoking a cigarette next to the station as Kath returned. She joined her under the tree as a fine mist started to descend.

'Marvin messaged me. They're on their way back.' Kath lit a cigarette and smoked quietly, her face stony, eyes gazing out to the trees.

'I know that face,' said Shirl. 'What's up?'

'Went to see Lenny.'

'Oh.'

'Yeah. Pretty much all I have to say on the matter.'

Shirl felt sad for her friend. Kath had finally got her act together with the love of her life after many years and it had all been going so well. Now they seemed farther apart than ever.

'If you need to sound off, I'm here for you.'

'Appreciated. Anything new?'

'Got the date through for our skydive.'

Kath's head cleared from the distraction of her own train wreck. 'When?'

'October twenty-sixth. Saturday before Halloween. It's an omen.'

'We'll all be there to support you, gazing up in wonder and cheering you on.'

'Let's hope the whites of your eyes aren't the last thing I see.'

Smoke streamed from Kath's mouth as a laugh turned into a cough. 'Don't be dramatic.'

'If you ever hear me say I'm going to Cassandra's for a drink, please lock me in a cell.'

'The woman's a goddess. I won't hear a bad word against her.' Kath's voice lost the jokey tone. 'She was amazing with Dylan.'

'Oh yes. What do we do about going back to the woods to see if we can find that ring?'

Kath raised an eyebrow and smiled.

Shirl ground her cigarette butt fiercely into the mud. 'Shit. Why did I even ask?'

Ruth and Marvin arrived back at the office, with little to report on Lane's condition. Ruth had left her on the sofa with a blanket, a piece of toast and the washing-up bowl placed next to her on the floor.

'I don't like leaving her,' Ruth said as she made tea.

'Agreed,' said Kath. 'Shirl and I are going to the estate to check out this metal ring next to the folly, if we can find it. We'll call in on her on the way back.' She looked at Shirl. 'I need to go to Tesco. Not much food in. I know Lane probably doesn't feel like eating, but she'll need more than toast and a Pot Noodle.'

'Woman cannot live by Pot Noodle alone, but I'd give it a go,' Shirl replied, finishing off the last of the biscuits from the tin.

'So, what's next?' Marvin asked, putting his mobile on the desk.

Kath suddenly remembered Richard's text, but he would have to wait for a reply.

'I had an interesting chat with Donvan B from the online forum last night.'

They all had a copy of the pages that Byron had printed out for Lane to read.

Ruth sat down. 'How did that come about?'

Kath gave them scant details of her trip to Bridgnorth, not ready to explain about their previous meeting in The Blasted Oak. Over plates of chips in the pub, he'd told her how Clarissa and Clemency had changed his life.

'So, Tom Devlin, a reporter for the Shropshire Star, just ups and quits his job, hides away for a few months and reinvents himself as Donovan Brightstone?' Marvin tried to wrap his head around the notion of such a huge life change.

'Yes,' said Kath. 'I thought I knew his face but couldn't place him. We've seen him at press conferences. He looked different then, suit and a short haircut.'

'Did they put some kind of spell on him?' Ruth said, ever the sceptic.

Kath smiled. 'In a way, I guess. He'd lost both parents within a couple of years of each other, his relationship with his girlfriend was chaotic and he was just generally unhappy with his life.'

'So, this transformation came from Clarissa?' Marvin asked.

'He said he didn't tell a lot of people about his story because, well, closed minds and all that. But, basically, he'd been sent to the manor to get an interview about the girls being found.' Kath exhaled heavily and her shoulders dropped. 'He said he felt different in the house, an energy that he couldn't explain at the time. Clarissa and Clemency saw something in him, a new way forward. They told him about the history of the estate. He was there for hours, he said. Clemency pulled out some Tarot cards. They helped him put his life into perspective and he saw a path of reinvention. He went home feeling better than he had in months. Next day, he quit his job, left his toxic girlfriend and went to some spiritual retreat. Four months later, he changed his name and opened the shop, The Bright Stone, in Bridgnorth.

'He also said there's a pathway from the front gates of the estate that leads into the woods, which means we don't have to announce ourselves.' She looked at Shirl.

'Great,' Shirl muttered.

Byron got up and gave each of the team a piece of paper with images on it. The four photographs showed small doll-like figures. One had the head completely bound with wool, one was blackened as if burnt.

'This is roughly what I think you're looking for when the break-in is... you know, anyway, there you go.'

Ruth studied the pictures. 'I was expecting something with pins sticking out of it.'

'That's more voodoo-based,' Byron replied, sitting down.

Kath smiled as she saw Ruth pull a that's-me-told face. 'Shirl, you've seen one room of Clemency's cottage. Any guess as to where this thing might be?'

Shirl thought for a moment, picturing the sparse lounge. 'There are shelves in the alcoves either side of the fireplace. It might be there. Also, there's a basket at the side of the sofa, full of bits of material.'

'Okay,' said Kath. 'Not a lot to go on, but it's something. If it is hidden somewhere, it's going to take longer.'

'So, how exactly are we getting it back?' Marvin asked.

'I'd like you all to come to my place later. I'll tell you then. I don't want to do it here.'

Ruth looked at Shirl. Marvin looked at Byron.

'Okay, Boss,' said Marvin.

Kath stood up. 'Right. Off to Tesco, then to the estate.'

Shirl grabbed her coat and bag.

'So, we'll see you at your place. You cooking?' Ruth smirked.

Kath shot her a look. 'It's not a dinner party. I don't think Lane would thank you for the smell of tikka masala wafting under her nose. I'll get crisps.'

'Whoopee,' said Ruth tartly.

Shirl gazed dolefully at Kath's basket. 'Bread, soup, milk, crisps. Is that it?'

'Like Lane, I'm not eating much at the moment.'

'I'm going to Greggs. Wait for you outside.'

Shirl had demolished two sausage rolls by the time Kath emerged from the supermarket. They set off in their cars for the estate, each lost in their thoughts.

The rain had held off and the sky was clearing, the temperature dropping. Kath pulled onto the grass verge as they neared the manor and Shirl tucked her car in behind

Kath's, hoping they'd get out again given the soft, muddy grass. They moved inside the gates and stood to the right. Kath gestured to the boundary wall, which was thickly overgrown with plant life.

'Donovan said if we stick to the wall and walk until we see the path, we'll be hidden from view. We'll come to the fork leading to the folly and Clemency's.'

'I'm guessing the last time he knew about this it was easier to get to.' Shirl pulled the collar of her waterproof jacket closer to her throat.

'It's worth a try. Come on.'

Kath led the way, holding back wet branches and trying not to let them spring back in Shirl's face. They both wore ankle boots, but Shirl was certain her socks felt damp as the undergrowth snatched at her feet. The sound of a car engine rumbled near the house and grew in volume as a Porsche shot down the driveway. Both women turned, seeing the flash of black through the foliage.

'Was that Rafferty?' Shirl asked.

'I believe it was. I wonder where he's going in such a hurry.'

| 26 |

The golf club bar was practically deserted as Rafferty strode in. Anger, fear and guilt flooded his body. He needed distance, a place to think where he wouldn't be disturbed. Or judged.

'Another.' The woman slumped on the bar stool flourished her tumbler at the barman, who took it from her shaky hand.

'Are you sure that's wise, Mrs Martin?'

'You want a job as my therapist now? Jack. Neat.'

Angela Martin had started on Jack Daniel's and Coke. Now the coke had been dispensed with, and her mood, like her body, was sinking. The barman put the glass of bourbon in front of her and nodded to Rafferty.

'Mr Quartermaine. What can I get for you?'

Angela Martin turned to him, her jaw tightening.

Rafferty barely acknowledged the woman, not even offering her a glance, and stood a few feet from her. 'Chardonnay, thanks, Mike.'

'Why aren't you in prison, you fucking creep?' Angela pushed herself upright with such force her body teetered on the edge of the bar stool. Mike reached out and grabbed her arm to stop her from cascading to the floor.

Rafferty noticed her now, recognition causing the blood to drain from his face. 'I-I haven't d-done anything,' he stammered.

Angela threw off the barman's grip and slammed her hands on the bar, angling her body, her bloodshot eyes boring into Rafferty. 'You murdered my child.'

'It wasn't me. I'm sorry...'

Rafferty's place of safety had now become another battleground, and he looked anxiously at the barman. Angela slid off the stool, and Rafferty took a step back.

'You're sorry? You hear that, Mike? Mummy's murdering son of a bitch is sorry.'

Mike moved quickly to stand next to Rafferty. 'Mrs Martin, why don't we go and sit down in the lounge—'

'We all know what you did.' She waved her hand at the empty room.

Rafferty shook his head vigorously. 'I didn't do it. I couldn't do that.'

She pointed a shaking finger at him, spittle flying from her lips. 'Her father and I saw you talking to her that night, at the anniversary party.'

'I did talk to her, yes.' Rafferty nodded, hoping to deflect her anger with as much honesty as he could muster. 'We were talking about art. I told her about my paintings—'

'Your paintings?' She looked him up and down and sneered at his simpering face. 'Don't make me laugh, little boy. Until your mother's dead, you own nothing. *Nothing.*'

Mike moved towards her, arms outstretched. 'Please, let's go somewhere else, Mrs Martin.'

She lunged, aiming her fist at Rafferty's face. Her diamond ring, made more prominent by her fist, split Mike's lip as his head snapped sideways. Rafferty stared open-mouthed and Mike held his cheek. Angela felt neither pain nor remorse thanks to the bourbon coursing through her body as she pushed Mike aside, determined to hit her intended target this time.

Rafferty did the only thing he could do.

He ran.

'Let's go into the woods, she said. It'll be fun, she said,' Shirl muttered under her breath as a branch caught her on the side of her face.

'We're nearly there.'

Kath moved into a clearer space. The fork in the path was visible now. They pushed ahead, the cold air tightening around their faces. They soon came to the folly.

Kath turned slowly, orienting herself. 'So, the house is back there... the boys would have come from this direction, I think.' She pointed straight ahead into dense woodland shaping into a skeletal landscape.

'What's the plan?' Shirl stamped her cold feet.

Kath pulled a pair of leather gloves from her pocket. Shirl plunged her hands into her own pockets, realising that her gloves were in her other coat.

'We just kick around the undergrowth until we find it. It's got to still be here.'

The folly loomed over them as they set about their task. They moved in parallel, a few feet apart, walking the grid like an active crime scene. The air, turning slowly colder, was so gradual that neither woman noticed the mist.

'I can't see my feet,' Shirl exclaimed. 'Where the hell did this mist come from? Maybe Clarissa sent it to thwart us.'

Kath laughed. 'It's not magic mist; it's called weather. Keep looking.'

Kath bent down at intervals, clearing away leaves and twigs and pressing her hand into the ground. She stopped. 'I think I've found something.'

Shirl joined her, and they kicked away the remaining woodland detritus.

'Oh my god.' Shirl stared at the metal plate in the ground, the large metal ring lying flat on its surface.

'Well, what do we have here?'

Kath bent down and pulled hard on the ring. The metal plate moved upwards, and she set it down, resting on the pile of leaves. Before them was a set of steps that led down into darkness.

Kath stood up and looked at Shirl. 'Bet the skydive is looking peachy now.'

Rafferty pulled the Porsche into a lay-by and turned off the engine. He could smell his body odour. He pushed the door open and stumbled out. A lone crow watched silently as he bent double, the pale bile splashing onto the grass. He wiped his mouth with the back of his hand and fumbled quickly with his trousers as the stream of urine mixed with his stomach fluid.

'I can't do this anymore, Mother,' he mumbled to himself, his body flooded with exhaustion from the double evacuation.

'It has to end now.'

'Hey you.' Lane slumped against the cushion, her mobile phone resting between her ear and the cushion. 'No, it's okay. I don't blame you for leaving. I'm not a good bed companion when my sleep's disturbed. I had a bad night, and my day's not good either. No, I'm not drunk.' She laughed. 'Mouth doesn't work well. Cheeky boy.' She sighed heavily. 'It's like psychic sick. Can't explain. I'm on the sofa watching Marvin's favourite TV show. I'm at Kath's.' She paused. 'It would be nice to see you, but I look a wreck... Don't know when Kath will be back... Okay. See you soon.'

Kath went first down the steps, testing each tread tentatively before committing her full weight. Once at the bottom, she clicked on her Maglite torch.

Shirl switched on the torch facility on her phone as she reached the bottom. 'You've seen *The Great Escape*, right?'

'Best bank holiday film ever,' Kath replied. 'Look at this place.'

She guessed the tunnel was a little over six feet high and about five feet across, the walls clad in wooden planks. The mist lay across the entrance like a damp blanket.

'Do we go?'

Kath nodded. 'Where there's an entrance, we have to assume there's an exit.'

'I refer to my previous comment. In the film, they didn't come out where they thought they would.'

They moved slowly, the beaten earth hard beneath their feet.

'I wonder how long it is.'

'We'll soon find out,' said Kath. 'Come on. Do you want to be James Garner or Steve McQueen?'

'Are you sure she's okay?' Ruth rolled her eyes and switched her phone to her other ear. 'No, you did the right thing. I can be there in half an hour. Give her some black coffee. Thanks for the call.'

'Trouble?'

Ruth swivelled her chair to face Marvin. 'Angela Martin's just punched a barman at the golf club.'

'Why did she do that?'

'She was aiming for Rafferty's face. This guy got in the way.'

'Oh, right. Does he want to press charges?'

'Don't think so. He found my card in her bag. She was sounding off about Rafferty murdering Sophia. Seems things took an alcohol-fuelled turn for the worse.'

'Where's Rafferty now?'

'Gone.' Ruth stood up and turned off her computer. 'Here's Kath's spare key. You and Byron go and look after Lane. I'll go to the golf club, make sure she's okay.'

She passed the key to Marvin and sent a text to Kath to update her.

Marvin was secretly pleased to play knight in shining armour. Lane really had looked dreadful and he was worried about her.

Byron picked up his coat and bag and stood waiting by the door. 'I hope Lane will be pleased to see us.'

'Of course she will.' Marvin said as he pulled out his car keys from his pocket. 'After all, she's stuck at Kath's. She must be bored silly by now.'

He kissed Lane on the cheek, closed the front door and guided her back to the sofa. Her body sank into the soft cushions, exhausted by the short trip to the door.

'I'm not given to professions of vanity,' she said slowly, 'but I didn't want you to see me like this.'

He smiled. 'You always look beautiful. It comes from in here.' He placed his hand over her heart, and she began to cry softly. He sat next to her and took her in his arms. 'Can you tell me about it?'

She knew her mouth wouldn't allow her to tell him everything, but she knew she could trust him with whatever information would come out, aware of his job and his background. Her slurred words fell as she tried to speak, him nodding, stroking her arm, her hair. She wasn't used to feeling vulnerable, and he sensed her fear.

She pulled back from him. 'I've made your suit wet.'

He shrugged. 'What's three grand between friends?'

| 27 |

An espresso cup and a glass of water sat on the desk next to Angela Martin's chair, her anger spent, body and brain tired. She groaned as Ruth walked into the office.

Mike pressed a packet of frozen peas to his cheek and extended his other hand to Ruth. 'Thanks for coming.'

Angela exhaled slowly. 'Are you pressing charges, then?' She looked at Mike, not really caring one way or the other.

'She's here for your welfare, Mrs Martin. It was an accident. I'm fine.'

'No accident. Meant to do it. You just got in the damned way. Wrong face.'

'I can't condone your actions, Mrs Martin, but I do understand. You have to let us do our job.' Ruth gave what she hoped was a stern but sympathetic smile.

'But nothing's happening; he's still walking around.'

'It's only been three days,' said Ruth. 'Just leave it to us. How are you feeling?'

'A bit sick,' Angela admitted.

Mike stepped back a pace, not wanting his shoes to be ruined as well.

'I think you should get a taxi and go home. We will let you know when we have any news.'

Ruth was confident there was nothing else to be done and looked at the wall clock. Marvin and Byron would be settled at Kath's.

'Are we good here?' Ruth looked at Mike.

'I'll see to it that she gets home.'

'Okay. Take care, Mrs Martin. No repeat performances. Alright?'

Angela leaned forward, her head in her hands. 'Fine. Just get that bastard.'

'You know when you asked me to join you in this cold case team?'

'Yes.' Kath knew exactly where the conversation was going.

'No more standing around in the rain at 5a.m., freezing our tits off, staring at some poor corpse in the mud. It'll be a change for all of us, you said. Regular hours, a cosy office, picking our own cases...'

'You want back on active cases?' Kath was teasing her now, light banter in the dark tunnel.

'I'm considering my options.'

'I hate to point it out, but you did choose this case.'

'Yeah,' Shirl muttered with an air of resignation. 'So I did.'

There were no other tunnels shooting off from the main route. Kath was beginning to wonder if the end was in sight. Then suddenly, their combined torchlight picked out another set of steps. They stopped and looked at each other.

'Our exit awaits,' Kath said quietly.

'If I don't make it, I bequeath my secret biscuit stash in my bottom drawer to Ruth. You first...Boss.'

Kath climbed the eight steps and was confronted with a large door. She put her ear to it.

'Anything?'

She shook her head. 'Here goes nothing.'

She grasped the metal handle and depressed it. The door swung silently open. She switched off her torch and placed it in her pocket, then stepped through the doorway into the smaller drawing room of Quartermaine Manor. After looking around the empty room, she beckoned to Shirl, who put her mobile away.

'What the hell? Are we in a Gothic novel?'

Kath put her finger to her lips and gestured to the hallway. 'I hear voices,' she whispered.

They stepped away from the door to close it, realising that the door was actually a huge oil painting of a young woman holding a small dog. Kath pushed the frame, and the door clicked into place.

'Now what do we do?' said Shirl.

Kath moved out of sight of the hallway and waved to Shirl to join her. Kath needed time to think but knew she wasn't going to get it as the sound of approaching steps grew louder.

'I'll deal with Rafferty when he gets back.'

Clarissa entered the room and her mouth fell open. 'How did you get in here?'

Clemency ran into the back of her and placed her hands on Clarissa's shoulders, eyes wide.

'We found something interesting that we'd like to discuss.' Kath moved to the painting. 'We've just had a trip through your secret tunnel.'

Their faces betrayed nothing.

'And?' Clarissa tilted her head, daring to be questioned further.

Kath suddenly felt like the proverbial wildlife in the headlights. She had nothing. Her mouth felt dry and her brain felt stupid.

Shirl cleared her throat. 'I bet a lot of these old houses have them. Who made it?'

Good cop to the rescue. Kath watched for reaction from the two women.

'Farraday's great-great-grandfather, Mortimer,' replied Clarissa. 'When he had the folly built, it was an easier way to access it instead of going through the woods.'

'Well, every man needs a hobby.' Shirl's humour hit the floor like a concrete block.

'How did you find it?' Clemency came from behind Clarissa and stood next to her.

'Accident,' said Kath. 'My foot caught in the ring.'

'I hardly think that's likely, but no matter.'

Clarissa held Kath's gaze but was the first to break away.

'I need to attend to Brocken.' Clarissa pointed to the hallway. 'You can use the door this time on your way out.' She turned and went down the hallway. Clemency gave the women a knowing smile and followed Clarissa.

'Byron was right.' Kath walked round the room, keeping her voice low, uncomfortable in the house but reluctant to leave it. 'I think each girl came here and, somehow, they were made to go through that tunnel. They were alive when they went into that folly.'

In comparison, Shirl was itching to leave. 'Completely plausible. And we have no evidence to support the notion.'

'Okay.' Kath's fingers twitched as she paced. 'Let's say each girl did actually come here. Why?'

'They were invited?'

'Why?'

Shirl shrugged. 'I don't know. Kath, why are we doing this here? Let's just go.'

Kath's mobile pinged, and she pulled it from her pocket and read the text. 'Ruth. Angela Martin's been kicking off at the golf club. She's going to see what's going on, then she'll be at my house. Marvin and Byron are on their way.'

Shirl walked out of the room, to the front door, and to her relief, Kath followed.

'They were here,' Kath said quietly. 'Those three girls walked into this beautiful house. I'm sure of it. We're close. I know we're close.'

'You have a plan, don't you?'

Kath closed the door, and they started down the driveway.

'I think I do. And now we have three definite suspects.'

| 28 |

Marvin was about to turn into Kath's driveway when he saw a car parked next to Lane's.

'That's strange.'

Byron leaned forward. 'Visitor?'

'Noone except us knows that she's here.'

Marvin coaxed the car past the house and pulled into a lay-by. The metal gate into the field was padlocked and rusting in places. Marvin couldn't make out any livestock in the mist as they got out of the car.

Byron clutched Marvin's arm, a look of panic in his eyes. 'Are you worried?'

He was, but he wasn't about to let Byron see it.

'Concerned. Come on.'

If this had been a scene in his favourite show, *Law & Order*, Detective Lennie Briscoe would have had his gun drawn, body crouched, using the hedge as cover. But he wasn't Lennie and he didn't have a gun, he just had a tech geek with an apprehensive frown and bad taste in knitwear. Marvin took Kath's front door key from his pocket and strode purposefully towards the cottage. He was about to put it in the lock when the door swung open.

'Detective Constable Marvin Henshall.' He held up his warrant card. 'Who are you?'

'Marvin?' Lane's weak voice floated to his ears from inside the house.

'*Lane.*' Marvin pushed past the man and rushed into the lounge.

'It's okay. He's a friend.'

Byron stood outside, not knowing what to do. The man beckoned him inside, then shut the door, following him into the lounge. Lane didn't look much better and her speech was still slow.

'Were you worried about me?' She patted the sofa cushion and looked up at Marvin.

He adopted what he hoped was an attitude of authority as he glanced at the tall, muscled man by the door. 'No-one knew you were here. But if she says you're a friend...' He sat next to Lane, and Byron took an armchair.

'We were going to meet for a drink. I phoned him to say I wasn't feeling well, and he offered to come over. Is that okay?'

'It's fine, Lane.' He looked back at the man. 'So, what's your name, then?'

They heard a car on the drive, and Byron craned his neck to see out of the window.

'It's Ruth.'

The man went to the door and opened it. Ruth stood next to her car, then walked towards the cottage, shaking her head and smiling.

'Well, well. Fancy seeing you here, Marcus.'

Kath squeezed her car into her driveway as Shirl went up the lane to find a parking spot. Lane and Ruth's cars had been expected, but she was shocked to see Marcus's black Lexus. She hadn't seen him since he'd rescued her from the hostage situation in which she'd found herself inside her home. Lenny's face came into her mind as she remembered him seeing her embrace Marcus in her doorway and jumping to all the wrong conclusions. Maybe that had been the slippery slope for their relationship. She suddenly realised she hadn't replied to Richard's text and was mildly annoyed to find that whenever she thought of either man, the other was never too far away. She retrieved the bag of shopping from the boot, and as she got to the door, there stood Marcus. Of all the surprises of the day, he was definitely the most welcome.

'And you're here because...'

He pulled her into a hug. 'I'll explain inside.'

Her cosy lounge was littered with bodies, some on furniture, some on the floor. Shirl's face was a picture of astonishment.

'So, we're all here.' Kath looked round at the expectant faces, and she suddenly felt bone-weary.

'Ruth, can you get everyone a drink? Shirl, catch everyone up on our little adventure. I need coffee and a smoke and Marcus.'

Ruth stood up, and they went to the kitchen. Kath filled the kettle as Ruth gathered cups from the cupboard.

'How's Angela Martin?' She added two hefty spoons of coffee to her mug.

'Angry, drunk and frustrated.'

'Must have been a shock for her to come face to face with Rafferty. We heard a car scream past us at the manor.'

'Barman said he ran like a frightened child. Mind you, apparently Mrs Martin packs quite a punch, so I think it was a wise decision.'

Kath poured water on her coffee and signalled to Marcus through the doorway. He walked into the kitchen, opened the back door for her and stepped outside.

'He was a nice surprise.' Ruth pointed at him, and he turned and grinned at her.

Kath went outside and lit a cigarette, the smoke mingling with the mist. 'So come on. What exactly are you doing here?'

Marcus leant against the doorframe, hands in his trouser pockets. 'Lane called me when she knew she was helping out on the case. We've been spending some quality time together.'

'Diplomatic as ever.'

'I'm concerned about her.'

Kath saw the worry in his dark brown eyes. 'Did she tell you what is going on?'

'Sketchy details. She said she literally can't talk about it.'

'I'll tell you,' said Kath. 'You won't believe it, but I'll tell you what's been going on.'

Ten minutes later, they appeared back in the lounge.

'Did you tell him?' Lane looked from Kath to Marcus.

'I did. Marcus has said he'll stay here tonight.'

There was relief in Lane's eyes.

'You have a habit of coming to the rescue of damsels in distress.' Kath looked at Marcus, and they shared the moment. 'Anyway, I don't want Lane in the room for what I'm about to say. Marcus, will you take her upstairs, please?'

'Sure.' He carefully scooped Lane up into his arms and carried her upstairs.

'Where's he been all my life?' Shirl muttered, watching them go and losing herself in a private fantasy.

'Marcus is a bodyguard for Pirate Sal.'

Ruth was already acquainted with Sal, the wheelchair-bound criminal living in the depths of the Worcestershire countryside. Shirl nodded, still smiling.

'Right, let's get on with this.' Kath stood by the window, all eyes on her. 'We're all caught up now, yes?'

Everyone murmured agreement. Kath kept her voice low as she outlined her plan for the retrieval of the poppet.

'So I'm effectively making you all party to an illegal activity.' Kath scanned each face. 'If anyone's got a problem with this, I understand completely. No judgement.'

'And you trust this Mikey?' Marvin asked.

'I do. Actually, I'm starting to trust the criminals more than law-abiding citizens at the moment. Present company excepted.'

'What do we do when we get this poppet back, then?' Shirl shrugged.

'Byron needs to lead on this.'

'We need to be very careful,' he said. 'We can't just destroy it or unwrap it. I think we need some kind of ceremony to release the magic.'

On any other day, there would have been jokes and comments, banter about the words he had just spoken. But they all felt the gravity of the situation.

'So, Mikey needs to get it and keep it safe?' Marvin said.

Byron nodded. 'Yes. I need to do some more research. It's not exactly an area of expertise for me.'

'What about your mum?' Ruth asked.

Byron shook his head. 'Like I said, she doesn't get involved in anything like this. She's not one for spells and hexes.'

Donovan Brightstone suddenly popped into Kath's mind. 'I think I may have a solution. Thanks, Byron. So, I will arrange for everyone at the Quartermaine estate to be at the manor after dark tomorrow. Ruth and Shirl, you'll be with me. We need to go in heavy and keep them talking. I want answers, and one of them, if not all, is going to tell us what happened to the girls.'

Disappointment clouded Marvin's eyes. 'Can't I be there too?'

'You've got an important job, Marvin. You'll pick up Mikey and take him to the estate and wait outside the gates for him. I need to know he'll be in safe hands when he gets out.'

Marvin's face brightened. 'Oh, okay.'

'If you think about it, it's barely breaking the law,' Ruth reasoned. 'I mean, if this poppet represents Lane, then we could argue it's her property. Plus, the fact that when they find it's gone, who are they gonna call? The police?'

'*Ghostbusters*,' said Byron and Marvin in unison.

The laughter broke the tension.

Marvin's face suddenly turned serious as he stared out of the window over Kath's shoulder.

'What?' She turned and thought she saw a movement past the hedge.

'Nothing.' Marvin's shoulders relaxed. 'Jogger with one of those headlamps on.'

Kath's heart rate increased. Could it have been Richard? She still hadn't replied to his text. Maybe he'd run past, seen all the cars and decided against knocking on the door.

'I'm going to break out the crisps.' Kath moved forward into the kitchen.

'Nothing more substantial?' Shirl asked hopefully.

Kath smiled. 'Can we stretch a Pot Noodle to serve five?'

Rafferty entered quietly through the rear entrance of the house. He heard chopping coming from the kitchen and peered round the doorway. Fenella was cutting leeks into small pieces, her paisley-patterned apron smudged with patches of flour.

'There you are.' Her eyes lit up at the sight of her husband. She'd heard the car screaming away and had run to the window to see his Porsche disappearing through the gates. 'Where did you go?'

'For a drink.'

'I was worried.' She gathered the leeks and dropped them, handful by handful, into the pan.

'Fenella, do you love me?'

She brushed her hands down her apron and moved to him, embracing his shaking body. 'Of course I do.'

He wrapped his arms around her and clung to her, breathing in the scent of her camomile shampoo and lavender face cream. It was the most contact they'd had since the night Brocken was conceived, and it warmed her heart.

'Do you think if we'd met under different circumstances, we would have been happy?'

She pulled back from him. His cheeks were pale, and she saw an echo of her son in his face. 'We're happy now, aren't we?'

Even as she spoke the words, she knew them to be false. Rafferty was away more than he was at home. When he did come home, he seemed overshadowed by his mother. Fenella cheered herself with plain cooking, the one thing she was good at, but Clarissa was the banquet, the feast for the eyes. Fenella was the uninspiring side dish that was traditional but that no-one really wanted on their plate.

'Has something happened?' She brushed his fringe from his forehead, and his voice quivered at her touch.

'I'm a bad person. I know it. My mother knows it.'

Fenella shook her head. 'I don't believe that.'

'I don't deserve you.'

'You're wrong,' Fenella replied, mustering a confidence that had lain dormant inside their marriage but was now rising within her.

'I have to tell someone what really happened.'

'Can you tell me?' She looked deep into his eyes, and as he opened his mouth to speak, Clarissa appeared in the doorway.

'There you are, Rafferty. Come to the drawing room.' She flashed a defiant look at Fenella and left quickly

Rafferty turned to watch her go and then looked back at his wife. 'I can't tell you, not yet, but I need to tell the story.'

'Tell who?'

Rafferty's hands fell to his sides. 'I need to tell the police.'

| 29 |

Kath waved the team goodbye as Marcus collected his overnight bag from the boot of his car and put it at the bottom of the stairs before taking his shoes back off.

'You're so prepared.' Kath smiled at him and shut the front door.

'Got to be in my line of work.'

They went into the lounge.

'I'm worried about Lane,' he admitted.

'I know. We all are.'

'This plan of yours, do you think it will work?'

She'd told him outside about Mikey and the retrieval of the poppet. He'd listened intently, taking in every bizarre detail.

'It's all I've got. It has to work.'

He nodded, his own brain having a lack of ideas to share despite the situation being stuck in his head. 'Do you need any extra help?'

'Thanks, but I think we're okay. You're helping Lane just by being here.'

He sighed. 'It doesn't seem enough.'

Kath pressed her hand into his arm. 'Believe me, it is. I guess Sal knows you're here?'

'She does, and she's got your back if you need her. As ever.'

Kath rolled her eyes and affected a bad Bronx accent. 'Jeez, you save a chick's life and you just can't shake her off.'

Kath had cost Sal her leg but saved her life. The criminal and the police officer gave each other respect and help whenever it was required.

Kath's mobile pinging broke the moment.

'I'll go up.' Marcus picked up his bag and went upstairs.

The text was from Richard.

I don't want to be that pushy guy but...

Kath smiled. Maybe she needed a distraction as the afternoon descended into twilight.

If you have alcohol, I can be there in an hour.

She didn't have to wait long for a response.

Then come on over.

Kath went up to Lane's room. The door was ajar. She pushed it the rest of the way open without knocking first.

'Hey, how are you feeling?'

'Alright,' Lane replied. She lay in the bed, Marcus on top sitting next to her. He'd changed into jeans and a sweatshirt, both items looking as if they cost more than Kath's entire wardrobe.

'I'm gonna grab a shower and go out for a while. There's bread in the cupboard and stuff going bad in the fridge, I'd order pizza.'

Marcus grinned.

'And yes, Marcus, you can clean my kitchen if you feel the need.'

Please clean my kitchen.

He put his hand on his chest in an over-the-top display of fake gratitude. 'Thank you.'

'Have a nice time,' Lane said with effort. 'Tell Richard I said hi.'

Kath's cheeks reddened, and she left the room quickly.

The front door opened, and Kath proffered a handful of decaying lavender stems.

'For me?' Richard stepped back and stood open-mouthed in fake shock. 'You shouldn't have.'

They laughed as she entered the house.

'You got me roses, after a fashion. Seemed only right I return the gesture.'

'I'll put them on my pillow to help me sleep.' He took the scrappy posy from her and walked through to the kitchen.

Kath followed him. 'Something smells good.'

Talk to me about food so I don't have to think about ripping your clothes off.

'Simple vegetable stir fry. We can eat whenever you like. If you want to, of course.'

Kath realised she hadn't eaten all day. 'That sounds great. So, was it you jogging past my house earlier?'

He opened the fridge to get a bottle of wine. 'Guilty as charged.' He poured the wine into two green glass goblets and passed one to her. 'Saw all the cars on your driveway, so I didn't stop. I was also quite sweaty. Not a good look or smell for a suitor.'

She sipped the wine and nodded appreciatively. 'This is good.'

'Organic and local-ish.'

'Of course it is,' she teased.

'So, was it a work meeting, or were you throwing a wild afternoon party?'

'No party.' Her face was serious now, and he moved to her side of the kitchen island. 'Can't talk about it. How was your day?'

He leant against the island, close enough that she could smell a citrus aroma clinging to his body. His green check shirt sleeves were rolled up to the elbows, revealing delicate arm hair. His green chinos clung to his thighs.

'Went to see Topiary Man.' He took a swallow of wine. 'He's talked the wife out of the swimming pool. We're going for a tasteful Mediterranean gazebo surrounded by palm trees.'

'Nice.'

I don't want to speak anymore; I just want to kiss him.

As if reading her thoughts, he put down his glass and took Kath's from her hand and placed it down on the marble top. The smell of him overpowered her as his lips brushed hers. His beard, like his lips, was soft and warm. He pulled away, not trusting himself to blow it and take the kiss too far too soon.

He looked at her. 'Any questions, Detective?'

'Just one,' she breathed. 'You going to do that again?'

Clarissa paced the floor of the grand drawing room. Rafferty stood next to the fireplace, watching her.

'So, they know? Now they've found the tunnel, they know.'

Clarissa stopped, her eyes narrow, thin lips set in a straight line. 'They know nothing; they can't prove the girls were here. Fortune thinks she's put the pieces together, but she's still empty. Just supposition. I still have the upper hand, and as long as you keep your mouth shut, it'll all be over soon.'

Rafferty kicked the stone fireplace with his heel. 'Yes, you've always had the upper hand, haven't you, Mother?'

She was in front of him so suddenly it was as if she'd teleported. 'You know what this place means to me. I can't lose it. I won't lose it. Do you understand?'

'Don't you feel anything for those girls?' His face flushed, and he was surprised to find himself with a new sense of urgency and confidence. 'They had their whole lives ahead of them.'

'Oh, stop with the fake emotion. It doesn't suit you.'

'They weren't meant to be found, were they? If those boys hadn't discovered them, you never would have told me.'

The slap across his face shocked him, especially after having avoided an earlier one from Angela Martin. As with his wife, physical contact with his mother was rare.

'You are correct; we would not have told you.' Clarissa stepped back, with no remorse for her action.

Rafferty had been a disappointment from an early age. Even though the Blackstock line ran through his veins, he showed no signs of the gift and the ways of the land. No connection. Brocken was different—bright and sensitive, attuned to Clarissa's thoughts.

'No doubt the police will be here again tomorrow. I think you should pack and go to London.' Clarissa folded her arms, signalling the end of the conversation.

Rafferty was torn. The overwhelming desire to tell the police what he knew fought against the damage he knew would be inflicted on his family with his confession.

'I need to see Brocken.' Rafferty started up the stairs leading from the drawing room.

'Leave him be. You have no connection with him.'

'And whose fault is that?' Rafferty turned so quickly he almost lost his balance. He put his hand on the wall to steady himself. 'You've poisoned him against me. That's what your obsession with this place has done.'

He marched angrily up the stairs and went to Brocken's room. He sat on the edge of the bed and began to cry.

'Again, any more questions?' Richard kissed Kath's bare shoulder.

'Just one.' She traced her fingers across his chest. 'Can we eat now?'

The sex had been slow, measured, satisfying and just what Kath needed. There had been no movie sex moves, no bodies crushed against the fridge in a frenzy of passion, no pressing of bare bottom cheeks against a marble worktop. He'd led her upstairs and undressed her with tempered anticipation. Kath watched him get dressed, admiring his lean body. Only briefly had she considered her stretch marks from where she'd lost weight around her middle. But his soft murmurs of delight had pushed all her insecurities away, and she was surprised that she hadn't thought of Lenny once.

'You should know that I'm not given to doing this after only three meetings.' She pulled on her underwear and jeans.

'Good to know. Of course, over dinner, I'll be expecting your full sexual history.'

'That'll be a short conversation and good luck with that.'

Over dinner, they grinned at each other between forkfuls of cabbage and bean sprouts infused with ginger and spices. The atmosphere was relaxed and easy. Richard had given her a small portion and she was warmed by the ginger and his consideration.

'So, date much?' He took a sip of wine.

'Not so's you'd notice. You?'

'Same. Worst encounter?'

She thought for a moment, chewing slowly. 'Nigel. The pathologist.'

'Nice pillow talk, I imagine.'

'It wasn't really going anywhere.' She swallowed her food. 'He had this knack of looking you up and down and correctly guessing weight and height. He said it came with the territory.'

'At least he didn't offer to weigh your liver.'

She didn't want to break the spell, but thinking about her previous liaisons had brought her back to Lenny, and she knew she had to address the issue.

'I spoke to Lenny.'

'Dover sole guy?'

She nodded. 'We had a chat... and that's it really.'

Chat? No. He behaved like a teenager and you flounced out of his office.

'Okay.' He saw by the look on her face it was not a subject to be pushed further. He poured more wine into her glass.

'Steady on. The car's outside.'

'You don't need to go.' He got up and took his plate to the sink.

'It's not that I don't want to stay...'

'But?' He turned to her, not wanting to hear the answer. *Open and honest, Fortune.*

'I'm not good at staying at other people's places, that's all.'

He gave a small sigh of relief. 'I get that. We all have our habits and routines and we have only known each other three days. Three really great days.' The teasing twinkle was back in his eye.

'Thanks for understanding. Also, I don't want to be away from home for too long at the moment.'

She told him brief details of Lane's situation.

'Sure. No problem. Is she going to be okay?'

'I have to believe so. Oh, and I must say that we have a mutual friend staying at my place, so if you happen to jog past and see me embracing him in the doorway, we are just friends.' Her tone was sharper than she intended.

Don't be petty, for Christ's sake. He's not Lenny.

Richard's brow furrowed slightly as he attempted to process Kath's meaning, then he turned the conversation back to before. 'When I was in the States, I took a lovely lady out to dinner. She was a make-up artist.'

'Oh, interesting. Movies?'

'Morticians.'

'Oh.'

'Mmm. Over the steak, she told me I have an amazing face and that I would be a beautiful corpse.'

Kath laughed, relaxing again. 'Bet that killed your appetite.'

'I didn't see her again. My imagination got the better of me.' He eyed her empty plate. 'Food was agreeable, then?'

'Very much so.'

His expression hinted at a more effusive answer.

'My whole visit has been more than agreeable. But I am going to go now.'

Exhaustion washed over her. The case plus Lane's situation, Lenny and his childish behaviour and the thought of what was to come tomorrow gathered together to cloud her brain.

'Okay. Take care driving back. I know it's not far, but this mist is getting thicker.' He cupped his hands to the glass panel in the back door.

'I'll be fine. I just need sleep.'

She gathered her coat, and he walked her to the door. The kiss was delicious, reminding her of what she was leaving behind.

| 30 |

April 2010

Jennifer's eyes flitted from the paintings to the chandeliers to the antique furniture. 'Oh my god, this is amazing.'

She picked up an ornate vase, and Rafferty quickly took it from her and set it down on the side table.

'Lots of expensive things in here. Don't want any accidents.'

He led her to the small drawing room, where a woman sat in an armchair, a sewing box on the floor beside her.

'Rafferty, dearest boy.'

She stood and enveloped him in a hug. She glanced at Jennifer over his shoulder, and a dark force twisted in her gut.

'Nanny, this is Jennifer.' He stepped aside. 'Jennifer, this lovely lady is Nanny Sighs.'

Jennifer shook the woman's hand. It was a firm grip and the woman seemed reluctant to let go.

Rafferty moved to a drinks table and separated two glasses from their neighbours. 'Nanny has looked after me my whole life,' he explained. 'She means the world to me.'

'He's my world, my universe.' The woman released Jennifer's hand and stared at her.

'I'm very pleased to meet you. This place is just so wow.' She looked around the room, aware of the woman's eyes still on her, and she wished she'd leave them alone.

'Rafferty, sit with your lady friend. I'll get your drinks.' The woman kissed his cheek as he passed her. She went to the table and selected a bottle of wine nestled behind the array of other bottles and glass decanters.

Rafferty sat on the sofa and patted the cushion. Jennifer sat next to him, wanting to kiss him again, as she had done when he picked her up in his car, more than anything. She wondered how long the woman was going to stay.

'Jennifer's very impressed with our little house, Nanny.'

'I'm sure she is.' The woman poured wine into the glasses, pulled a small vial from her pocket and discreetly added the contents to one of the glasses.

'Why are you called Nanny Sighs?' Jennifer asked.

'Oh, funny story.' Rafferty fondled Jennifer's bare knee. 'When I was little and did something a bit naughty, Nanny would take this deep breath and then her shoulders would drop and she'd let this breath go and say, "Oh, Rafferty." So, from when I could talk, I called her Nanny Sighs, and it stuck.'

The woman handed the glasses to both of them and pulled Jennifer up by her elbow. 'Let's leave Rafferty to have his drink in peace, and I'll show you the study. There's so much to see.'

Jennifer looked at Rafferty, unsure of whether to go.

He smiled and waved his hand. 'Yes, do what Nanny says. I'll be here waiting for you.' He winked at her and took a deep swallow of the wine. He sat back against the cushions and let his head fall back.

Ten minutes later, Jennifer and the woman returned to find Rafferty asleep. Jennifer went to open her mouth to speak.

The woman silenced her with a finger across her lips. 'Ssh, don't wake him.'

The woman guided Jennifer to a large painting on the wall, an oil portrait of a woman with a small dog. 'Has he told you about the surprise yet?' The woman's voice was low, conspiratorial. Her eyes sparkled.

Jennifer shook her head, her eyes wide. 'What surprise?'

'I'll show you, but you can't tell him you've seen it. Oh, it's so perfect. He likes you a lot, I can tell.'

Jennifer's vanity and curiosity blended together to wipe out her better judgement. 'He does?' she whispered. 'Wow. Well, I like him too. He's very special.'

The woman pulled on the frame of the painting. It swung back to reveal a door. 'Yes, he is very special. Come with me. It's a great surprise.'

The woman gestured to the darkness, and Jennifer took a last look at Rafferty as she stepped through the door.

11th October 2019

The team spent the day collating all their information and findings so far. Kath wanted to be prepared to present it all to the Crown Prosecution Service. She'd slept reasonably well. The kitchen was clean and tidy. Marcus had many talents in his arsenal, and Kath was glad he was around. She'd phoned Clarissa around eleven and told her she wanted everyone at the manor for six-thirty, when it would be dark enough for Mikey to get to Clemency's cottage. The clock on the office wall read just after three, and she was fidgety. She went outside, lit a cigarette and pulled out her mobile.

'Copper.'

'Mikey. We still on for tonight?'

'Course.'

'My DC, Marvin, will pick you up. Do you want him to come to your gran's?'

There was a pause. Kath knew he was uncomfortable with police cars outside his house, even if they were unmarked.

'Yeah. Give him the address.'

Kath outlined her plan and told him how to get to the cottage and what he was looking for. 'And don't look them up on the internet. I don't want you going in with preconceived ideas.'

'You don't know where this thing is, right?'

'It's a small cottage. You'll find it.'

'And this Marvin's gonna wait outside for me?'

'Yes. He'll be outside the gates to the estate.'

'Will he have my cash?'

Kath smiled. 'You'll get your money when we've got the goods.'

'Tell him to bring me fags, then.'

'Awful habit. It'll stunt your growth.'

'I'm tall enough. Concerned about me, copper? I can hear you've got one on. Maybe you should give up. Is that why you're such a short-arse?'

'Just be ready. Six o'clock.'

'I'll be ready.'

Kath ended the call, considering all the things that could go wrong as she watched the cars pass by.

<u>April 2011</u>

The cars passed by one after the other, and Layla shuffled from foot to foot. She'd blown off a shift in the pub to meet Rafferty and he was late. Three cars later, he pulled up and she got in, slamming the door.

'You're late.'

'Hey, princess. Calm down. When you see the dress I have for you, it'll make it all worthwhile.'

Ten minutes later, they were at the manor.

'Never thought I'd see the inside of this place.'

Layla was secretly in awe of the building, and the thought of the money that was coming her way warmed her. He led her into the drawing room. There was so much to take in. Her eyes picked out several small items that would fit easily into her bag. She reasoned he could afford it and probably wouldn't even miss them. This was turning into a very lucrative evening.

'Impressed, huh?' Rafferty took the coat from her shoulders.

'Maybe. Get me a drink.'

As he walked to the drinks table, Layla palmed a small silver trinket box from the edge of the shelf above the fireplace. As she was about to slip it into her bag, she heard footsteps in the hallway and turned to see a woman entering the room. Layla studied the box and placed it back on the shelf.

'And who do we have here, Rafferty?'

The woman went to Rafferty, and they embraced.

'Nanny, this is my new friend Layla. Layla, this is Nanny.'

'My, aren't you a pretty one.'

Layla tossed her hair over her shoulders and smiled at the woman.

'Layla's going to accompany me to the ball at the Stuart's house in a few days.' Rafferty poured wine into two glasses. 'Drink for you, Nanny?'

The woman circled Layla, looking her up and down. 'No dear. You go ahead. Lovely name, dear.'

'Thanks.' Layla felt like a prize cow at auction and was grateful for the distraction of the proffered glass.

'Sit down, Rafferty. Shall I show you around, Layla? We have many more lovely little things.' Her eyes flicked towards the silver box on the shelf, and Layla looked away quickly.

'Yeah, a tour would be great.'

The promise of the money had been enough to get her through Rafferty's door along with the dresses he said he would buy, which she could sell afterwards to add to her pot of cash. She followed the woman into the study. She knew she'd been handed a golden opportunity now to make even more money, as long as she could ditch the old woman for a while. Getting away for a new life was her only motivation, and she was prepared to do whatever it took to achieve her dream.

'Oh, I just need to tell Rafferty something. Look around. Help yourself.' The woman grinned knowingly and left Layla to admire the treasures in the room.

The woman pulled the glass from Rafferty's hand. 'Let me get you more wine, my sweetness.' She angled her body away from him and tipped a vial of liquid into the glass then swirled the contents around.

'I think this might be the start of something, Nanny.' He took the wine glass from her, and she brushed the fringe from his forehead.

'Do you think so, my sweet? Do you?'

11th October 2019

Marvin pulled up behind the Lexus. Marcus got out of his car.

Mikey shifted in his seat nervously. 'You know him?'

'Yes. I'm your backup, and he's your extra backup.'

Marvin and Mikey got out, and Mikey took in the stature of the black, muscled man before him.

'Glad he's on my side,' Mikey muttered.

Marcus approached the young lad, with his hand outstretched.

Mikey recoiled. 'Hey, man. What you doing?'

Marcus grabbed him and fastened something to the collar of his jacket. 'Relax. It's a tracking device. If you get lost in those woods, we'll be able to find you. Kath, Ruth and Shirl have just gone up to the manor. You're good to go.'

'You've got your instructions,' said Marvin, turning to face Mikey. He was feeling apprehensive about what the boy was going to do but tried to keep the note of authority in his voice.

Mikey sighed. 'I follow the wall for about eight minutes. I see the fork in the path. I take the right path, and the cottage will be just down there.'

'Good. Alright. Let's do it.' Marvin walked him to the estate gates as Mikey pulled a torch from his pocket. He took a last look at the two men watching him and disappeared into the undergrowth.

'We're pinning our hopes on a child criminal,' Marvin muttered.

Marcus put a hand on his shoulder. 'Kath trusts him. We trust her. Let's get in my car. Heating's better.'

| 31 |

Kath's eyes found the clocks in the large drawing room, and she registered that Mikey would probably be starting his foray into the woods. Rafferty and Fenella sat together on a sofa near the fireplace. Clemency had placed herself in a wingback chair by the window. Clarissa followed the detectives into the room and stood with her back to the fire, arms crossed. She didn't bother to indicate that Kath, Shirl or Ruth should sit down.

'Thank you all for attending,' said Kath.

'Ha. We had little choice, given that you threatened us with being marched down to the police station.' Clarissa's tone was full of agitation.

'Jennifer Blunt. Layla Mountford. Sophia Martin. Three girls. Murdered. Strangled with their own braided hair. Each one naked, chained to the wall in the folly.' Kath began pacing, watching each member of the household in turn. 'We believe that each girl entered this house, alive. Then taken, perhaps by force, through the tunnel that begins behind that beautiful painting in the other drawing room.'

Fenella gasped, and her hands flew to her face. 'That's horrible. It's not possible.' She grasped Rafferty's hand. His face was pale, dough-like, his body rigid.

'Yes, it is horrible and perfectly possible.'

Clarissa let out a bored sigh. 'You believe it, but you have no proof.'

Kath focused her stare on Rafferty. 'Some of you, or all of you, know it to be true.'

'I think you've been reading too many Agatha Christie novels, Detective.'

Kath looked towards Clarissa, saw the smirk on her face.

'Gather the suspects in one room and one of them will crack under the pressure. That's your game plan?'

Kath felt a flutter of panic. She looked over at Clemency, seemingly relaxed in the tense environment. Ruth knew Kath was struggling and stepped forward.

'Can I have a word?'

The three moved to the far side of the room.

'We need more time,' Ruth whispered.

'I know,' Kath retorted quietly. 'We need to go after the weakest of the herd.'

The three detectives turned together and looked at Rafferty.

Mikey had lost track of time and had no idea how much further he had to go. He cursed himself for wearing his best trainers as the roots and branches fought against his footsteps. Marvin had told him to leave his mobile phone at home, considering the worst-case scenario of any of his colleagues on the force obtaining Mikey's phone records. Marvin had assured him on the drive over that they would protect him. He just had to not get caught. The shrubs and trees started to thin out, making his transit a little easier, and he pressed on. The fork in the path soon appeared in his torch beam. He was cold and missing playing football online with his mates, but the thought of the cash made it bearable. He stopped. Was it the right path or the left? Right. He was sure they'd said right.

He set off at a quicker pace, not hampered as much by undergrowth and fallen logs. He was bothered by the fact that he wasn't as excited as he thought he would be and he'd realised, in the course of the car journey, that he was afraid. He was always the one up for a laugh, bold, adventurous. But the truth was not something he wanted to admit to anyone.

He didn't want to let Kath down.

He saw the lights in the cottage windows, curtains drawn. He turned off the torch, the muted glow giving him enough light to skirt the garden and make his way around the back to what he hoped was an unlocked door. The back door was solid. He tried to peer through the window, but the curtains were tightly pulled. He had no way of knowing what he was walking into, but he took a deep breath, pulled on the latex gloves that Marvin had given him and turned the heavy doorknob.

He stood just inside the kitchen and listened. No noise. He closed the door and stood for a moment, mesmerised by the lack of what he knew should be in a kitchen. A small door was on the left side. A strange-looking cooker sat against a wall, with some sort of metal canister underneath. There were no cupboards on the stone walls, just shelves housing plates and glass jars. A wooden table had a curtain across the bottom, and he moved the material to one side. More shelves with pans. He went to the door and opened it, finding a tiny shower room with a basin and toilet. He dismissed it as a hiding place and went through the tiny hallway, past the front door and into the lounge. The room was lit with lamps on various surfaces, and he stared at the shelves in the fireplace alcoves.

He smiled. 'There you are, you little fucker.'

He moved to the right-hand side of the fireplace and reached out for the small, doll-like figure. Before his fingers could touch it, he stopped. A noise. Was it in the house or outside? He listened for a moment. Nothing. He took a ziplock bag from his pocket, picked up the poppet and dropped it in, closing the seal, then put the bag in his pocket. He stared up at the shelves again and decided there wasn't anything worth nicking.

He turned to go and froze.

There was a woman in the doorway.

'Rafferty, where is your son?'

He stared at Kath, open-mouthed. 'He's, er, upstairs in his room.'

'Would you fetch him? I think we need to talk to him.'

Fenella stood up, her hands clasped in front of her. 'My son has nothing to do with this awful business.'

'Of course not,' said Kath, smiling.

Shirl leaned into Ruth and whispered in her ear, 'Where is she going with this?'

'Beats me.'

Clarissa held up a hand. 'Leave this to me, Fenella. Sit down,'

Kath's demeanour remained confident and serious, holding back the excitement that she had got the exact reaction she wanted from the lady of the house.

'I will not have Brocken interrogated.' Clarissa moved from the fireplace, closer to Kath, eyes blazing.

Kath returned her stare. 'Oh, but he may have heard something relevant, don't you think?'

'He's a little boy,' said Fenella. 'Please don't do this.'

'Do sit down, for heaven's sake,' Clarissa snapped.

Fenella remained defiantly standing, in a switch from a manipulated mouse of a woman to a protective mother. 'Brocken is my son; I say what is best for him, Clarissa.'

Rafferty stood up and took Fenella's hand, his eyes unable to meet his mother's glare. 'Our son is our responsibility, and my wife is right. Don't speak to her that way.'

'Look who just grew a pair,' whispered Shirl.

Kath continued smiling. This was a good result. Division in the house.

'Perhaps I ought to alert social services. This doesn't constitute a safe place for a child, as there is clearly information being withheld about a serious crime.'

Fenella collapsed back onto the sofa, and Rafferty joined her, still clasping her hand. Clemency and Clarissa exchanged a glance, and Kath caught it. She averted her eyes to the nearest clock and wondered how much longer she could keep up the charade.

Shirl went to Fenella's side. 'Are you alright?' The woman looked pale and fragile, and Shirl was afraid Kath had gone too far.

Fenella let go of Rafferty's hand and pawed at Shirl. 'They won't take my boy, will they?'

The bracelet sparkled, and Kath found her next mode of attack.

'Did you know that your bracelet is identical to the one that Jennifer Blunt had?'

Fenella looked at the bracelet, then back at Shirl. 'No, I didn't. Why should I?'

'Quite a coincidence. I believe your husband gave it to you as a wedding present.'

Rafferty rose and started to speak, but Clarissa got in first.

'I think you need to leave.'

Ruth put her hand on Kath's shoulder. It was time.

'Very well. Don't be surprised if I call you one by one down to the station tomorrow. I can send marked police vehicles for you. I think we need to address this on a more formal level.'

'Again with the threats, Detective?'

'No threat, Mrs Quartermaine.'

Kath turned and walked down the hallway.

| 32 |

Mikey's heart was racing. It wasn't just the shock of finding out there was someone in the cottage, it was the fact that the old woman was blocking his only exit and she looked mad as hell.

'Who are you, and what are you doing here?' Her voice was raspy, beady eyes looking him up and down.

'None of your business, old lady.' His voice quivered, but he stood his ground, staring at her.

'I think you're going to tell me what I want to know.' She moved further into the room. The fireplace was at his back. There was no option but to go towards her.

'Let me leave and you won't get hurt.'

The woman laughed. 'I can hurt you in so many ways, child. Come here.'

Her speed surprised him. As she grabbed his coat, he pulled back, cornering himself even further.

'Get off me, you witch.'

The shove was harder than expected, adrenalin fuelling his fear. She fell backwards with a yelp. Mikey shot round her and ran through the doorway into the kitchen. He fumbled with the door handle as he heard the woman cursing him. He ran outside and round to the front of the cottage. His foot caught against a large stone, and he stumbled, trying to right himself whilst still in motion. He went down, landing awkwardly on his side. His breathing came in ragged gasps. He scrambled to his feet, finding his rhythm and running through the trees.

In the darkness, he had no idea he was going the wrong way.

'Park on the road outside the gates. Then we'll talk,' Kath ordered, getting into her car.

Shirl and Ruth followed suit, all three vehicles speeding towards the gates. Marcus and Marvin watched as the cars sped past and stopped further up the road. The three women joined them, and they stood in a huddle.

'Do we know how Mikey's doing?'

'He should be back soon,' said Marvin, trying to convey confidence.

Kath rubbed her face with her hand. 'I couldn't keep it going any longer. I hope we've given him enough time.'

'Fenella's been quite a revelation,' said Shirl. 'I think she found her backbone in one of those boxes she unpacked.'

'The family can stew in their mess for tonight. Right now, our focus needs to be on Mikey and Lane.' Kath looked at Marcus, anxiety in her eyes. 'Did you plant the tracking device?'

'I did.' Marcus looked down at his phone.

'Tracking device?' Shirl looked at Ruth, who looked equally blank.

'Oh. That's not good.' Marcus stared at the green dot moving quickly on the screen.

'Not good how?'

'He's gone the wrong way. He's heading deeper into the woods.'

Mikey was really scared now. He knew the streets of Broseley and the lanes and villages surrounding the small town. He knew how to guide stolen cars around the twists and turns in the roads, speeding through the countryside, egged on by his friends. He was in control then. Now, he was just a lost child in the dark woods.

Fear poked at his bladder, and he unzipped his trousers and let out the urine, the stream steaming as it left his body. Night sounds caused his head to turn from side to side, his imagination bright with possibilities. He was used to the sounds of engines, machines. Those he could identify. Nature was a blur to him.

He zipped himself up and felt in his pocket for the torch. It wasn't there. He moved to a huge tree, the thick ridges of the bark harsh against his fingers. He put his back against it and tried to think, tried to slow his breathing, get his bearings if that was even possible with no light. He realised the undergrowth and collection of trees were thinner, more space to move between them without branches reaching out to grab him like the old woman's arms. Then he remembered the tracker and prayed that Marvin's friend would come and get him.

'I'll go in after him,' said Marcus, looking up from the green dot that seemed to be slowing its movements.

Marvin turned to him. 'But what if you get lost in there?'

'It's okay. Marcus has a background that...' Kath fought for the right words to reassure him.

'That makes me perfect for the job,' Marcus finished.

'Go in the easy way.' Kath gave him the directions past the manor house.

'So, what do we do?' Ruth asked. She was getting colder and that always made her grumpy. Like Shirl, she'd been glad to join the new team with the regular hours and no late-night calls to crime scenes. Now, it seemed as if she'd gone back in time.

Kath watched Marcus run through the gates. She lit a cigarette. She felt she was losing her grip on the case. Unable to get a confession or anything concrete about the killer, a lost teenager, a friend disabled by magic.

'I'm going to call Donovan Brightstone when Mikey's safe. He's the closest to an expert we have in how to handle this poppet business.' She looked at Ruth and Shirl, sensing their irritability. 'Why don't you two go home? Marvin and I will wait here. I'll get Donovan to come over to mine and Marvin can take Mikey home.'

'If Marcus finds him,' Ruth mumbled.

Mikey was seeing shapes in the darkness and thought he might be going mad. He'd never feared the night before. It had always been his friend, hiding him as he crept around gardens looking for items to steal to make more money to give to his gran and maybe buy some cool new clothes. And then he spotted something and frowned, certain his brain was playing tricks now. He moved slowly towards the huge structure, unsure of what was emerging from the woodland. What the hell was a fairground carousel doing in the woods?

His feet found steps, and he climbed. His grandmother's friend had taken him to the fair once with her grandkids and he'd been on the horses. What was it she'd called them? Gallopers. That was it. He ran his hands across a flank, remembering the whirling sensation and throwing up when he was finally allowed off. Now they posed no threat, and Mikey thought it might be a good place to stay until Marcus found him.

| 33 |

Lenny turned the engine off and stared at the cottage. The other car on the driveway was unfamiliar, and his stomach lurched as he thought it might belong to Kath's new friend. Boyfriend. Man friend. There was no real terminology for his age group relating to romance. The lights were all on, and he realised he was being an idiot. Kath's car wasn't there. So where was she? He was torn. The mystery man could be inside. She could have gone out to get food. A thousand scenarios pushed through his brain, but his curiosity got the better of him. He picked up the bouquet from the passenger seat, got out and knocked on the front door. He faintly heard movement coming from inside, then a key turning in the lock.

'Hello, Lenny.'

He almost chuckled with relief. 'Hi, Lane.'

'You shouldn't have.' She pointed to the flowers, and he laughed.

'I'm guessing Kath's not here.'

'She's working the case, but she should be back soon.' Heat billowed out from the interior of the cottage, but Lane pulled the blanket tighter around her shoulders.

'Are you okay?'

Lane was slurring her words and her face looked gaunt. She nodded, fed up with people asking her how she was. 'Come in. She won't be long.'

He followed her through to the lounge. The atmosphere in the cottage was stifling and the electric fire was pumping out even more heat.

Lane sat down. 'Sorry. Not a good hostess. Help yourself to whatever. I'm sure Kath won't mind.'

He stood in the middle of the room, feeling like a delivery man not knowing where to deposit his goods. He noted the bowl at the side of the sofa.

'I'll put these in the kitchen.'

He placed the flowers on the worktop then went back into the lounge and sat in an armchair.

'Can I get you anything?'

Lane's words were slow and ragged. 'No. Might throw up and I don't think we're close enough for you to be holding my hair back.'

His smile was genuine. He'd always been uneasy with Lane and her involvement in police business. Not just with her, but with supposed psychics in general. He'd been furious when Kath called her in a couple of years ago, although he'd known once Kath had been approached to lead the new cold case team that she'd involve Lane. Her call and he had to respect that. Then there was the fact that Lane had helped solve the team's first case, the murder of five-year-old Daisy Prospero. He relented a little when she'd produced results. But the woman sitting in front of him bore little resemblance to the one he'd previously met.

'So, what's going on with you?'

She looked as if she might have had some sort of stroke.

'Kath will fill you in,' Lane said, shifting her position and encasing herself further inside the blanket despite the heat. 'I'm not being evasive; I really can't tell you.'

'Okay.' He waited to see if she was going to say anything else.

'You thought Richard was here, didn't you?'

So that was his name. Lane obviously knew all about him. He shrugged. 'Maybe.'

'Do you not think you're being a giant arse?'

He bristled at the attack. 'What's this Richard like, then?'

She shook her head. 'Haven't met him, but he's put a twinkle back in Kath's eyes.'

His face crumpled a little at her words. 'I'm going to get a beer.'

He went to the kitchen and took a beer from the fridge. He didn't want to have this conversation, particularly with Lane, but it seemed there was little else to fill the time. He headed back to the lounge. The TV was on, sound low.

'Any good?' He gestured to the screen.

'It's Marvin's favourite show of the moment. *NCIS*. I'm watching back-to-back episodes. My brain's not really following stories, but it's full of cute guys, so that's a bonus, although I don't think that's why he watches it.'

'So, how long have you been like this?'

'Couple of days. Kath's fixing it.'

He was intrigued but didn't want to dwell on her circumstances. 'Say I am being a giant arse'—he looked at her and smiled—'what do I do about it?'

'Have you tried talking to her?'

'Sort of. We didn't really get past point scoring.'

'You or her?'

'Me, I guess. It's complicated.'

'No, it really isn't.'

'Am I making it complicated?'

'Now you're getting it. Christ, Lenny. Do you love her?' Lane tried to push herself further upright but gave in.

'I do.'

'Then stop being a dick, tell her and do whatever you need to do to fix it, and that includes doing whatever the hell she wants. Simple.'

'Is that what your crystal ball tells you?'

Lane sighed. 'Jesus, Mary and Joseph and the wee donkey...'

The dot had stopped moving. Finally, the lad had seen sense and stopped running.

Marcus moved swiftly through the woods, taking the path as directed by Kath to Clemency's cottage. He skirted the building. It looked as if Mikey had just taken the wrong direction when he'd come out. He had to hope Mikey had retrieved the goods. He carried on until the trees thinned out, and he saw what looked like a carousel in the distance. He had no time to consider the strangeness of the fairground ride. He approached the horses quietly

'Mikey?'

'Here.'

Marcus heard the relief in the lad's voice as he wound his way through the horse bodies. Mikey appeared from behind one of the gallopers, looking small and child-like, the bravado of the criminal teenager now gone.

'Fuck, am I glad to see you.'

'Are you okay?'

'Yeah. I got the thing.' Mikey patted his pocket.

'Thank god you stopped running. Let's go. Stick close; I don't want to lose you again.'

The way back seemed quicker, Marcus not missing a beat as he negotiated the terrain. They hugged the tree line as they passed quickly by the manor house and made it to the car, where Kath was pacing. She threw her cigarette down and fought the urge to hug both of them.

'Christ, you scared us.'

Kath got in the back of Marvin's car, with Mikey and Marvin in the front. 'What happened?'

Mikey passed her the bag with the poppet inside. He held onto the bag as she grasped it. His bottom lip quivered as he fought back tears.

'There was someone in the house. I think I did a bad thing.'

| 34 |

'*Rafferty, stop.*'

Fenella stood and watched as her husband threw open wardrobe doors and drawers. Two leather holdalls sat on the bed, open and ready to receive the clothes.

'We can't stay here. Help me, Fenella.'

He pushed jumpers into her arms. She let them fall onto the bed.

'But we can't just leave. What about Brocken? Where will we go?'

'Keep your voice down,' he barked. He stared at her crumpled face, tears about to spill down her cheeks. He went to her and placed his hands on her arms. 'I have to get away from this place. I want you and Brocken to come with me. We'll go to the Bahamas or the Cayman Islands.' His eyes begged for acceptance of his plan.

Fenella's shoulders sank. 'We can't do that. Brocken and I don't even have passports.'

That was the really big detail Rafferty had overlooked in his haste and the frustration built within him. 'Well, we'll go to Scotland, the Highlands, anywhere that gives us time to think, to make a plan.'

Fenella struggled to find the strength she had shown in front of the detectives. 'Rafferty, tell me the truth. Do you know something about those poor girls? Were they really here in this house?'

Rafferty slumped onto the bed. 'I don't want you to hate me. I couldn't bear that.'

She saw the little boy in him, exposed, afraid, and her resolve tightened. 'I don't hate you,' she said quietly. 'I love you. It's been hard to cling onto that, living here. You seem to have lost yourself.' She held out her hand, and he clung to it. 'I want to help you find your way back, but you need to be completely honest with me. Can you do that?'

He shivered at the sight of her steady gaze that reminded him of his mother. 'If I tell you, then you're implicated. If you don't know the details, the police can't get it out of you.'

She stood up straight. 'I'm stronger than you think I am, Rafferty. I always was. I too got lost in the essence of this place.'

She looked around the room. Wealth was everywhere. In the paintings on the walls, the silk wallpaper, the precious china vases and silver candlesticks. 'Money can't make up for the burden of a secret. So you need to tell me. Start at the beginning.'

'What do you mean, you've done something bad?' Kath said the words slowly, as if they didn't want to leave her mouth.

'There was this woman. She, like, just appeared, and she came at me, grabbed me. I pushed her.' Mikey's hands were visibly shaking.

'And what happened then?'

'She fell over and I ran. That's it. I had to do it. To get out.' Mikey folded his body further into the car seat. He hadn't wanted to hurt the woman. She was old. He'd nicked stuff with no problem, but he'd never hurt anyone. Until tonight.

Marvin half-turned in the driver's seat and looked at Kath. 'What do we do?'

Kath was conflicted, but her priority had to be Lane. 'Did you see if she hit anything as she fell? Did she bash her head on the way down, anything like that?'

'I… I don't know…' Mikey shook his head hard and fast, his hands reaching up to clutch the hair at the sides of his head. 'I don't think so. It was all really fast. I panicked. I just wanted to get out of there.' He paused, then looked at Kath in the sun visor mirror, which was always kept open, his eyes showing his hurt as he quietly said, 'You said the place would be empty.'

She patted him on the shoulder, swallowing down the upset she felt at how she'd unintentionally made him feel. 'I'm sure she'll be okay. You did great. This is really so important.' She shook the plastic bag. 'Marvin, get out, please.'

He didn't question her and got out of the car.

Kath reached into her coat and pulled out an envelope. 'There's your money. Thank you, Mikey.'

The lad was obviously feeling guilty about what he'd done, but Kath now detected an element of pride in his completed mission.

Mikey took the envelope and stuffed it into his pocket. 'Ta.'

'Marvin will take you home now.'

Kath tapped on the window and beckoned Marvin back into the car. She opened the rear door and made to get out.

'Wait.' Mikey reached for her across the seat. 'Will you let me know she's okay?'

Kath leaned into the car and smiled at him. 'I will, of course. Don't worry.' Then she closed the door and stepped back.

She watched Marvin execute a perfect three-point turn and drive away.

Marcus got out of his car. 'What's next?'

Kath pulled out her phone. 'I need to talk to Donovan Brightstone.'

Kath was surprised to learn that Donovan lived in Restonfield, in practically the last cottage on the way out of the village, just past The Blasted Oak. She told him what she needed. He agreed to help and told her he'd be at her cottage in half an hour.

The biggest surprise, however, was seeing Lenny's car in her driveway.

'Perfect.'

She got out as Marcus pulled up behind her and exited his vehicle. He saw the anxious look on her face.

'Problem?'

'Yes, Marcus. Very probably.'

The heat inside was welcome, if a little overpowering. Lenny jumped to his feet and smiled as Kath entered the lounge, his smile falling as Marcus followed her.

'What are you doing here?' She didn't wait for an answer but sat down next to Lane, taking her hand. 'How are you doing?'

Lane managed a crooked smile. 'Lenny's been keeping me entertained.'

'I doubt that,' Kath grunted.

'He bought flowers and everything.'

'He does that.' Kath sighed. 'Lenny, Marcus. Marcus, Lenny.'

'Hi.' Marcus nodded at Lenny and went to the kitchen. He seemed at ease in the cottage, and Lenny resented it. He recognised him as the man who had hugged Kath in the front doorway a few weeks ago. When he'd been spying on her. When he'd got it all wrong.

'He's my lover and Kath's friend, in case you're wondering,' Lane said, sensing Lenny's unease.

'I've come at a bad time, it seems.'

'As usual,' Kath muttered, folding her arms.

Lenny stood quickly and moved to the doorway. 'Maybe we can catch up soon.'

'I'll walk you out.'

Kath pushed past Lenny, making her way to the front door. 'Why did you turn up unannounced? I've got a lot going on with this case.' Her voice seemed tinny and sharp, and even she didn't like the sound of it.

Did you hope to catch me with Richard? Maybe in bed?

'I thought we could talk. Properly. Can we do that?' His eyes searched hers hoping for some kind of acquiescence.

'Yes,' she said impatiently, opening the door. 'But not now. Marcus? Can you move your car so Lenny can get out?'

Marcus appeared and pushed gently past both of them.

'I'll see you soon, then.' Lenny wanted to kiss her cheek but thought better of it. It seemed there was never a right moment to resume any kind of physical contact between them.

'Yes. Fine.'

She left the door ajar and went back to Lane, glad to let out a little heat.

'He loves the bones of you,' said Lane, tilting her head. 'Just saying.'

'My bones are not the issue, you are, and I've invited a man round to fix you. Sit tight.' Kath walked into the kitchen.

'Who's gonna fix you, sweetie?' Lane shouted from the lounge.

Kath grabbed her cigarettes and opened the back door. 'No fucking idea,' she muttered.

They arranged themselves in the lounge, looking like four new Tarot card characters—the Detective, the Bodyguard, the Healer and the Psychic. Marcus sat next to Lane, Kath in the chair, Donovan on the floor.

Lane stared at the poppet in Donovan's hands. 'They could have made a bit more of an effort.'

Marcus held Lane's hand. Kath knew Lane was masking her fear with levity.

'So, what do you want us to do?'

Donovan's curly hair encroached across his face, but he didn't seem bothered by it. He gave off an air of quiet confidence, and Kath was grateful she'd run into him that night in Bridgnorth.

'This is all quite new to me really, but I'm just going to go with what I feel is right.' He looked at each of them and felt the weight of expectation. When Kath had called him for help, he'd been unable to mask his surprise. He had felt the power of Clemency and Clarissa, the power that had steered him towards a new life and some kind of salvation. He was having trouble connecting the force of goodness with the power of evil intent. He reluctantly believed what the detective had said as being the truth. Having studied Lane as he'd walked into the cottage, he knew he was right to want to help.

'I'm going to unwrap the poppet and say some words, a kind of prayer if you like, and I want all of you, Lane included, to close your eyes and see Lane as you have done in the past. Picture her laughing, walking, eating, whatever sends out positive vibes. This is how I know her, this is how I see her. She will be this again. That kind of thing.'

'Don't picture me naked.' Lane looked at Marcus, and he grinned.

'Actually, that's fine,' said Donovan. 'We're aiming for normal. How she is, the essence of her in your eyes. Ready?'

They all nodded.

Donovan carefully unpicked the knot that held the string around the head of the poppet and began to unwind it.

'*Wait.*' Kath held up her hands. 'Diana. They may have named it Diana. That's how Shirl said she introduced Lane to Clemency.'

'Good. Okay.' Donovan took a deep breath. 'We call upon the spirits, the ancestors, the Universe, help us to release Diana from that to which she has been bound.' The top of the head appeared. 'She is free, she is whole. She harms none and none shall harm her. We ask that the life force be restored within her, that she may move easily, speak freely, love unconditionally with an open heart. Her natural state is freedom, and we ask for this now.'

Kath opened one eye to watch Donovan, the pale string in his hand, his eyes closed, the poppet now free from the binding.

'Open your eyes and give thanks.'

The group muttered incantations of gratitude, and all eyes turned to Donovan.

'Kath, I need a fireproof bowl and your lighter.'

She got up and went to the kitchen, her stomach churning. She found a garish patterned bowl in the cupboard and passed it to Donovan, who had followed her. He took the bowl and lighter and went outside, then put the bowl on the small patio table. She watched him place the poppet and string in the bowl and set them alight. He raised his hands to the sky and muttered words that she couldn't make out. The fire died quickly, and he returned inside.

'In the morning, bury the ashes somewhere down the bottom of the garden where the earth won't be disturbed. Extra precaution.' He winked, and she smiled, nodding.

'That's it, then?'

He shrugged. 'I think so. Let's keep the faith that it worked.'

Kath went back into the lounge. 'How do you feel?' she asked Lane. 'Is anything happening?'

Donovan put his hand on her shoulder, and she jumped. 'It won't be that fast. I suggest sips of water and bed.'

Lane got to her feet, helped by Marcus, his eyes full of gratitude. They went upstairs, and Donovan perched on the edge of the sofa.

'Well, that's one for the memoirs.' Kath sat opposite him. 'Thank you. I can't tell you what this means.'

'I hope I've done enough, sorry, *we've* done enough. Joint effort. All about the collective energy.' He stood up.

Kath walked him to the door and clasped his hand. 'Sorry to break up your evening. Thank you again. No parking tickets ever in your lifetime.'

They both laughed. 'Why thank you. I think I've earned a pint in The Blasted Oak.'

Kath smiled. 'I'm heading for the last beer in my fridge.'

He drove away, and Kath went to the fridge, soon realising that Lenny had consumed the beer she had been saving.

'Give me a break.' She slammed the fridge door and set the kettle to boil.

12th October 2019

Kath assumed Marcus was the early bird in her kitchen and was shocked and elated to find Lane setting out mugs.

'Oh, look at you. How do you feel?'

Lane, in a green silk dressing gown, looked much like her old self. The two women embraced, Kath fighting back tears of relief.

'Hey, no tears, sweetie.'

'No, really. Tell me how you feel.'

'No sickness. I've slept, I've drunk lots of water and my speech seems back to normal.'

'You know we were all really worried.'

Lane heaped coffee into the mugs, felt Kath's eyes on her and added another spoonful to Kath's mug. She poured on the water and pushed the mug into Kath's hands.

'Coffee, smoke, talk.'

Lane stood in the doorway as Kath lit up on the patio. She glanced at the pile of ash in the bowl and remembered Donovan's instructions.

'Your man Donovan is a cutie.'

Kath blew out smoke. 'Yep, you're back to normal.'

Lane's smile faded. 'I was scared, Kath. Clemency has real power.'

'I get that,' said Kath. 'I don't understand it, but I accept it.'

'So, what exactly happened last night?'

Kath told her everything. She'd not slept well, worried about Mikey, guilty about involving him.

'Sounds like the woman Mikey encountered was the one I felt was watching us when we first went to the cottage.'

'I missed a trick,' Kath admitted. 'I was so focused on getting Clemency to the manor that it never occurred to me that she might be in the house.'

'And you have no idea who this sick friend is, as Clemency described her?'

Kath shook her head. 'We took the story at face value. But maybe there's more to this woman.'

Another reason sleep had not come for Kath. Was the woman that Mikey pushed over still lying on the floor of the cottage? She knew Mikey had only resorted to the action because he was threatened, had no choice but to get out of there with the poppet. At the end of the day, he'd done it for her.

'What are you thinking?' Lane tilted her head.

'That I've been completely bloody selfish and I feel guilty about it.' Kath pressed the cigarette butt into the ashtray, being careful to avoid the bowl with the poppet ash. 'I don't know how to find out about this woman without going back to the cottage.'

'What if I went back?'

Kath's eyes widened. 'That's a shit idea.'

'Hold on.' Lane held up her hand that wasn't holding a mug. 'They're not going to try this again. They will know what has happened.'

'Forget it. I'll find another way.'

'I know you will. Look, it's Saturday. I'll get out of your way. Marcus can take me back to the hotel. You need some downtime.'

'No, I want...' She stopped. She needed to stop making snap decisions. 'Go back in. I'll have another smoke and talk things over with the girls.'

Kath pointed to the cows at the bottom of the garden, heads peering over the fence.

Lane laughed and went inside. Kath lit another cigarette and walked down to the fence. Three cows stared at her through the morning mist.

'So, here we are again, ladies.'

Six eyes looked at her, waiting for the next words.

'What is it I'm not seeing?'

Steam rose from their nostrils.

'Should I stand Lane down? Is that the right thing now?'

One cow shifted, turned its head and meandered back across the field. The other two followed.

'Thanks for the chat. Big help.' Kath pulled her dressing gown tighter and went back into the cottage.

| 35 |

The workshop doors were open, and Roy watched Kath emerge from her car as he wiped his hands on a towel.

'Morning.'

'Hi, Roy. How's it going?'

'Good. Busy. Car trouble?' He pointed to the Audi.

'People trouble.' Kath leant against one of the wooden doors.

'Ah. Can't fix that. Coffee?'

'Great, yeah.'

He disappeared inside, and Kath walked to the edge of his driveway and looked up and down the main street of the village. A woman and a young girl approached on two horses, the sound of the hooves echoing on the tarmac. She envied them, not for the fact they were riding, as she had no interest in getting onto something that high up with no pedals. It was their easy movements and smiling faces—carefree, no murderer to catch, no thoughts of corpses running through their heads.

'You look miles away.'

Roy pushed a mug into Kath's hands and lit his roll-up. She placed her mug on the ground while she lit a cigarette.

'Case. Girls found on the Quartermaine estate.'

Roy's face darkened. 'Nasty business. How's it going?'

'Frustrating. Suspects coming out of my ears, no confession and no evidence.'

She sipped her coffee. Good and strong. Roy had been supplying her with coffee and wise words for many years, along with his expertise with car engines. He'd come to her aid a few weeks ago when she had been forced off the road. She trusted him. He was a good sounding board, and she needed that right now.

'I guess you're looking at the four living up on the estate?'

Kath shook her head. 'Fenella's not on my radar.'

'I didn't mean her.'

Kath stared at him, the cigarette an inch from her lips. 'Who exactly am I missing?'

Roy blew out a plume of smoke. 'Clemency's friend. The woman that lives with her.'

'Hush now. Lie still.'

Clemency unwrapped the bandage from the woman's wrist, applied the warm poultice and rebound it.

'How did they know? How did they know to send the boy here?' The woman thrashed in the bed, the patchwork quilt tangling in her limbs.

Clemency struggled to pin the bandage back in place. 'We came against worthy opponents. We have to respect that.' Her rage seared her guts, but she knew inflaming the woman further would prove too much.

'They'll come again.' The woman moaned, throwing herself back against the pillows. 'Come again, come again.' Her voice faded as she slid into a fitful slumber.

Clemency walked to the window and looked down at the chickens strutting in the garden. 'I fear they will,' she said quietly.

The mist was lifting. It hovered over the tower of the fifteenth-century church. Kath pulled the car against the perimeter wall, Roy's revelation circling round her brain.

'When I've got a problem, I go and sit in the churchyard and pray,' he'd told her. 'I usually get the answers I need.'

Kath was willing to try anything. She walked through the lychgate. It was certainly a peaceful place to come and think. Splashes of colour adorned many headstones. It was the only nod to ostentation. She strolled along the designated pathway—a ribbon that ran around the church. There were no big stones or marble statues or angels weeping over the earth. All the grave markers were simple and modest. At the rear of the church, another small pathway led down to what appeared to be a walled garden. A lone bench was positioned on the right-hand side. On it sat Donovan Brightstone. He looked up as she passed through the low gate and moved towards him. Yew trees flanked the separate cemetery on the left, with open pasture to the back and the right.

'Hi. How's Lane?'

'Better, so much better. I can't thank you enough. I was going to call in but thought it might be too early.'

He stood up and shook out the blanket he'd been sitting on to protect himself from the damp wood. He lay it back down, spreading it across the seat so she could join him. 'I'm glad to have helped.'

She sat next to him.

'So, my parents are buried over there.' He indicated to the left side of the church, the main cemetery. 'But why are you here?'

'A friend told me to pray for answers.'

He smiled. 'How's that going?'

'Haven't started yet. This is where the Blackstocks are buried, isn't it?'

'Yes. Four centuries of ancestors. Quite remarkable.'

Kath stared straight ahead, sensing he had more to say.

'They must have felt threatened.'

'Explain.'

Donovan blew out a breath and turned to face her. 'From what you've said about Lane and what I've read myself, the poppet must have been a last resort.'

Kath looked at him. 'I can tell you're conflicted, and I understand that. Those women effectively gave you a new life.'

He nodded.

'But they still know what happened to those girls. One or all of them may even be murderers.'

His cheeks coloured. 'But I can't believe that.'

'You don't want to believe it, and that's understandable. You went digging for the truth when you interviewed them for the paper.'

'I was doing my job.'

'And I'm doing mine. Someone in that house is a killer, I'm convinced of it, and the others have covered it up. That's all I have to go on. I *feel* it.' She pressed her hands against her stomach.

Donovan bit his lip, still trying to push away the possibility. 'Middle-aged women don't kill young girls and I doubt Rafferty could manage it. He doesn't boil an egg without Clarissa telling him the water's ready.'

'He's definitely the weak link,' Kath admitted.

'He's been dominated by women his whole life.'

'Yeah, Clarissa and Clemency are quite the double act.' Kath rolled her eyes at how much harder they'd been making her job.

'Teddy has always been on his side, though.'

Kath's hands tensed around the blanket-covered wood beneath her. 'Who's Teddy?'

'His nanny. Have you not met her?' He frowned. 'She's still at the estate. Never left.'

'Does she live in the house?' Kath asked slowly, her stomach churning.

Donovan shook his head. 'She lives with Clemency, in her cottage.'

Clarissa stood in the doorway of Rafferty's bedroom. The holdalls and an assortment of clothing lay on the bed.

'Damn that boy,' she whispered.

She moved to Fenella's room and opened the door.

'What are you doing?' Fenella pulled the quilt up to cover her naked chest, her cheeks flaring.

Rafferty sat up, clasping one of his wife's hands tightly

'So, here you are,' Clarissa said flatly, covering her irritation. 'We need to talk, Rafferty.'

'I'm done talking, Mother. Leave us alone.'

Mother and son locked eyes.

Clarissa's mouth twitched in annoyance. 'Fine. I'll leave. For now.' She slammed the door.

Rafferty rubbed his face with his hands.

Fenella caressed his bare shoulder. 'What do we do, my love?'

He took her hand and kissed it. 'We need to get out of here.' He sighed. 'And then I'll tell you everything.'

| 36 |

The lights were off in Richard's cottage and Kath saw movement through the window. She knocked on the door and waited for it to open.

'Hello and good morning.' He ushered her in and shut the door before kissing her, but she only pecked him back.

His brow creased. 'That's a distracted kiss. Coffee?'

He went into the kitchen and put the kettle on, and she followed him.

'Sorry, and yes, please. Strong and black.'

'Are you okay? Do you need anything?' he asked as he got out two cups and made the drinks.

'No, I'm alright. I think.'

He handed her a cup.

'Thanks. I was on my way home. Thought you might be up.'

'How did yesterday go, or can't you talk about it?'

'Good and not so good. I'm trying to deal with the not so good.' She pulled her cigarettes and lighter from her pocket and pointed to the garden.

He nodded, opened the back door and joined her outside.

'Don't even think about nagging me, Mr organic jogger at one with nature.' She'd meant the comment to be light-hearted, but the words sounded harsh to her ears. 'Sorry. I'm grumpy.'

Richard laughed. 'I can cope with grumpy, Mrs smoking, coffee-drinking workaholic.'

Kath forced a smile that morphed into a genuine one.

'I mean, it's been five days. In some cultures, we're practically married.'

'Wow. If that's your idea of a proposal, it needs work.'

He put an arm around her shoulder. 'Don't panic. We haven't even been on a proper date yet.'

The banter was easy, and Kath's mood lifted a little, assisted by the good coffee. She walked to the planted area of the garden on the right-hand side and crushed her cigarette butt into the soil. The garden was small and manageable, the left side flagged with an array of coloured pots standing proud, displaying their bright pansies—the only flower she could identify other than roses.

'So, what are your plans for the weekend?'

She turned to him. 'I haven't really got that far.'

She'd planned on phoning Mikey and checking in with him. Beyond that, she hadn't a clue. Donovan's revelation of the now-named mystery woman at Clemency's cottage was at the forefront of her mind and she had been debating whether to go to the manor. But was she going to go to the cottage and demand to see this Teddy woman? Clarissa and Clemency would find another way to wrong-foot her, of that she had no doubt. The team needed their downtime and the girls couldn't be any less dead.

They went back into the cottage.

Richard pulled eggs and spinach from the fridge. 'Fancy breakfast?'

She grimaced. 'It's a little early for me, but thanks for the offer.' She leant in to kiss him, and he responded, still clutching the egg box.

'I need to get back to talk to Lane.'

'Okay. Call me if you want to catch up later. Maybe a drink?'

She nodded. 'Enjoy your eggs.'

As she got into her car, Richard blew her a kiss from the doorway. 'Missing you already.'

She grinned and got in. Five seconds later, the grin disappeared and the weight of the case settled upon her.

Fenella pulled the cream wool scarf tighter around her throat and stared out across the lake. 'So, that's everything? No more surprises?'

Rafferty shook his head. 'I've told you everything.'

Her silence threatened to strangle him, and he was scared now. Not for himself, but for his marriage. His son.

'Say something. Shout at me. Hit me.' His hands flew up then fell limp at his sides.

Fenella continued looking at the lone fisherman on the other side of the lake. 'I have so many questions.'

'I'll answer them,' he said quietly.

'Why those girls? They were so young. You were twenty-six, twenty-seven... Whatever, it doesn't matter. You were so much older than them. And we'd been promised to each other,' she added quietly, as if the last part didn't matter as much, though Rafferty could hear the pain in her voice. She toyed with her scarf, loosening it from her throat.

'Honestly, I wasn't ready to have my life mapped out for me. It was bad enough that Mother had pushed me into my godfather's company. Then my marriage was being arranged. I needed some release, to have some freedom back.'

'So, you didn't sleep with any of them?'

'No, I told you, I never got that far.'

'But you were going to.'

The words stung him harder than a physical slap. 'Yes, my love,' he admitted. 'I was going to. I'm ashamed of that.'

Fenella let out a long breath.

'Go on,' he urged. 'I can take it.'

'It's just... I know we didn't really know each other that well before we married...we'd had a few dinners and social engagements.' She laughed at the absurdity and crossed her arms. Rafferty wasn't sure if she was trying to keep warm or put somewhat of a barrier between them. 'But I have to ask you...what did you think had happened to each of those girls after they entered your house?' She turned away from the lake and the lone fisherman to look at him.

'You can't make me feel any worse or ashamed than I already do. I just believed what I was told. They each had to leave suddenly. Naive, I know. Then each one was all over the news, missing... I didn't know what to think. I knew Layla was planning to leave at some point, Spain I think she said, so I just thought she'd gone and maybe not told her parents. The other two...' His voice trailed off. 'I just didn't know and I suppose I didn't really care.'

'I forgive you,' said Fenella. 'I do. We all do stupid things that we regret.'

Rafferty bared his teeth as if looking in a mirror and hating what he saw. 'This is going to land me in prison.'

'But you didn't kill them.'

'Yes, but I've known who did for seven years and I've done nothing about it. I've kept it hidden. That's bad, Fenella.'

'Oh god.' Fenella put her head in her hands as she realised she was now in the same position. 'What about me?'

Rafferty shrugged, calmer than her. 'Well, I'm an accessory after the fact, I believe, and I guess you are too now that I've told you.'

Panic was spreading through her body. She felt a twisted knot in her stomach and her heart beat seemed to be thundering in her ears. 'What about Brocken?'

'I think you should take him to stay with your parents. You stay together, safe, away from my mother. I'll protect both of you from this shit storm. I'll tell the police the truth. That I've only just told you. I don't think they'll come after you. It's my family that will take the fall, and rightly so.'

'I hope you're right.'

They turned to get back in the car as the fisherman drew up his line to find a fat fish dangling from the end.

'I have to agree, there's not a lot more I can do to help you.' Lane gave Kath a hug. 'Thank you for healing me.'

Kath laughed. 'Are you sure you're okay to drive?'

Lane nodded. 'I'm ninety-eight percent there, the other two percent might have to be provided by this guy.'

'Two percent?' Marcus raised one eyebrow playfully. 'A guy could get offended.'

'So, you'll be at Sal's?'

'Yeah, just for a few days. Make sure I'm completely myself.'

'Text me when you get there.'

'Yes, Mom.'

Kath waved the two of them off and shut the door. She wandered back into the kitchen. Marcus had put Lenny's bouquet in her only vase, and she allowed herself a sad smile.

She went into the lounge, picked up a pile of CDs, then put them all back. The silence, usually welcome, was now too much. She turned on the TV. Cookery shows and *Murder, She Wrote*. Great. She turned it off. She reached for her phone, then saw the time. Mikey would still be asleep. Tough.

'What the fuck, copper?' he answered with a huff.

'Good morning to you, too. How are you?'

'I'm okay. How's your little dolly?'

'Burnt to a crisp, thanks for asking.'

Mikey paused. 'What?'

'Never mind. You did a really good job. Just wanted to check you're okay.'

'I was 'til you woke me up.'

He sounded wide awake, and Kath wondered if he had actually slept much.

'I looked up them doll things.'

'Mmm.'

'That's some weird shit. Do you know if that woman's alright?'

'I honestly don't know, but I don't want you to worry about it.'

'Is she, like, a witch, then?'

'I would hesitate to use that word, but... maybe.'

'Will she curse me?'

Kath tried not to smile. 'You'll be fine. Now, go back to sleep and keep out of trouble.'

'You too, copper.'

She went into the kitchen and looked around. It was clean and tidy, thanks to Marcus. She went upstairs, cleaned the bathroom and stripped Lane's bed. When she'd finished, she realised that only half an hour had passed. She was bored, restless. She went downstairs, made another coffee and phoned Byron, Shirl and Marvin to update them on Lane and Mikey. Then she called Ruth.

'Hey, how are you doing?'

'Bored, you?'

Ruth snorted. 'Roger is doing my head in.'

'Let me guess, something he said or something he did.'

'He's talking about retiring and taking up fishing.'

Kath laughed. 'Ooh, worms in the utility room. Nice.'

'Don't. Any news?'

'Mikey seems fine. Lane is much better and has gone with Marcus to stay at Sal's for a few days.'

'Good. All going to plan, then?'

The silence piqued Ruth's interest.

'What are you not telling me?'

'Well, I did threaten to pull someone or all of them down to the station,' Kath said. 'Feels like I should make good on it; otherwise, they'll think I'm not serious.'

'Want some company?'

'Actually, yes. Come to mine?'

'Be there soon.'

'How is she?' Clarissa twisted her fingers together, her body taut.

'It's just a sprain. It's her mind I'm concerned about.'

'It was obviously a setup.' Clarissa began pacing Clemency's small lounge.

Clemency looked up at the ceiling. 'I could take her somewhere?'

Clarissa shook her head. 'If you disappear, they'll know they're onto something. That bloody detective.'

'We need to stay calm. If she sees we're agitated, it can all go wrong. We stick to the plan. We say nothing. Still no evidence. How's Rafferty this morning?'

'He and Fenella have gone out.' Clarissa listened for a moment for any noise from the kitchen, but Brocken seemed quiet and happy with his pencils and paper.

Clemency tapped her forehead, as if trying to quieten her racing thoughts. 'The shift has happened with Fenella. She took in everything that detective said. Rafferty's fear leeches out of him. He needs to be contained.'

'I agree,' said Clarissa. 'We just have to figure out the best way to go about it.'

|37|

'And, Byron? This stays between you and me, okay?'

'No problem. I'm on it.'

'Good. Thanks.'

Kath ended the call as Ruth's car pulled into the driveway. She made them drinks and then went out onto the patio for a smoke. Ruth stood in the back doorway, blowing on her hot tea. Kath told Ruth about her early morning conversations with Roy and Donovan. She also elaborated on Mikey's encounter.

'So, this woman isn't the sick friend that Clemency said she was. She's been living there for years?'

'Exactly.'

'I haven't told the others about this woman yet.'

'Do you think she's okay after the fall?'

Kath smoked quietly for a moment. 'I don't think they'd take her to hospital unless it was really serious.'

'Good point. We could always check the hospitals.'

'Mmm, maybe.' She turned to Ruth. 'You've known me a long time. Have I lost my edge? I feel like I haven't handled this right. Would you have done things differently?'

'No, you haven't, and no, I wouldn't. With what we've had to go on, I think you've done it right.'

Kath nodded, grateful for the reassurance. Ruth didn't lie or flatter and she'd pulled her up before now if her behaviour was less than correct.

'I thought cold cases would be easier. It seems they get harder.'

'No, you're wrong there. We've cleared two cases in as many months. We're doing a great job. I know you feel guilty for what happened to Lane.' She paused as Kath was about to protest. 'Yes, you do. But it could have been any of us with that poppet, you included. Lane had them on edge because they know she sees things that we don't, however the hell they do that. Keep the faith and keep doing what you're doing and the way you do it.'

'Are you done?' Kath grinned at her.

'Yes.'

'Okay, then. Let's go be great detectives.'

Rafferty loaded the bags and boxes into Fenella's Peugeot.

'As much as I hate us being apart at the moment, I'm proud of you for doing the right thing.'

He closed the car door and pulled her into a hard embrace. 'I should have done it sooner.'

She ran a hand through his hair as his head nestled into her shoulder. 'No time for regrets. What's done is done.'

He pulled away and stroked her face. 'You've been so strong. You're amazing. I don't know if or when I'll be able to talk to you.'

'They won't keep you in custody, will they?'

Rafferty shrugged. 'I don't know.'

'Give the police my parents' address. You'll stay with us if they let you out. Which I'm sure they will,' she added quickly. 'Do you have a solicitor?'

He nodded. 'We have a family firm, but I know another guy, friend of an acquaintance. Might be best if I remove myself from my mother and Clemency and...' He couldn't finish the sentence. 'What will you tell your parents?'

Fenella gave a staccato laugh. 'As little as possible at the moment. About you, anyway. Something to the effect that we can't live here due to family differences.'

'You've got it all worked out, haven't you?'

She kissed him lightly on the lips. 'Planning ahead has kept me sane.' She looked up at Brocken's bedroom window. 'I better go and get him.'

He held onto her arm, and she stopped moving. 'I don't advocate violence, but please feel free to punch my mother in the face if she tries to stop you.'

Clarissa smiled to herself as she listened, hidden by the half-open rear door. 'Not if I punch you first, sweet Fenella,' she whispered.

Kath parked as close to the woods as possible. They set off quickly down the path. She thought a bony hand might reach out and stop them at any moment, but it seemed the manor was quiet, although she thought she heard low voices in the distance.

'And what's the golden rule when we get to the cottage?'

'We don't let anyone touch us,' Ruth replied.

'That's the one.'

They walked in silence for a moment.

Kath pushed aside a skeletal branch and shuddered. 'Mikey really came good for us. He must have been crapping his pants out here in the darkness.'

'Character-building exercise, as my mother would say.' Ruth smiled. 'Any plans for the rest of the weekend?'

'Apart from harassing women in the woods, not really.'

'Not seeing Richard tonight, then?'

'Well, we might meet...' Kath stopped and stared at Ruth. 'How the hell do you know about him?'

Ruth laughed as she ducked below a branch, glad to have caught her out. 'I'm a detective, remember? Come on. Keep up.'

'It's early days. Don't interrogate me.'

'It's gentle questioning from a friend.'

'A nosy friend.'

Ruth stepped around the body of a dead bird and grimaced. Well? 'Where did you meet him? Have you slept with him yet?'

'What happened to gentle questioning?'

'I lied. Sue me.'

Kath let out a laugh, which faded as the cottage came into view. 'Here we go.'

They approached the front door, both looking up at the bedroom windows. There was no movement.

Kath knocked, and Clemency answered almost immediately.

'Again, Detectives?' She crossed her arms and stood upright, filling the doorway.

'We'd like a word with your sick friend. Teddy, isn't it?'

The colour drained from Clemency's skin. 'She's still sick. In bed. She can't be disturbed.'

'We won't disturb her. Can we come in? It won't take long.'

'No.'

'It would be in your best interest to cooperate with us,' Ruth said sharply.

'No.' Clemency uncrossed her arms, her hands rolled into fists at her sides.

'I can have you arrested for obstructing a police investigation.'

Clemency smirked and wagged a finger at the two detectives. 'Be gone with your idle ramblings. Clarissa and I will be lodging a formal complaint against you for harassment. Your chief superintendent will be hearing from us.'

Kath's hand twitched, and she fought the urge to slap the woman across her smug face.

'Let's go,' said Ruth. She looked at Clemency. 'We'll be back.'

'I don't think so; you're done here. Oh.' She held up her hand. 'One more thing. Don't send any more little boys to assault my friend. I believe that is an arrestable offence.' She smiled and shut the door.

Ruth pulled Kath from the door, Kath's nostrils flaring with internal rage, and they made their way down the path.

'If she talks to Lenny, we're screwed.'

'In more ways than one,' Kath muttered.

***

Kath picked up the kettle to fill it but slammed it onto the work surface. 'Fucking woman.'

'Calm down.'

Kath turned on the tap and held the kettle underneath the stream of water. 'They just exist to piss me off.'

The kettle overflowed, the jet stream splashing against her jumper and spraying water across the sink and the draining board. Ruth rushed forward and rescued the kettle, turning off the tap as she pushed Kath out of the way. 'Let me do that.' She emptied out some of the water and set the kettle to boil. Kath watched her, tapping her fingers on the table. Dozens of scenarios ran through her head like a herd of deer as she watched Ruth mop up the excess water.

'What if they do go to the police about Mikey? This Teddy woman can identify him.'

'We are the police.'

'You know what I mean.'

'They're not going to do that. It's an empty threat designed to rattle you, and it's working really well, so stop it.'

Ruth made herself a mug of tea and a coffee for Kath. She pushed the mug into her hands and opened the back door. 'Go and smoke. Calm yourself down a bit.'

Kath paced across the patio. Her eyes fell on the patterned bowl. 'I have to bury the ashes. I'll do it when I've had this.'

'This Donovan came up trumps, then? With this ritual stuff for Lane?'

'Yes, he did. It was quite simple and actually quite... serene is the wrong word, but... I don't know what I was expecting, but it was a lot quieter, no fuss. And it's worked, so whatever he did, we did, it worked and that's all that's left.' She pointed at the bowl.

Ruth looked out over the field and sipped her tea.

'What do we do next?' Kath asked. 'Any suggestions welcome, as I'm all out of ideas.'

'I think you need to take the weekend to cool off. Have sex with Richard, drink wine, eat steak. The women that exist to piss you off are not going anywhere.'

Kath snorted, and smoke issued from her nostrils.

'You do know you look like a dragon when you do that?'

Kath laughed again, and her shoulders relaxed. 'Stop trying to make me feel better.'

'I'm guessing Richard doesn't know you can be a right stroppy cow.'

'No, he doesn't, and he's not going to find out.'

'Then, put your face straight and call him. I'm going home.'

Ruth disappeared, and Kath picked up the bowl. She walked down to the bottom of the garden, across the overgrown grass, moss, weeds and dandelion leaves that passed for a lawn. She found a patch of soil underneath a shrub she couldn't name and then realised she had nothing with which to dig any kind of hole.

'Oh, what the hell.'

She bent over and scraped at the wet earth with her fingers, tipping the contents of the bowl into the depression and covering it over, pressing the earth down with her fist. She took the bowl back to the kitchen and washed it.

Her mobile pinged, and she looked at the text from Byron. She smiled and dialled Richard's number.

'It's me.'

'Glad you called,' Richard replied.

'Take me somewhere nice and feed me.'

'Yes, ma'am. Pick you up at seven?'

Kath smiled. 'Good for me. Not The bloody Mallard's Rest though.'

'I'll surprise you.'

'And I've got one for you.'

'Now I'm intrigued.'

She laughed again and ended the call.

Clarissa stood in the middle of the galleried landing. Fenella clasped Brocken's hand, only realising the strength of her grip when her son crinkled his face and winced.

'Where are you going with my grandson?'

The look in Clarissa's eyes told Fenella she was acutely aware that they were leaving for good.

'Get out of the way, please.'

'Brocken, tell me where you're going.'

The boy looked up at his mother, then at Clarissa. 'We're going to my other grandmother's house.'

'I see. And why is that?'

'Let's not do this in front of him,' Fenella snapped.

'You can go. Leave Brocken with me. He belongs here, don't you, Brocken?'

Fenella tried to edge past, but Clarissa moved to further block her exit.

'Mummy says it's for the best.'

'Well, I disagree and I think you do as well.'

Fenella placed a hand on Brocken's head. 'Stop it. We're leaving.'

Clarissa gave a derisive laugh. 'Bravado does not sit well with you.'

'Shut up.'

Brocken jumped at the harsh tone of his mother's voice. Fenella hated what her son was witnessing, but she knew she had to be strong, or she would never get away.

'Last chance, Clarissa. Move.' She had one more weapon up her sleeve, which she was reluctant to use unless it was absolutely necessary. She was close to it.

'He stays here and you can go.'

Fenella took a deep breath to calm the rage inside her. 'You leave me no choice but to do this. Brocken?' She bent down to his level. 'Shall I explain to you why we really have to live somewhere else?'

Clarissa's eyes flashed, and she wondered what nonsense was about to spill out from her daughter-in-law's mouth.

'Yes, Mummy.'

Fenella tried not to smile. 'I know you're a big boy now that you're seven, so that's why I can tell you that you can't stay here because Grandmama is probably going to go to prison.'

Brocken's eyes grew big, and he shook his head. 'No. That's where bad people go.'

Fenella stood up, enjoying the look of horror on Clarissa's face.

'Shut your mouth. You're scaring him.'

'He's right to be scared. Brocken, your grandmama has done a very bad thing, and the police are going to come and take her away.'

Tears formed in her son's eyes. Fenella knew she'd pushed the situation to its limit, but it was too late to go back now.

'Is that true?' Brocken looked again from his mother to Clarissa.

'It is,' said Fenella. 'I never lie to you. We shouldn't tell lies to children.'

'You silly little bitch.' Clarissa raised a hand.

Brocken screamed, and both women reeled at the sound.

'Don't say that to Mummy. That's a bad word.'

Suddenly, Fenella knew she was doing the right thing. 'You're right, it is a bad word to call someone, but how do you know that?'

The boy trembled, and Fenella smoothed his hair with her fingers. 'You can say, my love.'

His voice was small. 'Grandmama said it and I heard it, and she said I wasn't ever to say it.'

Clarissa felt the fight drain out of her as Fenella pushed past her. She put her hand on Fenella's arm. Fenella looked down at it, and Clarissa slowly removed it.

'You may have won the battle but not the war,' Clarissa whispered.

Rafferty appeared in the archway to the stairs. He smiled at Fenella and nodded. She returned the smile and turned back to Clarissa.

'The victory is in knowing you're doing the right thing. Goodbye, Clarissa.'

They walked down the stairs, a united family. Clarissa went into Brocken's bedroom, lay on the bed and let her failure wash over her.

| 38 |

The restaurant was tucked down a side street, away from the centre of the small town, but it was already half full. Couples sat at the window tables inside, holding hands, smiling, laughing. The wall lights cast a romantic glow across the diners as their waiter seated them.

'Italian. Nice.'

'Good choice this time?'

Kath smiled. 'Yes, if you want to watch spaghetti sauce dribble down my chin.'

'I can't think of anything I'd rather watch.'

He didn't want to allow himself to believe it could be this easy as he watched her studying her menu. It wasn't even a week and he had caught himself entertaining the idea of a future with her.

'How do you even know about this place?' She knew he was looking at her and she didn't want him to stop. 'I mean, you've only been in the area three months.'

'Well, I did several trips around the county when I was thinking about relocating. I liked what I found. I still do.'

She returned his smile. 'So, what do you recommend, Hector?'

'Ach, no.' He put his menu down and shook his head.

'I told you I'd find out.' She was enjoying her victory and his mock embarrassment. Byron had worked his magic.

Richard held his hands up. 'Guilty as charged. But you can see why I go by Richard.'

'I can't believe I've been intimate with a Hector. You're my first.'

He rested his elbows on the table and steepled his fingers. 'I hope I'll be the last.'

They both let the implication hang. Richard broke first. 'So, is there anything you don't like to eat? Do you have any allergies I should know about?'

'Stuffed marrow, and no.'

'Marrow?'

The waiter came over with a carafe of water and set it down on the table. 'Any drinks for you?'

'I'm good with the water, thanks. Kath?'

Drink wine, have sex, enjoy yourself.

She glanced at the list of drinks on the back of the menu.

'We have glasses of elderflower cordial and Prosecco. It's very popular,' offered the waiter.

'Okay, yes. Lots of ice, please.'

'Are you ready to order food yet?'

Richard looked at Kath and knew she was struggling with the thought of huge platefuls of food. He'd noticed her looking at the dishes in front of the other diners, plates and dishes overflowing with pasta and sauces.

'Give us a minute with that,' said Richard.

The waiter moved away to another table.

'Tell me more about the marrow conundrum.'

Kath grinned and poured them both some water. 'My grandmother used to make it. It was her speciality dish. My grandfather grew them and was unfortunately very successful. I don't think she knew what else to do with them. I had it a lot growing up. What's your food nemesis?'

'Do not laugh. Haggis.'

She laughed, and he looked sternly at her. 'Really?'

'I know. Weird. Can't stand the stuff. Excuse me for a moment.'

He got up and stopped the waiter as he was about to enter the kitchen. The waiter nodded as Richard spoke and wrote something down on his pad, then disappeared through the swing doors. Richard sat down.

'So, best Bond.'

'Craig.'

'Connery.'

'Figures. Scottish thing.'

He took her hand and rubbed his thumb across her fingers. 'Name of first pet.'

'Desmond. Ginger and white cat. Stray. Mangy thing with chunks missing out of his ears, but I loved him.'

'Kip. Springer spaniel.'

They released hands as the waiter returned. He placed the plates in front of them, a dish to the side along with Kath's drink. 'Anything else I can get for you, sir?'

'No, that's great. Thank you.'

'This is…interesting.' Kath studied the small plate with the cannelloni roll nestled in sauce in the middle of the white china. She tilted her head as she looked at the small tureen of fresh vegetables, steam misting her water glass.

'They're very generous with the portions here. I ordered one dish between us so you don't feel overwhelmed. We can share dessert as well, if you like.'

A warm glow spread through her as she watched him shake out his green napkin and lay it across his lap.

'What?' He stopped cutting into his pasta and looked at her.

'I'm just touched by your thoughtfulness, and I really appreciate it.'

He chewed slowly and smiled. 'It's really good. I hope you don't mind me ordering for you. Seemed a bit forward, but hey, we're practically married.'

She speared a stem of broccoli and added it to her plate. 'It's fine. Perfect, actually.' She closed her eyes as she savoured the taste of the meat and pasta. She found his care and attention so endearing that it seemed to make the food more appealing, and she thought dessert might be an option.

'Apart from my name, what else did you find out about me?' Curious. No guilt. No demand.

'Nothing. You're safe. I'm afraid it's pretty standard procedure when police officers date. I just had my colleague check you don't have a criminal record. It's sort of frowned upon.'

'I stole some sweets from our local shop when I was eleven. Charges were never brought against me, but the owner told my mum and I got a severe reprimand. Better than any telling off from a policeman.'

'Quite right too. What sweets did you steal?'

'Liquorice Allsorts.'

'Urgh.' She pulled a face, and he laughed. 'I only like the round coconut ones and I leave the horrid black middle bit.'

'Ah, we've found something you don't like.'

'Well, it wasn't on the menu, so I didn't bring it up.' She sipped her drink, wrinkling her nose at the bubbles. 'This is good. Could be my new favourite drink.'

'No sweet stealing for you as a kid, then?'

'Certainly not.'

He waved his fork at her. 'But there's something. Come on, spill the beans.'

She remembered the incident quite clearly, ten years old and being sent to her room. 'My mum and our neighbour had a row, don't really know what about. She was a horrible woman, mean face, beady eyes. Anyway, my mum was upset, so I snuck out when it was dark. She was so proud of her roses, this woman. Won prizes at the local show every year. I got my dad's shears and I cut the heads off every one of the bushes. Every last one. I denied all knowledge the next day, but my mum went to put my cardigan in the wash and a damn rose petal had got stuck in the pocket. Got a big telling off, but I could tell my mum appreciated the gesture.'

'Wow. Impressive.' Richard wiped his mouth with his napkin. 'So, have you done anything bad since that you've actually got away with?' He averted his gaze as a woman squealed at a table near the back of the room. Two waiters presented her with a chocolate cake with candles on the top. A chorus of "Happy Birthday" was started, and the rest of the diners joined in, much to the recipient's delight.

Kath heard nothing. The food rose up her gullet, and she fought the urge to vomit. Reg Miller's bloodied face filled her brain. Images coming so fast. The lipstick. The dancing. The humiliation she had been too young to process.

Richard turned back to see her pale face looking down at her plate. 'What's wrong? Is it the food?' He reached for her hand, and she snatched it away.

'I need to go to the toilet.'

She got up quickly and made her way to the rear of the restaurant. Once inside the bathroom, she darted into a cubicle, slammed the door shut and vomited into the toilet bowl. Red sauce and pieces of pasta clung to the porcelain and the white plastic seat. She stood upright and pulled some toilet paper from the roll, dabbing her lips. She heard the door open, and someone stepped into the adjacent cubicle. She listened to the stream of urine. The woman hummed to herself as Kath's mouth filled with saliva again. She heaved and spat out the remains of the food.

'Are you alright, love?'

'I'm okay. Bad prawns yesterday.' Kath listened to the woman adjusting her clothing.

'Oh, poor you. I'm just glad it's not the cannelloni. I've just had far too much of it.'

Kath flushed the toilet at the same time as the woman next door and waited while she washed her hands. When she heard the door close, she leant against the wall and tried not to cry.

***

'You're leaving too, then?'

Clarissa watched her son come down the stairs with two holdalls.

'Will you be with Fenella's parents as well?' Clarissa assumed her daughter-in-law and grandson had gone back to Fenella's childhood home as Brocken had said.

'You don't need to know where I'm going.'

He walked through the drawing room and down the hallway to the front door. Clarissa followed him.

'Bring Brocken to see me tomorrow.'

'No, Mother.' Rafferty opened the door and strode off, not bothering to look back.

| 39 |

14th October 2019

Kath stared at the whiteboard and sipped her coffee. 'I'm close, girls. Just keep the faith. I'm so close now.'

She heard Ruth's heavy tread on the stairs.

'Morning.'

'Hey.'

Ruth put her bag under her desk and took off her jacket. 'Did you take my advice and see Richard?'

Kath didn't see the point in lying. 'Yes, we went out for a meal, but I didn't feel well. Cut the evening short.'

Ruth raised an eyebrow. If the woman didn't get some decent food inside her, she was going to fade away. She seemed reluctant to eat in front of anyone else. Ruth hoped Kath's relationship with Richard, as new as it was, would reignite her appetite. She looked pale and tired, but Ruth kept her thoughts to herself.

'You're alright now, though?' She set the kettle to boil.

'Yeah, I'm fine.'

Ruth dismissed the previous idea of keeping her mouth shut. 'You don't look fine; you look dreadful.'

Richard had accepted the bad prawns explanation. She had been quiet on the journey home and deferred the goodnight kiss. She'd spent Sunday fighting between frantic bursts of activity, cleaning out old paperwork and doing two loads of washing against slumping onto the sofa and watching reruns of *Columbo* on the television.

Byron arrived in another bright hand-knitted jumper, Shirl and Marvin soon after. When everyone was settled, Kath summed up their visit to Clemency's cottage—Lane was okay and had gone to Sal's, the woman Mikey had knocked over was seemingly fine, but she and Ruth were barred from entering the cottage. Kath added the fact that the woman, the visitor, had actually been living there for years as part of the Quartermaine extended family. Byron was typing as Kath talked.

'This woman isn't on any census,' he said.

'Didn't think she would be,' Kath replied. Her desk phone rang, and she snatched up the receiver. 'DCI Fortune.'

'Kath.'

'Oh, morning, Len… sir.'

Everyone looked at her.

She perched on the edge of her desk. 'What can I do for you?'

'You can stop harassing Clarissa Quartermaine and her family. I've just had her on the phone and she's very upset.'

'I'm not harassing her, I'm trying to close a murder case.'

His tone bothered her. She picked up a pen and clicked it on and off, ignoring Ruth's glare.

'She said you've been up at the estate every day and night, snooping around, as she put it.'

'Not snooping,' Kath spat the word back at him. 'She gave us permission. I know we're close to finding the killer—'

'Well, you'll have to do it some other way. She has withdrawn her permission for you to be on her land, so unless you're going to arrest her, you'll have to take a new approach. Do you have any evidence the girls were there?'

Kath stood up, her hand shaking as she gripped the plastic receiver. 'You mean apart from the two skeletons and one decaying corpse? No.'

'This isn't good,' Ruth muttered.

'Don't take that tone with me, DCI Fortune. Do you understand your position?'

'With the case or with anything else?'

She stared at the dead receiver and slammed it down. 'Bastard hung up on me.'

'He's in a difficult position,' said Ruth.

Kath threw her a sarcastic smile. 'Yeah, he's a man on the edge, and if he's not careful, I'm gonna push him right off it.'

Marvin looked at Byron, who shrugged and returned to staring at his monitor. 'I'll put the kettle on.' He busied himself with mugs and spoons as Shirl fought to dispel the tension.

'It's like a bloody soap opera in here with the kettle always on. Have you noticed how they all flock to the local cafe for a coffee when they live next to it, or over the road? I mean, save the money, people. Go home and fire up the kettle.'

'What's a soap opera?' Ruth asked.

Marvin turned round. 'Hey, I watched some *Columbo* episodes yesterday. They are so cool.'

Kath couldn't help but smile. 'What did you think, from a professional perspective?'

'I really enjoyed them. It was weird, though. No mobile phones. Forensics was pretty bleak too.'

'Hey, that's our lives you're talking about.' Ruth snorted. 'I have to confess, crime was different in the seventies.'

'He kind of reminded me of you.' Marvin looked at Kath.

'You need to look up flattery in the dictionary,' Ruth said, glancing at Kath but seeing nothing but an amused smile.

Marvin waved his hand. 'No, sorry. I mean, he never gives up. Keeps on at the suspects.'

'Stop now,' Ruth warned.

'Would anyone like some good news?' Byron asked.

'That would be great.' Shirl beamed, glad to deflect attention from shabby detectives and displeased chief superintendents.

'You and Mum have reached eleven grand so far for your skydives.'

'Oh wow.'

'Great news.'

'Crap,' said Shirl. 'I really have to do it now, don't I?'

'Twelve days to go.'

'Cheers, Ruth.' Shirl reached into her drawer for a bag of crisps, sighed and threw them unopened onto the desk.

'Training session Saturday, don't forget.' Byron ducked in case Shirl decided to throw something at him.

Kath's desk phone rang again. She stared at it, wondering if Lenny was coming back for another round.

'DCI Fortune. Hi. Yes. What? Cheers. I'll be right there.' She looked around the room, all eyes on her, expectant and hopeful. She replaced the receiver and rubbed her hands across her face. She took a deep breath.

'We just caught a break. Rafferty is at Malinsgate and he's asking for me. He has a solicitor with him.'

'This is big,' Ruth stood up and pressed her hand into Kath's shoulder.

The fact that Rafferty had voluntarily walked into the main Telford police station was unsettling and gratifying at the same time.

'It's bigger than big,' said Kath. 'He's just said he wants to confess.'

Kath walked into Interview Room Three. Marvin and Ruth went next door to watch. Shirl had offered to stay behind with Byron, as she could see Marvin was itching to go with Kath. Rafferty's face was drawn, hair limp, shoulders slumped. He and his solicitor stood up as Kath approached. Kath extended her hand to Rafferty, who touched it briefly, and then the solicitor, who shook it and sat down.

'Mr Quartermaine. I'm told this is your solicitor?'

'Brent Delaney,' the solicitor said.

Kath sat at the opposite side of the table. 'You've been through the protocols and your solicitor has advised you accordingly?'

'Yes,' said Rafferty.

'This interview is being video recorded and you are not under arrest. Do you understand?'

'I do.'

'I believe you are here to give us information regarding the murders of Jennifer Blunt, Layla Mountford and Sophia Martin. Is that correct?'

'Yes.'

'Start when you're ready. If at any time you want to stop, please tell us and we can take a comfort break.'

Rafferty looked at Brent, who nodded for him to begin.

'I wasn't entirely honest when I gave my statement seven years ago...'

| 40 |

Marvin wanted to hold Ruth's hand. This was it, this was what they'd been working towards, but he fought the impulse and crossed his arms. He stared through the two-way mirror as he leaned towards Ruth, his voice low, although he knew they couldn't be heard. 'This is like in *NCIS* when Leroy Jethro Gibbs is interrogating suspects.'

'Take it easy, cowboy.' Ruth smiled, not having a clue what he was talking about. 'Just watch and learn.'

Rafferty cleared his throat and spread his hands on the table. 'The girls were at the house, with me. I picked them up in my car, took them back to the manor.'

'You wanted to impress them?'

'Yes.'

'Were you planning to have sex with each of them?'

Rafferty's cheeks flared. His hands twitched. 'Yes. But I wasn't going to force them. I wanted them to like me.'

'So, each girl went to the manor with you, and in the following twenty-four to forty-eight hours, each one was declared a missing person.'

'Yes.'

He brushed his hair back, just as he'd done seven years ago. This time, the arrogant air was gone and Kath could feel the genuine desire for him to unburden himself.

'Go on.' She sat back a little in her chair.

'I actually lived in the cottage next to the main house and that's where I was planning... to spend the night with them. But, like I said, the manor is impressive and I wanted to introduce them to Nanny... I mean, Teddy.'

'You wanted her to approve of your girlfriends?'

'I did. My mother was just as difficult as she is now, when I was growing up. Distant. Hard.' His face clouded at the memories of Clarissa and her mode of parenting. 'Clemency was always kind to me, but Teddy adored me. I felt she really loved me, you know?'

Kath nodded encouragingly.

'I guess the other reason for wanting them to be my girlfriend was to piss off my mother. She'd already set things in motion for me to marry Fenella. I wasn't ready for that but knew I couldn't stop it. What my mother wants, she gets.' He smiled knowingly at Kath.

'I can see that,' said Kath.

'But I was telling the truth when you interviewed me after each girl went missing. I didn't know what had happened to them. I didn't find out the horrible truth until the boys found...' He hung his head and sighed sadly. 'When they went to the folly that night. Then I was told everything, and I had to keep the secret. I'm not proud of what I've done.'

Kath looked at Brent Delaney, his face showing no emotion. Kath pointed to the plastic cup of water on the table.

'Take your time. Have a drink.'

Rafferty picked up the cup and stared into it. 'She drugged me. Teddy. Put something in my wine. I have no idea what it was. I woke up each of the mornings with a blanket over me, passed out where I sat.'

Kath took a deep breath. In the other room, Marvin clutched Ruth's arm.

'So, Teddy drugged you and took each girl through the tunnel from the drawing room to the folly?'

Rafferty nodded. 'Yes.'

'So, Teddy—your nanny—killed Jennifer, Layla and Sophia?'

'Yes.' Rafferty nodded slowly as if not believing the words he was speaking.

Kath pressed her hands into her thighs underneath the table, trying to slow her breathing. 'For the benefit of the recording, can you give me Teddy's full name?'

Rafferty took a sip of water, his hand shaking. 'You have to understand...she's not well. Her mind is broken.' Tears filled his eyes as he drained the cup. 'She did it to protect me. To save me.'

Preaching to the choir.

'Her name,' Kath pressed.

Rafferty stared at her. 'Theadora Blackstock. My aunt.'

| 41 |

Ruth and Marvin followed Kath outside to the rear of the station. Kath stood against the wall underneath the No Smoking sign and lit a cigarette.

'I feel a bit sorry for him, in a way,' said Marvin.

Ruth raised her eyebrows and opened her mouth to speak, but Kath jumped in.

'Ruth, call Shirl. Tell her what's happened. She and Byron should be here for the next bit.'

Ruth stepped away and pulled out her phone. Kath had arranged for two cars and uniformed officers to pick up Clarissa and Clemency and bring them to the station. An ambulance was to accompany them for Teddy. As well as the mental health issues, Kath wanted to make sure any injuries sustained from when Mikey had pushed her were treated. The psychiatric team at the hospital would assess her accordingly.

Ruth wandered back over. 'They're on their way. Pretty shocked.'

'We all are,' said Kath, blowing smoke away from Marvin.

'So, Clarissa's sister didn't die in that fire?' Marvin said. 'How did they manage to cover that up?'

Kath's eyes narrowed. 'Clarissa's going to tell us *everything*.'

Kath walked round to the front of the building and lit another cigarette. Through the smoke, she watched shoppers going into the large Asda store across the road. Ordinary people buying their potatoes and pyjamas, picking out Halloween decorations. Normal people living normal lives.

That could be me. Shopping, working, cooking. Maybe not the cooking.

But her past made her a hypocrite. A liar. A criminal. Kath didn't want to admit it in front of Ruth, but she felt the same way as Marvin. Rafferty had finally done the right thing, throwing himself on the altar of truth to offset the years of domination by the women who surrounded him. She thought also of Donovan, another man who had been affected by the women, albeit in a more positive way. He would be shocked by the revelations.

She moved to the entrance as the police cars pulled in. Clemency exited the rear vehicle. She glanced at Kath, then looked away quickly. She was escorted inside, staring straight ahead. Clarissa got out of the other car and glared at Kath, who moved closer, blocking her path.

'Nice to see you on my home turf, Mrs Quartermaine.' Kath acknowledged she was being petty, but she was past caring.

'You've got nothing.'

Kath smiled and walked away to the edge of the building. 'I've got your son.'

She turned the corner, resisting the temptation to look back at Clarissa's face.

Half an hour had passed whilst they waited for Clarissa's solicitor to arrive. Clarissa sat upright, hands clasped on top of the table in the interview room. Kath and Ruth introduced themselves for the recording, as did Rupert Penhale. Clarissa stated her name and stared straight ahead at her reflection in the mirrored glass.

'Where is Teddy?'

'She's been taken to hospital for assessment.'

Clarissa's knuckles appeared as white clumps against her mottled skin.

Kath cleared her throat, more for dramatic effect than anything else. 'Why don't you tell us what you know of the murders of Jennifer Blunt, Layla Mountford and Sophia Martin?'

'I'm telling you nothing.'

Kath shrugged. 'Fine. Your son, Rafferty, has made a full statement.'

'Has he now?'

'Yes.'

'So, you have all your little breadcrumbs in a neat pile.'

'There are still some details I'd like to clarify,' Kath said, ignoring the barbed comment. 'For example, did you know immediately what your sister had done to Jennifer, or did you stumble across her body nine years ago?'

Silence. Kath had a game plan. She knew she'd get nothing from Clarissa and Clemency, but she didn't need it. Rafferty had given a full account. She'd felt his remorse, his shame, and that was something she could give to the families.

'Okay, what about a year later when she killed Layla? Find the body? Did she tell you about it?'

Clarissa's face remained a stony facade.

'Did you not think that your sister might benefit from the correct medical care that she so obviously needed? Perhaps in a psychiatric facility? Oh no, wait. You tried that, didn't you, and apparently, she died.'

A twitch in the corner of Clarissa's eye.

'Do you have any relevant questions for Mrs Quartermaine, Detective?' Rupert Penhale tried a polite smile that fell short of its objective.

'Yes, I do, actually. Who's buried in your sister's grave?'

Clarissa pressed her lips together.

'Or perhaps it's just an empty coffin? I'm sorry, did I hear a "no comment"?'

'You need a career change,' Clarissa spat out.

Kath smiled. 'Rafferty has shown remorse and empathy with respect to this situation. I'm guessing he gets that from his father.'

'*Pah.*'

'Is that confirmation?'

'Farraday had a weak constitution,' Clarissa growled.

'And a weak heart, apparently. That was what killed him... we are led to believe, anyway '

'Another Agatha Christie moment for your memoir. You should call it Fortune and Glory.'

'Glad you can find the humour in the murder of three young girls. I wonder what Clemency will tell us?'

'I think you'll find "no comment" are the only words she'll utter.'

'Why do you hate your son so much?'

In a nearby room, Rafferty watched the monitor, his fists clenched.

Clarissa looked at Kath with a bored expression. 'I don't hate him, Inspector. He's just not what I wanted from a child.'

'I'm sure you're not what he wanted for a mother. And it's Chief Inspector.'

Clarissa's eyes roved across Kath's body. 'You do like to keep reminding me of your title. Do you feel that extra little word commands you more respect?'

'I think we're going a little off topic.' Ruth shifted in her seat, feeling tension leeching from Kath's rigid body.

'Tell us where you were when Rafferty brought the girls to the manor house on the three evenings.'

Clarissa placed her hands in her lap. 'I was in bed. I didn't know the girls had been in my house.'

'But you knew your sister had killed them and you did nothing,' Ruth pressed.

'I did what I needed to do to protect her.'

'Which is morally wrong and a criminal act,' said Kath.

'I have to protect my sister. She's delicate. The world outside is too much for her. You come across as an only child. You wouldn't understand.' Clarissa waved a hand dismissively.

Kath saw herself reaching forward to scrape away the superior look from the woman's face. 'If Rafferty was such a disappointment, why didn't you have any more children?'

'That's not relevant.' Penhale glared at Kath.

'Just trying to get a deeper understanding of the family dynamic.'

Kath watched Clarissa's shoulders tense as she brushed away imaginary hair from her face. Rafferty leaned forward in his chair, and Shirl wanted to put an arm around him.

'Poor little Rafferty,' Kath went on. 'Surrounded by women and the only one that could care about him was the crazy lady.'

Clarissa half-rose, her hands white and flat on the table. Penhale pressed his hand into her arm, and she sat down slowly.

'She cares for him more than you know.'

'Tell me. Just tell me why you haven't an ounce of affection for him.'

Clarissa stared at Kath and sighed, too tired to fight anymore. 'Because I'm not his mother. He's Theadora's child.'

Shirl watched open-mouthed as Rafferty's eyelids fluttered and he fell to the floor.

| 42 |

They sat at a corner table in an almost empty pub. The drinks were tainted with sadness rather than celebration.

'I just didn't see it coming,' said Shirl for what seemed like the hundredth time since they'd left the station.

Kath had spent the last few hours contacting everyone who needed to know the result. Lane was shocked, the families of the girls relieved to have some measure of closure at last, Mikey thankful that no serious harm had come to Theadora. No jokes or banter from him. Donovan was the hardest call, a sob in his throat as he acknowledged what she was telling him.

'What about Theadora, though?' Marvin asked. 'Will she stand trial?'

Kath shrugged. 'Psych services will be involved in the process.' She looked down at her blackcurrant and soda water. 'Let's all take a personal day tomorrow. We'll regroup on Wednesday.'

'I feel so bad for Rafferty,' said Shirl, and everyone nodded.

Clarissa had finally reluctantly relented and told Kath what she wanted to know. She'd been desperate for a child but unable to conceive. Farraday and Theadora had come up with what seemed a perfect solution until the post-partum depression took hold of Theadora. The rages and violent outbursts were too upsetting and too immense to cope with, so she'd been shipped off to Derbyshire. The idea for faking her death had been Clarissa's. She realised quite quickly that she had no maternal instinct whatsoever, so Theadora returned to the Quartermaine estate, her mind seemingly calmer, and was allowed to care for Rafferty. Her love for the boy acted as the perfect panacea, but as he grew into a man, her obsessive desire to protect him overwhelmed her damaged mind.

Ruth lifted her glass. 'To a great team.'

They all clinked glasses.

'So, who gets to pick the next case?' Marvin asked tentatively.

'Let's visit that on Wednesday.' Kath gave him a reassuring smile.

'Yeah, okay.' Marvin's confidence level rose. He looked at the blackboard at the side of the bar. 'It's only just after five. We could stay and have another drink and then get some food—it's curry night.' He pointed to the board and the attempt at fancy chalk writing.

'I'm gonna go. Not really hungry.' Kath stood up. 'Have a good night and a restful day tomorrow.'

Ruth touched her arm. 'You okay?'

'Yeah. Just need to be on my own. See you soon.'

Once home, Kath put on all the lights and drew the curtains. It was that strange time of autumn day between late afternoon and early evening, a time that had no definitive name. It wasn't yet fully dark, but thick, grey clouds brought the night in closer. She went to the patio and lit a cigarette, the smoke rising straight up in the still air. She pulled her other mobile from her pocket.

'Hey, you. Alright?'

'I guess.'

'Obviously not, which is why you're phoning me.' Sal chuckled, and Kath grinned. 'Lane said you caught another bad guy...well, woman.'

'We did. How is Lane?'

'Fine. Nice eye candy to have around the place. I keep telling her it's okay for her to wander around in her underwear, but she keeps covering up that fabulous body.'

'Watch it. Zelda will get jealous.' She flicked her ash into the bowl on the table, imagining Sal's face.

'Ha. New interest. She's bought a potter's wheel and a bloody kiln. I hardly see her. I think she's going to have to build a new shed.'

'Every girl needs a hobby.'

'Talking of which, how's your new man?'

'It's only been a week.' Kath told her what had happened in the restaurant, the one person who would get it.

'I told you, you can't just kill someone and think it won't affect the rest of your life. I thought you got that by now?'

'You manage it.' Kath said tartly.

'I don't get my hands dirty. It's a job. No emotional involvement.'

'But I've been okay for thirty years, Sal,' Kath heard her own whining tone and closed her eyes.

'Okay, but in the last few months, your situation has changed, hasn't it?'

Kath opened her eyes and drew heavily on her cigarette as Sal continued.

'Reg Miller came slap bang into the middle of your head because he was a cold case, alongside the fact that you now have an emotional involvement with Lenny and now Richard.'

'I see it...'

'Yeah, but you don't want to confront it. How's things with Lenny? Do you still love him?'

'I do,' said Kath, tapping her cigarette more vigorously. 'But it's different now. He's acting like we're back at school. It's as if he's got this romantic notion of us moving in together and getting a dog and a greenhouse...'

'Really?' Sal laughed.

'Well, no, okay, but you get the idea.'

'And Richard?'

Kath smiled at the mention of his name. 'Whole new ball game. It's like that Craig David song. I met him on Monday, took him for a drink on Tuesday etcetera.'

'I get it, but yet, after a few days, an innocent comment from him has you throwing up out of guilt because of what happened in your past.'

Kath pulled hard on her cigarette and coughed. Sal waited for her to stop.

'Sounds to me like you have three choices. Visit a priest for absolution, confess and face a prison sentence...'

Kath was struggling to think of a third option. 'Or?'

'Retire and come over to the dark side properly with me. The job offer is still open.'

Kath crushed her cigarette butt into the ashtray as the night closed in around her. 'Great choices. Cheers.'

'Happy to help. Let me know what you decide.' Sal ended the call, and Kath pocketed the phone.

She felt eyes on her from the cows staring from a distance as she pulled out her regular mobile and dialled Richard's number.

'Hello. Happy one-week anniversary.' She could hear the smile in his voice.

'Not fed up with me yet, then?'

Richard laughed. 'Let's give it another week. Want to celebrate tonight?'

'Wrapped up the case today. Don't feel much like celebrating, if I'm honest. Even with you,' she added.

'Are you alright? You sound a bit... I don't know, strange.'

'All this death makes me sad.'

'Of course. I mean, it must. I can't imagine doing your job, but at least you get justice for victims and families.' He desperately wanted to see her. She sounded all wrong and he was worried.

'It comes at a price. Sometimes I just feel—'

A shot rang out, fracturing the silence.

Kath's body shuddered and dropped to the patio. Her phone flew from her hand and landed on the edge of the lawn, the screen a bright light in the darkness. Her mouth opened and closed quickly as if her face could not process what had just happened. She thought she heard the sound of a shot being fired but, lying shivering on the cold slabs, she wasn't trusting her brain to give her the right information. She thought she'd put her hand to her head, but her eyes fluttered and she saw her arm pinned beneath her. Her eyelids felt twisted, her cheeks slapped by tentacles of cold air. She could see the blood leeching from the bullet wound in her thigh, spreading across the mismatched paving slabs. Her heart hammered in her chest whilst all around her the air seemed to slow and settle upon her prone body. She could just make out the sound of hooves thundering across the meadow in the distance.

Not like this...not ready...need to tell... need to tell the cows...

Richard's voice was tinny, distant. 'Kath? Kath! Are you there? What's happened? Kath?'

Also by Julia Vaughan

<u>Daisy Chain – A DCI Kath Fortune novel, Book 1</u>

In 2009 the body of five-year-old Daisy Prospero was found in Shropshire woodland. Her killer has never been caught. Ten years on, Detective Chief Inspector Kath Fortune and her new Cold Case team are on the hunt to find the truth. Alongside the new investigation into his daughter's murder, Todd Prospero has his own mystery to solve. Who is the woman he finds in his garden in the middle of the night on the brink of death? A chain of secrets and lies leads the team to uncover connections that no-one could have imagined. Can the killer be brought to justice?

Grave Issue – A DCI Kath Fortune novel, Book 2

Who killed Abraham and Esther Downing in the 1970s?

What is the significance of the seven tiny skeletons unearthed in the garden of the Downing's cottage?

And why does no-one care?

As DCI Kath Fortune and her Cold Case team dive deep into their second investigation, they come up against a wall of silence surrounding the reclusive couple. With Kath trying to piece together the clues and keep her personal and professional relationships on track, her past comes back to haunt her with time running out on all counts.

About the author

Julia Vaughan is a Medical Secretary living in Shropshire with her husband and two cats. As a youngster, she wanted to be Destiny Angel or one of Charlie's Angels. Neither came to pass. Julia completed a degree from Worcester University in English & Literary Studies with Associated Drama and has been writing crime and mystery fiction for years, with the odd short story published. She's happiest when watching Columbo, Law & Order and Midsomer Murders.

Julia would be very grateful if you can submit a review wherever you can. If you post it on social media please use the hashtag #trmjv so Julia can find it.